GREETINGS
FROM TUCSON

Peter,

Thank you for the support! I truly hope you enjoy the story.

Cherie L. Genua

GREETINGS FROM TUGSON

A NOVEL

CHERIE L. GENUA

ISBN: 978-0-578-97608-2
LCCN: 2021917089

Cover art, illustrations, and book design by
Jordan Bernard

Dedication

To the inspiration behind this story: My grandmother, Loretta, and her sisters, Nancy, Josephine, and Dolores— Four strong women who taught us the true meaning of family and to never, ever give up no matter what life throws at us.

Grandma (my real-life "Cookie"): Every so often a red cardinal comes to visit and reminds me that you're always here with me.

Grandma

Prologue:
Eulogy

December 2012

Hi Arizona family,

I hope all is well with everyone. I wanted to reach out and thank all of you for your support during these past few days [and weeks]. I know my grandpa appreciated you all lending your ear and sending your prayers our way——he needs comfort right now and you guys have provided just that. I'm attaching the eulogy I wrote for my grandmother's funeral in case you wanted to read it:

On behalf of my family, I would like to thank you for coming today to share in the sorrow of the loss of our mother and grandmother, Loretta, but also to share in the joy of celebrating her wonderful life with all of you.

Some of you might know her as Coach, Cookie, or "the lunch lady"— but my family will always know her as our guiding light in a dark and unknown world. My grandmother was a kind, gentle, and strong woman, who lived a rich life——not in material possessions——but rather rich in love and family. As the years moved along, we could always fall back on the fact that she was always there for us, even if it was just to listen about our workdays, discuss the winner of "Dancing with the Stars," or plan for our futures. She was quieter than the rest of our loud, Italian family, but always spoke powerful words that made us stop and listen. With any heartbreak or disappointment, she whispered "it is what it is" and gently pushed us to keep moving forward. She went through more in her early years than most people have to deal with in a lifetime, but she never let life knock her down.

In the 28 years that I have been alive, I have never once heard her yell, which is very telling of the woman that she was——especially having to deal with all of us. What we will always remember about her was her beautiful and inviting smile and her deep brown eyes that sparkled when she talked about anything she loved. Wherever I am in the world, all I have to do is close my eyes and I can see her watching her favorite soap opera on television like it was pure magic, even though she'd seen a similar scene play out over and over again over the years. I can hear her belly laughing at the movie "Home Alone" whenever the criminals succumbed to Kevin's zany mischief. I would do anything to hear that belly laugh again. It assured me that everything would be alright in the end.

My grandmother has shared many milestones and memories with us as a family. She loved road trips—my grandparents took my mother and aunts across the country to Arizona and California when they were just toddlers, which is a story in and of itself. And they never went a year without visiting the Cape, and we continued these traditions well into my childhood years. There, she would take me to the five-cent candy store and get a pile of salt water taffy for my grandpa to chew when they watched their programs together after a long day at the beach. And I think I can speak for all of my family when I say, some of our most favorite memories come from recent trips to Newport, Rhode Island, Saratoga Springs, New York, Boston, and Atlantic City, New Jersey, and, of course, her beloved casino. She would sit at a machine for hours, while playing slow and steady. While others around her lost their money, she would always bet small but come out ahead. The times we all shared as a family will always be in our hearts and, on bad days, we will have those times to get us through.

Fifty-five years of marriage to my outstanding grandfather, three sisters whose bond was unbreakable, four children, and four grandchildren later, I can confidently say that she lived a long, fulfilling life full of joy and laughter. She and my grandpa held hands while sleeping and rarely would venture out without the other. He cooked and she cleaned the stove after he was done without saying a word about how dirty he made it. A girls' day would almost always include my grandpa, because she didn't want to leave him home. And that was more than okay with us.

I hope in the future when I'm faced with darkness, I will handle it with the grace and composure that I observed in her over the years. Even over the last few weeks of her life when her body grew tired, she giggled at Lucy and Ethel's shenanigans on the small hospital room television screen as she and my mother watched "I Love Lucy."

Grandma, I will always be grateful for the lessons that you've taught me and I promise to make you proud.

Love,
Cherie

This was the eulogy I gave in front of family and friends at my grandmother's funeral on December 14th, 2012. Her name was Loretta. We will always remember this date, both because it was the date of my grandmother's funeral and, also, because it was the day of one of the most horrific school shootings in recent history at Sandy Hook Elementary School in Newtown, Connecticut.

It was a mild December morning, much warmer than I expected it to be in mid-December. Overdressed in a wool winter coat and tights with sweaty knees and clammy hands, I stood with my family in a semi-circle around her overly expensive white casket. My grandpa chose it because he wanted the best for her, his lifelong best friend. He wanted her to rest in peace, eternally, and thought the cushiony casket with a velvet interior made it a bit easier to do so. Who knows, maybe he was right.

In front of her casket stood two young girls, maybe 14 or 15 years old. One of the girls, tall with long limbs and frizzy brown hair, put a flute up to her lips and began playing, as the moisture from her breath caused condensation on her instrument. The music was choppy at first but became smoother as she continued to play. The other girl began to sing along as her braces reflected the light from the sun. My grandma's favorite song, "Ave Maria," cut through the soft sniffles of the crowd. The two girls knew her from their time at the elementary school where she worked as a lunch lady. They even volunteered at the cafeteria a few days a week once they went to middle school, just to keep in contact with my grandma. I remember her talking about them. She even kept the notes each of them wrote her tucked in her jewelry drawer amongst the neatly packed boxes of costume jewelry she collected over the years. My grandpa had his head lowered as they sang, one hand on the casket as he balanced himself, trying his best not to cry.

After the girls were done singing, I made my way to the

casket and put my hand on my grandpa's shoulder. Behind his glasses laid drooping skin that showed the signs of almost eighty years, but also the bluest eyes I've ever known. With a squeeze on the arm and a gentle smile, he watched as I dropped a deep scarlet carnation on her casket, which was the moment everything felt so final. As hard as it was to think about my grandma being lowered into the ground, I was all cried out and numb from the pain of watching her deteriorate for the past eleven weeks after the heart attack that brought her to the hospital in the first place. She was at peace now, but she was gone. There were no tears left.

I glanced at some of her old friends who worked with her at the elementary school over the years, their eyes pink and swelled with tears, as they said their final goodbyes. Around my grandmother's age, I could tell that this wasn't the first time they buried a close friend. My lips turned upward into a semblance of a smile; her friends from the elementary school were so treasured. Being a lunch lady was her retirement job, but she took it as seriously as a doctor performing surgery. Her plan to work five more years turned into ten. Ten turned into twenty. She only stopped when her knees started giving her trouble and she could no longer spend all morning on her feet.

She was my lunch lady in elementary school. When I switched schools in second grade to the school where my grandma worked, she made the transition so much easier.

But, the thing about my grandma is that although I was her one and only grandchild at the time, she didn't favor me over the other kids in school. She was fair and equal to all of us. But every once in a while, I would find a cookie wrapped in a thin paper napkin in my lunch box next to the thermos of Spaghettios that my mother packed for me. I was always so proud that she was my grandma. It was no surprise that the kids and teachers referred to her as "everyone's grandma." I didn't mind sharing her, especially after seeing how her brown eyes lit up under the fluorescent lights of the otherwise dingy cafeteria as she placed warmed-up meals and cartons of chocolate milk on the kids' trays.

As my family and I began our slow trod back to the black Lincoln Town Cars on the windy roads of the cemetery, we heard a gasp from the lingering crowd. Someone received an alert about the Sandy Hook shooting, which was about 15 miles west from where we were standing that day. I could barely comprehend the nightmare that occurred.

After I wept and prayed, and later reflected on the unspeakable loss that took place, a thought entered my mind: my grandma was taken from us when she was because someone needed to comfort those poor, innocent souls in heaven. She was a lunch lady and everyone's grandma. Most importantly, she was the most kind and patient soul I've ever had the pleasure of knowing. If those beautiful children needed a lunch lady, then Loretta was the woman for the job, and she would do it without hesitation as her new purpose in the afterlife.

The weekend after my grandma's funeral, my mom, aunts, and I went to my grandpa's house to begin organizing some of her belongings. I always wondered what the rush was, but my grandma was his best friend and his whole world. Although he appeared strong outwardly, I knew the rush was because he couldn't bear to see all of the precious memories as a reminder to him that she's no longer with us. I recall walking into their bedroom and seeing only his side of the bed turned down—her side was perfectly made and untouched—and it hit me like a ton of bricks how precious life truly is. One day, you could be sleeping soundly next to your adored husband, and the next day, in a hospital, frightened and wondering if it's your time to go, never returning to the home that you knew for over fifty years.

I opened the cedar pocket door to my grandma's half of the closet and was hit with her signature perfume scent, Red Door. Even though I knew I would not wear her clothes, I took a few pieces out to bring home with me, simply so I could have the scent of her mixed in with the clothes in my closet. A few homes and a few closets later, I still have these two pieces of clothing bookending the clothes in my closet, and her scent still lingers. I gently touched her soft sweaters and noticed a little section carved out for her uniform as a lunch lady—a simple white crew neck sweatshirt and navy pants—ironed and ready to go, even though she stopped working a few years prior.

It was then that a floral shoebox sitting on the top shelf of her closet caught my eye. It stood out amongst the Reebok and other sneaker boxes alongside it, and I had a feeling it was special. I pulled it down and sat on the bed to open it and begin going through it, while my mom and aunts were busy in the hallway closet admiring her doilies and handkerchiefs that she collected and neatly stored for so long. When I opened the box, a pungent scent filled my nostrils... the smell of floral perfume and finishing powder mixed with the stale smell of mothballs. Handwritten letters and postcards filled the box to the brim, the yellow and brittle paper indicating these were decades old. The once vibrant colors of the envelopes, in varying shades of pink, yellow, and blue, had faded into pastel hues that were almost indistinguishable in color from the others.

I gently picked up one of the envelopes to open it, realizing the return address on the back was her late sister's address in Tucson, Arizona. I thumbed through a few more of the letters still in the box. They were all letters from her sisters, many of which were over sixty-five years old. I was fascinated—I've been in my grandma's closet many, many times, and I never once noticed this floral box holding my grandmother's story. It's almost as if she was trying to tell me something and placed the box right in front of my eyes to see it that day.

At that moment, one by one, I consumed each captivating letter. For the first time, the jigsaw came together to complete my grandmother's intricate backstory. Like many of our lives, hers was riddled with tragedy, love, heartache, treasures, and surprises; but one theme emerged that overshadowed the rest. My grandmother and her three sisters had an unparalleled connection, a true love story of our time.

Although they lived across the country from one another, they never grew to be strangers. There was no social media or text messaging. They conveyed their deepest secrets and celebrated their wondrous journeys through the art of letter writing, far before technology made it simpler to maintain a relationship. I thought of these letters often, until one day, I was inspired to write this book. A story loosely based on the lives and love of four sisters.

A story that taught me sisters could be soulmates, too.

1

The Accident

Dear Diary,

I only have a few minutes to write tonight. My sisters were
tired and fell asleep on my bed with me. I'm tired, too, but I
hear Mom crying through the walls. She's in the bathroom.
I can smell her cigarette smoke through the window.

Sometimes I wonder if she's going to leave us all behind.
Dad came home drunk tonight and he's passed out on the
couch. Drunker than usual, if I'm being honest. I hate when
he comes home before the girls are asleep——it scares
them. Frankly, it scares me too, but I never show it because
I want to make sure they are okay. Tonight, though, something was different. He had a look in his eyes that I have not
seen before. I love him——I love him so much. I do.

But something has to change. Someone is going to get hurt.

Scared and sad,
Cookie

June 27th, 1945. There hasn't been a day that goes by that I don't think of that day or the days leading up to that day. In fact, I have thought about the events of June 27th, 1945, every single day for the past sixty-six years. But even though I think about it daily, I have never talked about it. Not even with my husband of fifty-seven years. Not with my four children. My best friends and I talked about anything and everything over the years, but we don't talk about this.

One time, my eldest granddaughter was sitting at our kitchen table after school. She was putting together a family tree for her fourth-grade project. Like any other curious child, she asked me some questions and I politely answered, but I didn't tell her the whole truth. I could never be honest about what happened that day—June 27th, 1945.

So, I changed the story. I pretended things were different. I'm not a liar, but I guess you could say I lied. I lied to everyone I knew.

There were only a few other people who truly knew what happened that day. Me and my three sisters: Frankie, Dottie, and Connie.

I will tell you, though, that my sisters and I had different memories of what happened for many years after that day in 1945. I saw the angst and forewarning behind my mother's eyes that day—they were dark and clouded like a premonition. I was the oldest sister and I was confident for so long that I saw things pretty clearly at the time. I always looked out for my sisters and I assumed I had shielded them from a lot. But now I know that they shielded me from some of the lasting pain, too.

1945 was the year that both of my parents died. They did not die at the same time, but they died the same day. Over the years, we all maintained that they died together in a catastrophic car accident. Certainly, that was not the case, but it was believable to most. People didn't ask follow-up questions about a tragedy like that.

A few moments ago, I was sound asleep in the same full-size bed my husband and I slept in for decades when I jolted awake. My mother's face appeared in my dreams—her face was a mix of my sisters' faces and mine. Soft and rounded like my face, but with a button nose and big round eyes like on my sisters' faces. I wanted to save her, and I hope she knows that. Her expression looked relieved. Or scorned. I couldn't quite tell. I slipped out of bed and headed to the bathroom mere steps away from our bedroom. I tried to shut the door, but it never stays shut. I don't think it has since we moved into this house, but it had never bothered me until this very moment. After splashing water on my face, I stared in the mirror.

I think about my mother. I think about my father. I think about my sisters.

I think about what our lives could have been.

The morning our mother died was sunny and clear. It was one of those perfect days where the cotton candy clouds crawled through the powder blue sky. It was a memorable morning; much like the day itself, I'll never forget it. Me and my sisters—Frankie, Dottie, and Connie—woke up early that Saturday. Dad was awake, which was a bit of a surprise, as he often slept in on non-work days because he drank the night before. He was grinning and singing an old Italian song from the 1930s as he moved across the kitchen from side-to-side. Grease and pancake batter splattered onto the wall and the counters as he prepared breakfast. Mom walked by and shut a cabinet or two that he left open with a huff. She didn't say a word to him but smiled at me when she saw me watching.

My middle sisters, Frankie and Dottie, played jacks at the table and giggled. They were still wearing their nightgowns—Dottie's was a hand-me-down and slid down her shoulder a bit. Frankie swayed along to the song that our father was singing. Connie, my littlest sister, walked in to join us, yawned, and slumped down on the empty chair next to me. She was moody in the morning and didn't like to talk much when she first woke up. As soon as she sat down, Dad flopped a large plate of pancakes on the table. Mom followed behind him with four small plates, forks, and a tin of syrup. She sat down with us but didn't touch the pancakes; instead, she looked around the kitchen at the mess and let out a sigh. Dad was sweaty as he walked back over to the stove and poured some more batter into the sizzling hot pan. He wiped the sweat off his forehead with a mappine on the counter. I'm pretty sure he made a hundred pancakes that day, but neither he or Mom had even a bite.

We ate and laughed and talked about nothing until Mom interrupted us. "Guess what girls? We're going to the beach. Be ready in fifteen! Cookie, help your sisters." She smiled at me, but her eyes appeared distant and blank. Something felt off, but maybe she was just mad at him. She's been mad at him a lot, lately.

Frankie, Connie, Dottie, and I got ready in record time. We put on our bathing suits, wiped the syrup from our face and hands, and grabbed towels from the chest. We ran to the car, tripping over each other to get the best seat. Dad and Mom were already sitting in the front waiting for us. They still weren't speaking to one another—it must be because of last night.

When we arrived at the beach, the sun was warm and the parking lot was still rather empty. Mom opened the door to let us out of the backseat and we piled out. Dottie, who had started to whine just a few minutes before we arrived, was now skipping and smiling wide as we made the trek down the sandy walkway towards the beach. Dad walked a bit behind us with his head down. He seemed tired and frustrated that Mom wouldn't even look his way.

Frankie picked the perfect spot near the shore—we were

close enough to take a dip when the sun started to heat up, but we weren't too close that we would need to move when the tide rolled out. The four of us each took a corner of the blanket and positioned it on the sand. The seagulls flying overhead cast a slow-moving shadow over us. Connie squawked to mimic their shrieking cries. Meanwhile, Mom took a towel out of her straw bag and laid it out about ten feet away from us girls. Dad put his hand on her shoulder as if to offer help, but she shook it off and continued setting up herself. With a huff, he sat down on the blanket and unbuttoned his shirt. Mom slipped off her shorts but was wearing a linen button-up top over her bathing suit and kept that on. She applied sunscreen to her legs, which looked almost translucent in the sunlight. She then motioned for me to take it and share it with the girls. Sitting down on the blanket, she grabbed the hat and sunglasses from her bag and laid back on her perched elbows. Sand stuck to her legs and tumbled off her body with each subtle movement, as the sounds of the wave rolled into the shore.

My sisters didn't notice but she seemed more upset than usual at Dad... agitated... quiet... even cold. Mom and Dad fighting was nothing new, especially after a night of drinking. But today was different. It's almost as if you wouldn't be able to tell they were even married if you didn't know they were. Sure, they were sitting next to each other. But they could have been actual strangers sitting there and no one would be the wiser.

Mom lowered her glasses and waved her hand at me. I didn't realize it, but I must've been staring at her for quite a while. "Go play with your sisters," she said. "We're at the beach to relax and enjoy. Nothing to see here, Cookie."

My sisters had already run to the water. They splashed water at each other with their feet and ran in circles as the waves crashed on the shore. The sea spray glistened in the sun and the golden sand felt warm under my feet. All three were howling with laughter as I jogged to catch up with them. An older man tipped his hat to me as he walked by and let out a soft chuckle as he watched my sisters play.

When I made it to them, Frankie immediately reached down towards the water and splashed it my way, soaking the front of my bathing suit and legs. It felt good against my sun-kissed skin and I smiled at her, joining in on the fun. Dottie and my littlest sister, Connie, were already chest-deep in the water. They held hands and hopped up every time a small wave collided into the sand. Being that we were in Milford on the Long Island Sound, the waves were not huge, but it never mattered much when we were little. You would think we were in South Miami where the waves were big and mighty by the way we got excited to jump in and out of the spraying water.

Before joining them, I looked back at Mom and Dad. They were talking, which was almost shocking to see at this point, but their body language was harsh. My father was speaking sternly to her with his hands as her head hung down low. He kept pointing a finger on his right hand and plunging it into his other palm. It was hard to know what they were saying, but it didn't seem good. I heeded my mother's words and tried to enjoy myself, so I dove under the waves to meet my sisters in the deeper water.

We played and swam for what seemed like hours in the surf. There was barely anyone else around and our voices echoed up and down the coastline. There was more seaweed than usual and it was starting to feel slimy and sticky against my legs. I told the girls I needed a break and they agreed to get out of the water, too, so we could have a snack and try to build a sandcastle with the pail that Frankie found in the trunk of Dad's car.

"Hey kids, you havin' fun?" Dad asked as we ran back up to our beach blanket, his hands in a funnel around his mouth so we could hear him over the melodic sounds of the water. Dottie had to use the bathroom and Mom offered to take her. She was still visibly agitated, so a few minutes away might do her good. I watched as they trudged through the sand to get there. It seemed to be miles away.

"Yeah!" Frankie, Connie, and I replied in unison.

"Can we bury you in the sand soon, Dad?" Frankie asked with a giggle. He shook his head to say "yes" and that he'll be over in a minute. They were so innocent and assuredly unaware of Dad's shortcomings. I loved how their eyes sparkled when Dad played with them. He always seemed to do no wrong, in their eyes anyway. I was at an age where I was starting to see his faults, but I still loved him and Mom more than anything. Mom stopped looking at him the way she used to. Her skin used to glow and her eyes would light up when he entered a room, but that light lost its flame. I hoped they would find happiness again in each other. I hoped Mom would look at him with the love and affection she showed when she looked at me and my sisters.

A few minutes later, Mom and Dottie emerged in the distance as they headed back. Dottie's little legs were struggling to keep up with Mom's quick pace. Dad rose from the blanket and removed his shirt as he made his way over. He bent down and helped us dig a large hole in the sand, where he would soon lay to get buried. He always let us bury him in the sand; one time, he even fell asleep halfway through. The girls and I always thought it was so funny to see Dad in the sand with only his face peeking out. Sometimes, he would pretend to be a monster and pop his arms out of the packed-down sand. It scared us every time, no matter how often he played this trick on us in the past.

Dad sat down in the gigantic hole we dug and closed his eyes to shield them from the sun. Dottie returned in time to help as we worked together to cover his legs with sand. Frankie ran back and forth between the shore and the sand. She filled the pail with water and dumped it near Dad to make the sand sticky. She must've spilled half of it running back from the water, but that didn't stop her from having fun.

As Dad's legs became completely covered with sand, Mom pushed herself off the blanket and laid her cover-up over Dad's shirt. She marched towards the water and stretched her arms over her head. She appeared to be preparing for a swim. Mom loved the water but wasn't a particularly good swimmer. It never stopped her from wading in the water, though.

Before she stepped into the water, she looked up at us with a broad smile on her face and waved, her long fingers mimicking the waves behind her. Now that her sunglasses were off, I could faintly make out that she had been crying. Maybe she was still crying. Just like that, she put her arms up over her head and dove into the water—like a mermaid, I imagined—her black hair glistening like silk as she came up for air. Dad's belly was almost covered with sand and his eyes were still closed. The water was over Mom's head but she stayed there for a few moments, treading water and looking into the distance. She began swimming further and further away towards the bright haze of the horizon, further than I've ever seen her go before. I felt extremely uneasy. I stood up and put my hand over my eyes to try to block the sun, squinting to see where she was as she swam away. Little did I know that would be the last time I saw her alive. Just as if the image of my sisters splashing in the waves is ingrained in my memory, the image of my mother waving and crying is an image that I would never be able to forget.

"DAD," I shouted. "GIRLS! Everyone get up. Mom swam out really far and I can't see her anymore."

Dad sprung up, as sand poured onto the ground around him. He trotted to the water and began screaming her name. I ran in tandem with him and told him I had seen her swim towards the marshy area of the water, where the seaweed was thick and murky. I pointed to the area and he jumped in without saying a word. He no longer looked tired to me, but instead like a true hero, his arms and feet splashing as he swam with all his might.

My sisters had caught up to us by this point. Connie was crying and I put my arm around her and pulled her close to me. I turned my attention to my other two sisters whose eyes were fixated on Dad as he bobbed and weaved through the sea like a dolphin. After about a minute or two, which felt like an eternity to us, he reached the marshy part of the shore. At this point, other adults were gathering around us at the shore. Two men started taking off their tee-shirts and threw them on the sand and went into the sea, following Dad's path. Another woman started running towards a house near the shore to call for help. My sisters and I stood there, stunned, and unaware of exactly what would happen next.

A few seconds later, we heard an ungodly scream from the marsh. "NOOO!!!!! Oh my God, no," he bellowed as he looked to the sky, grabbing something that I couldn't make out. My face was flush and I was dizzy with fear. I somehow managed to take a few steps into the water, thinking I could see what was happening better from here. Dad turned around and faced the crowd that had gathered on the shore. He was holding my lifeless mother in his arms. He was treading water as he attempted to give her mouth to mouth. Finally, the other two men reached Dad's whereabouts. They supported her body as he continued to try and breathe air into her lungs. I felt like I was in a bad dream when I saw him stop breathing into her mouth. He put his hands over his eyes and laid his head on her chest, as the two strangers held onto her. They struggled to stay afloat but ensured neither she or Dad sunk even further into the depths of the water. They all started swimming back to shore, holding our mother who was floating on her back. She looked like she was sleeping but we all know she wasn't.

As they neared the shore, the incoming sirens from police cars and an ambulance jolted me back to my senses. The two men who helped carry her placed her on the sand and rolled on their sides. They were breathless. Our father hovered over our mother's face, looking for any sign of life. The crowd shifted as the policemen pushed through to get close to our mother. Their pant legs became soaked as they kneeled down into the shallow water.

Dad's usual ruddy appearance had turned stark white. His eyes were glossy as he stared through everyone. Another pair of policemen stood in front of me and my sisters. They crouched down to my youngest sister's level in an attempt to shield us from our mother's dead body. They turned us around and ushered us towards the parking lot, where the red and blue lights filled up the sky. I could hear deep breaths of air followed by slaps onto Mom's wet skin as the medics performed mouth-to-mouth behind us with no luck.

Our mother was dead. We'd never see her face again. We'd never grin at her contagious smile or hear her chesty laugh. Laughter made her whole body—specifically, her shoulders— shake, but we'd never see that again, either. We would never feel the silkiness of her black hair under her soft bristled brush as we combed through her hair at night before bed. We'd never smell the cigarettes through the bedroom window when she secretly smoked in the bathroom. How would we feel safe without her calmness or her strength? Who else's sparkling brown eyes would assure us that a bad grade on a test or a skinned knee will be okay? I can't wrap my head around it. From the looks on my sisters' faces, they certainly can't either.

Did our Dad do this to her? He did not physically kill her, but did he somehow bring her to this moment? I was so angry, I could scream. I didn't want to go in the squad car... I wanted to fight it, but I had no energy and no will. I sat down in the car next to my sisters and I squeezed Frankie's hand. The cops were speaking to us but none of us were listening. They cracked the windows and shut us inside. The warm summer air became thick and stifling in mere moments but none of that mattered. I looked out the car door and saw the gurney carrying my mother. A sheet laid over the outline of her lifeless body as they lifted her into the ambulance and shut the door behind her. The girls saw this, too, and I realized I could no longer protect them forever.

Dad was walking towards us, alongside a police officer. Another officer tried to calm the crowd and seemed to be asking them questions. Someone else had brought up our belongings from the sandy shore and left them on the pavement. Mom's hat crumpled underneath her bag. Dad looked defeated and tired and lifeless himself, as if he knew he was the reason this happened today. He saw us in the car but didn't come talk to us right away. Instead, he spoke with the officers for a while longer. One officer filled out paperwork on his clipboards as Dad answered questions. Somehow he showed no sign of emotion and every emotion at the same time.

It felt like their conversation was never going to end. My sisters sobbed and sniffled next to me, but I couldn't cry; I had to be strong. I stared out the window and waited for any sign of someone coming to let us out of that car. A mixture of sadness and rage rose up my body, making me feel flustered while my stomach tied itself deeper into knots. Finally, Dad started walking towards us with a policeman, who unlocked the door to let us all out.

"Come here, girls." He leaned down to embrace us as we poured out of the car, sweaty and breathless from the hot air, our hair sticking to the back of our necks. We hugged him. No other words needed to be spoken. We all knew our mother was not coming home with us that day. "C'mon...get in the car," he whispered as he let us go. "Time to go home."

The silence on the 40-minute car ride home was deafening. I could hear the pavement underneath the tires and the ticking sound of the car's blinker with every turn. My sisters' eyes were swollen from crying. Tears and snots ran down their faces as they wept. It was about six o'clock and my youngest sister, Connie, had somehow fallen asleep. I wondered if I would ever sleep again. How could I when every time I shut my eyes, I saw my mother's forlorn face? She was crying when I last saw her and I hadn't thought to save her before she plunged into the sea. I had to live with that. I stared at Dad's reflection in the rearview mirror as he drove us home. His eyes didn't move from the road once. His hair stuck to his forehead and his face was still white. There seemed to be no blood left in his body.

When we pulled into our driveway, our father put the car in park without turning it off completely. He looked back at us. His face was serious, but soft for the first time in a long time. "We are going to get through this together," he assured, "but it's not going to be easy. Cookie, I need you to take care of your sisters tonight. Go on, now, go to the house. I'll be home soon." We crawled out of the car and went inside. I watched as Dad drove away towards the main road. When we shut the door behind us, the four of us hugged so tightly that I don't remember breathing. We stayed like that for a long, long time. There were no tears left. All we had was each other.

Dad came home about an hour later. He was carrying a large brown paper bag and his breath already smelled like liquor. He sat on the couch and started drinking right from the bottle without speaking to any of us right away. The bottle gurgled as brown liquid drained into his open mouth. I led the girls into the bedroom. I didn't want them to see him like this, not even after the day we all had. He stopped us before we got to the hallway. "I'm so sorry about what happened today. I want you to go to bed and remember I love you more than anything." His words haunted me as I stared into his lifeless and worrisome eyes. Something told me that today was only the start of the bad days that were to come and, boy, was I right.

I was the first to wake up the next morning. My sisters were still sleeping and cuddled up to each other. I hoped that they were dreaming of anything except this real-life nightmare that was only about to get worse. I snuck out of the room and out of the living room. And that was when I found him. Slumped off of the couch, near the same spot where we left him the night before. On his back. Covered and choked in his vomit.

The next moments and hours were a blur. Calling for help. Waking up the elderly neighbor that lived upstairs. Waiting on the cops to show up, again. My sisters waking up and watching the scene unfold from the hallway. The same spot where our father told us he loved us, mere hours before.

Dad. Our biggest hero. Our only parent. Dead.

Dead.

Dead.

We were orphans. No parents. No relatives. No one to take care of us. No one but each other.

We never spoke of that day to anyone, ever. And, unfortunately, the days and weeks that followed were as bad—if not worse—as the day the accident happened.

2

This House Is Not Our Home

Dear Diary,

It's me, Frankie. I know I haven't written in a while but times have been hard. Being away from Cookie is the hardest part of being in this new house. I overheard these foster parents talking and it seems as if me, Dottie, and Connie will only be here for a short while longer until we get our permanent placement. Hopefully, that means the four of us will be together again soon. The way things have been going though, I won't hold my breath.

Yours,
Frankie

There is a part of me that thinks we are all going to wake up soon. Our hearts will be beating out of our chests as we look up at the ceiling from our beds. We will all realize these past few weeks have been a horrible, horrible nightmare. We would sit up and look at each other, disoriented and breathing heavy, and we'll realize our parents are still here and we are still to-gether. We'd smile and turn to our sides and fall back asleep, and wake up restful and ready for our family trip to the beach. We'd all sing together in the car on our way. Mom and Dad would be holding hands and Mom would be nestled close to Dad's shoulder. She'd look at him like he was the most perfect man in the world. He'd look back at us in the rearview mir-ror and then he'd glance down and kiss Mom's forehead. "Hi, sweetie," he'd say. "My little bride." She'd laugh at the senti-ment. He'd smile big and turn the radio up as he sang along with us to the music—some new Italian song none of us quite knew the words to. We would play and laugh at the beach all day and fall asleep on the way home. Dad would carry our youngest sisters while Frankie and I groggily walk beside him to get inside. We'd pile into the bed with our salty tangled hair. The heat from the sun would still feel warm against our skin as we dreamt of ocean waves. And bits of sand would trickle off the bed in the morning as we climbed out. That's how you know the day before was perfect in every way. We'd have our memories from the beach, our tight-knit family, and most im-portantly, we'd have each other.

Instead, our lives have been flipped upside down. We are living a real-life nightmare and the past few weeks have been hell. In fact, right at this very moment, I am laying in the bed of some kind strangers I met last week. They are fostering me. My sisters are living with Janet and Michael Thompson, another couple kind enough to take in Frankie, Dottie, and Connie temporarily. We have been in touch often, thankfully, but we are all terrified of what's to come.

Our parents were buried two weeks ago. We have no family here, so there were no traditional funeral services. With the help of a priest, the kind policemen put together a quick service at the chapel in the hospital right before we were able to say goodbye to them. It was so last minute, in fact, that we were wearing our ratty play clothes. Frankie's dirty shirt had a small hole on the sleeve, which caught my attention as she kneeled down to pray. Dad always got upset when we wore clothes that were torn. He once lost his temper at me for having a hole in the elbow of my uniform. "Why the hell would you disrespect your mother and father like that and show up to school looking like a hobo?" he yelled from the front seat of the car.

In their caskets, Dad wore the cashmere sweater that Mom bought for him last Christmas when things seemed good between them. Mom had on a dress we picked out—it was lavender and cheery, but seemed very out of place amongst the dark wooden tones of the chapel. Music crackled over the loudspeaker—it was distracting as I tried to listen to the priest's monotone reading of a Bible verse about heaven. I glanced over at Dottie who was staring straight ahead, the candles illuminating her face like a still oil portrait. One of the hardest moments of my life was watching my littlest sister cling onto Dad's body before the detective removed us from the room. I tried my best not to cry, but I lost it. I don't know how I will ever be the same again.

The weeks that followed were a blur, as you would imagine. We talked to detectives, lawyers, judges, social workers, and several foster parents. A week ago, we went home to gather some more belongings. I say home lightly because it's no longer our home, just a place where our stuff still is. We stuffed our lives into tiny canvas bags and said goodbye to our home where we spent our entire childhood. As I packed up my belongings, I looked out the window and saw Frankie sitting on the tire swing that Dad made us. She was looking at the ground and kicking her feet into the muddy puddle on the ground. She wasn't swinging; she was just sitting there. I wondered to myself if she'd ever smile again.

Frankie was the type of little girl who was reserved. Other people would look at her and think she was sad or depressed, but I don't think she was. She was a deep thinker and observant, much older and wiser than her years. She was stoic at times, often not showing emotion, even when something was bothering her. And the girl was as honorable as could be and was always on my side. I really liked her—not just as a sister, but as a friend, too.

When I was in eighth grade and Frankie was in seventh, I

would wait for her to get out of class so we could walk home together from school. I would often sit on the pavement walkway, reading a book as I so often did. This one particular day, her class bell rang and the kids started pouring out of her classroom. One of the boys—a red-headed kid with freckles and a huge, goofy grin—ran over to me and snatched the book out of my hand and threw it into the grass. Looking back, I think he had a crush on me or Frankie, but at the time, it seemed like he hated us. Without skipping a beat, Frankie waited behind him and clocked him right in the cheek when he turned around. I can still remember the way he cried and cried. I also remember how mad Mom was when Frankie got suspended from school because of that incident. Dad secretly gave her a high-five when Mom wasn't looking. It was then that I realized my little sister was brave and honorable and would always have my back.

So, when I saw how melancholy she looked on that tire swing, it hit me like a punch to the gut. I worried that my brave little sister would be broken. I knocked on the window to get her attention and she lifted her head. The smile I once knew was now a permanent frown. She jumped off the swing and came inside, first stopping to wipe her muddy shoes on the mat at the back door like Mom always instructed her to do. It didn't sink in yet for Frankie that this was no longer our home and our mother was no longer here to remind us to use our manners, like the way she always ensured we helped carry the elderly neighbor's groceries inside. She grabbed a few more items from her bureau and out of the closet. Dottie and Connie were hand selecting the toys and dolls they wanted to bring along, knowing they only had room for just a couple. Connie had been throwing fits lately, so I'm happy the two of them were able to divvy up some toys without fighting, including a soft gray bunny and a clown doll that always looked a bit scary to me even though Dottie loved it. After I packed some clothes and several books that were probably too heavy to bring but that I couldn't part with, I snuck into Mom and Dad's room.

Their usually bright and cozy room felt so cold to me that day. The bed was made with a white quilt and pale blue pillowcases. Their buttercream headboard that I adored because of its intricate carvings now looked chipped and cracked in the light of the day. One of the drawers on the matching dresser was ajar. Mom must've pulled her swimsuit out of it that fateful morning. She didn't have much but she had a few pieces of jewelry that were special to her. One was a pearl bracelet with little blue stones connecting the pearls. It was her "something blue" from her wedding day. Although she never wore it much after that day, she always cherished it. She once let me wear it when we were playing dress-up but made me promise I wouldn't tell my sisters I got to wear it. Even though the detectives already gave us Mom and Dad's wedding rings, I put a few of her precious pieces into my knapsack. What would happen to all their stuff? Would it vanish into thin air like they never existed?

I opened the drawer where she kept some of her most special silk scarves and doilies. I put one up to my nose as I closed my eyes and thought of her wide smile. Her perfume reminded me of fresh-cut roses from a plentiful garden—ones that were dewy from the afternoon rain. I'll never forget that smell. I put a few of the dainty, floral scarves into my bag as well, hoping I would be able to hold onto them forever. I noticed a few folded-up, handwritten notes at the bottom of the drawer. Although I didn't have time to read them, I took a few of those, too. I hoped they would hold the answers to some of the questions swirling in my mind. I looked up at their dresser and stuck in the mirror was a photo of the four of us that I had never seen before. We were sitting near the Christmas tree that was strung with big and bright colorful bulbs, covered in tinsel with wrapping paper lining the floor. Our pajamas all matched, even though Connie's looked a size too big. I tugged it off the mirror so I could take it, as well as a photo from Mom and Dad's wedding day. As I closed the door behind me, I thought about all the precious things our mother had saved over the years and how it would all be thrown away now that she was no longer here.

I walked into the girls' bedroom, and they were finishing up gathering their things. The detective put down the newspaper and sprung up to help us carry our stuff to his car. Our most prized possessions fit inside eight small canvas bags. The rest was all left behind. And this was the last time we would be inside the home where we grew up and lived together as a family of six.

I woke up to the sound of my foster mother announcing dinner was on the table. Although I have no appetite or desire to make small talk with adults who I barely know, I put on a smile and take a seat at the table. This couple is doing their best and taking a teenager into their home had to be a tough decision. I can't fault them for trying to help me out, so I help myself to the pot roast and fixings on the table. It feels good to have a warm meal in front of me for what feels like the first time in weeks. My mind wanders to my sisters for a moment. Are they sitting around the table about to have supper as well? I hope they are laughing again and their foster parents are treating them as well as mine are right now.

"How's the food, dear?" asked my foster mom, Annette. She was a tall, thin woman with olive skin and a long neck. Pearl studs dotted her ears and she wore a short-sleeved black top with a white collar and cropped cigarette pants. Annette had dark hair and short bangs, her hair tied back in a ponytail. My hair was also tied back in a white ribbon. She actually could have passed for my mother if no one knew better. I reached up to untie it and let my hair down as soon as I noticed the similarity.

"Oh, it's fine. Thank you for your hospitality," I responded by looking at her in the eye and then moved my gaze to Arnold. Annette and Arnold, my foster parents. I let out a little sigh and covered it up with a cough, hoping they hadn't noticed. Arnold was around 40 years old and sat extra straight in his chair. He had tortoise rimmed glasses and wore a plaid short-sleeved button-up shirt with khaki pants.

As we continued to eat, I wondered how I would feel about having Arnold and Annette as my new parents. Would they eventually want to take my three sisters in with them, too? Would they talk to me about the books I read and listen to stories about my favorite authors, like Louisa May Alcott or Edith Wharton? Would we go on family vacations together in the summer to Cape Cod and walk on the beach at dusk collecting sea glass together for the bowl on the dining room table? How would I feel having Arnold walk me down the aisle one day and give me away to the man I was to marry? Would I visit Annette at the nursing home when she was old and gray, and reminisce about my high school and college days? Well, none of that matters because I know this is only temporary until we find our new homes.

"Arnold is going to take you to visit your sisters tomorrow at the Thompsons' home. How does that sound?" Annette cheerfully asks as she folds her napkin onto her plate, interrupting my thoughts once again.

"Oh, great. Thank you," I respond. I push my chair back and stand up to start clearing the table since everyone has finished their meals. I realize I didn't eat much but my stomach was in knots like every other night since I lost my parents and have been apart from my sisters. I pile the dishes into the sink and start wrapping the leftover food up for the refrigerator. Annette follows me to the kitchen and tells me to go relax on the couch, but I'm happy to help. Arnold pulls his pipe out and lights it up while reading paperwork of some sort. The sweet but stale nicotine smell reminds me a little of our father; he didn't smoke pipes often but on special occasions or celebrations he would take it out to enjoy.

As promised, the next day Arnold drove me over to the Thompsons' house so I could see my sisters. When we pulled up, the door sprung open and my three sisters piled out of the house with smiles so genuine I almost forgot what was happening in our worlds. I jumped out of the car to meet them and we collided in the grass. We fell to the ground and hugged while we rolled around. I was laughing and couldn't hold the tears of joy back from my eyes. We held onto each other for what felt like hours until the shadows of Arnold and my sisters' foster parents fell over us and brought us back to reality. We brushed ourselves off and followed Janet and Michael, their foster parents, inside the house. Luckily, we were in the same town, not too far from each other and a quick car ride away.

When we went inside, the Thompsons had a beautiful spread of fresh fruit and homemade loaves of bread on the table served alongside lemonade in pretty pewter-rimmed glasses that looked like they were used for fancy dinner parties, not for us girls who were just rolling in the grass a few moments ago. Steam rose from the bread after Janet unfolded the black and white gingham towel it was wrapped in. Dottie's eyes lit up at the sight of food; she always loved to eat and help Mom bake. When Dottie was about 4 or 5, she stood up during supper and proudly exclaimed that she wanted to be a baker when she grew up. She put her finger above her lip to make a mustache and talked in a French accent for the rest of supper, which made Mom and Dad belly laugh. Almost five years later and she hasn't yet let go of her dream of baking in Paris.

As we gathered around the table, the four of us were so excited to see one another that we all talked at the same time. Others would have found that to be chaotic, but we all knew exactly what the others were saying. Frankie couldn't wait to tell me about the neighbor's dog, Rufus. She loved animals even though Mom would never let us get one of our own. Dottie was talking about the peach and berry pie she helped Janet make last night. Connie had a bit of a stutter but I always understood her. She was so excited to share the news about the secret door she found on the third floor of the Thompsons' house. She said her stuffed animals used that little room as their bedroom at night so they had their own space to sleep. I wanted to tell them about the street I lived on and the colorful flowers that lined the road, which reminded me of Mom. She loved bright, fresh-cut flowers—hydrangeas and daisies were her favorites. But I stopped myself from telling them because I didn't want to ruin the mood. I wished for someone to come along and put us in a little bubble where we could stay forever and ever.

As we continued to update each other on the seemingly insignificant days since we've been apart, Arnold cleared his throat to speak. "Girls, tomorrow is an important day. It's the day we've been talking about. Tomorrow you're going to find out where your permanent placements are. We are praying you'll all be together again, but we can't make any promises. We just know it's been a pleasure caring for you. Do any of you have any questions?"

"I do," volunteered Frankie. "Will our new parents love us or will they want to leave us like our real parents did?" The smiles wiped away from our faces and we jolted right back into the dark places we knew all too well.

3

Judgment Day

August 7, 1945

From: The Honorable Judge Edward Mason
Topic: Adoption Hearing
Re: The Cipriani Sisters
Identification Number: CT-1510009
Start Date of Respite Wardship: 06/25/1945
Close Date of Respite Wardship: 08/14/1945
Adoption Trial Date: 08/15/1945

To Whom This May Concern:

A Letter from the Honorable Judge Mason for the case involving the following four minor children: Loretta [Age 14], Frances [Age 13], Dorothy [Age 10], and Concetta [Age 9].

This letter is to confirm that the four minors listed above are a "ward of the court" as their parents were recently deceased on June 27th, 1945. The court has placed them in temporary foster care; however, the judge will determine their permanent placement on August 15th, 1945. Please note the preference is to keep the siblings together with adoptive parents.

Your presence is required at the date listed above.

Sincerely,
Judge Mason

I tossed and turned in bed as a memory from last Christmas flooded into my mind. I was standing in the middle of a department store with our mother and three sisters when I heard Connie's little voice. "Mom! Mom. Look at this doll. I NEED her!" Connie demanded as she stomped one of her tiny mary-janes on the shiny tiled floor.

"Not today, dear," Mom whispered while touching the sleeve of a black cashmere sweater with her gloved hand. "Put it down and come help Mommy." Connie placed the yellow-haired doll with freckles back on the shelf and shuffled over.

The five of us were in Howland-Hughes downtown and the store was buzzing. Men, women, and children filled up the spaces between the racks of clothes, toys, and home furnishings. A Christmas tree stood tall in the center of the room.

Delicate glass ornaments, twinkling lights, and mounds of tinsel covered each evergreen branch. Snowflake cut-outs dangled from the ceiling and twirled around as people floated throughout the store.

Everyone seemed happier than normal. It was the week after Thanksgiving and it seemed like everyone was in the holiday spirit. People anxiously awaited Christmas and the New Year, and all of the hope the holidays promised. After Dad left for work that morning, Mom told us we were going on a special shopping trip and had us put on our favorite dresses and patent leather shoes. Although we didn't have much money and didn't own many fancy clothes, Mom always encouraged us to dress to impress. I loved that about her; even the simplest outing seemed extravagant when we were with her. She was wearing a three-quarter sleeve wool coat with high gloves. Her dark hair was in an up-do straight out of a magazine. She looked like she could be a model for the clothes otherwise on the mannequins. She was in search of an extra special gift for Dad, something she thought he might keep for years to come.

Meanwhile, my sisters were prancing through the store, trying so hard not to run. They didn't want to get in trouble by Mom or the store worker who would shoot them an evil glance whenever they seemed to move too fast. They touched every toy in their paths—Frankie thumbed through some painting supplies, Dottie grew intrigued with the caroling figurines within the tiny Christmas village, and Connie clutched onto the baby doll with a realistic-looking bottle. They wished that they would find one of each wrapped under the Christmas tree in a few weeks.

"Now, *that's* a shirt," a man muttered to our mother as she continued to admire the sweater. "Is that a gift for your father?" He asked, raising his eyebrow as he brushed the hair back out of his forehead. Men admired our mother's effortless beauty wherever we went. She never seemed to pay much attention to it.

"It's for my husband," she quipped without looking him in the eye. "Their father." She motioned to the four of us as I shot Mom a grin. He nodded at us and swiftly turned around to walk away. Mom smiled at us and held the sweater up to her torso. "I think this is it!" she exclaimed. "Now...who wants to go downstairs to meet Santa and get some hot chocolate?"

The rest of the day was magical. Mom drove us around town, hot chocolates in hand, as we admired the decorations and lights strung across the city. Flurries fluttered through the sky and it felt like we were in our own transparent sphere made of glass. Our own snow globe enclosing a wintry, snowy scene with the five of us secured in the center. I always loved shaking snow globes and watching as the snow fell

through the water.

How I longed to be in that snow globe.

My eyes shot open and I stared at the ceiling, my body frozen. I slowly opened my eyes and I swore I saw remnants of snow sprinkling through the air. Sunlight peeked in through the drapes as I snapped out of it, remembering I was no longer in our cozy snow globe and instead in the spare bedroom of a stranger's home on the morning of the trial that would determine the fate of my sisters and me.

I crept out of bed and got dressed for the day, putting on the same dress and shoes that I wore for our most recent Christmas trip, without the coat and tights though, as it was summer. I didn't have any nice summer dresses, so this would have to do. There was no day more important than today to dress to impress. I hoped my sisters remembered Mom's words that morning, too, as they decided on what to wear. I combed my hair and put a barrette through it, ensuring my appearance was neat. I hoped that a neat appearance would lead to a nice family taking us in as their own.

When I went into the living room, I found Annette and Arnold sitting quietly on the sofa, waiting for me. Annette was fidgety, brushing her skirt down as if she was trying to iron out non-existent wrinkles, while Arnold had his hands neatly folded in his lap. They both sprung up to greet me, asking how I slept and how I was feeling, amongst a stream of other questions. I was barely listening, but nodded and smiled as I often did. Instead, I was thinking of my sisters and how they were feeling about the day that lay ahead. It was hard to be away from them, not being able to see their facial expressions and body language, since I knew their every gesture all too well. The way Connie crossed her arms and stomped one foot on the ground when she couldn't get the words out or how Frankie pursed her lips when she was trying not to cry. I knew when they were pleased or upset, when they were indignant or dejected, and mostly, when they needed their big sister. I'm sure they need me today, more than ever before.

As I stared out the window of the car on the way to the courthouse, a wave of grief rushed over me. It's true what they say, grief comes when you least expect it; however, it also comes on the way to find out your and your sisters' destiny. I thought about our father and how happy he was to open the sweater that Mom picked out for him that day at How-land-Hughes. They were getting along so well then—I think it's because he took a break from drinking and was so present with us. It didn't last long, but I think he tried. He held the sweater up in front of his face in admiration as Mom gushed over how soft and delicate the material was. He was buried in that sweater, too, and I know that was not the occasion Mom had in mind when picking it out for him. Dinner parties, celebrations, holidays, and birthdays, sure. But his own funeral just a few months later? No, that was not where she wanted him to wear his cashmere sweater. I wiped a single tear from my warm cheek and hoped for the best that day.

We arrived downtown in no time, cars starting to trickle into the parking lot. I wondered what others were there for that morning: a parking ticket? A divorce, perhaps? A murder...? No, I don't think a murderer would be at this courthouse. Maybe other orphaned children looking for their next set of parents? Sigh. I hope not for their sake. We parked near the car of my sisters' foster parents, so they must be inside already. Annette hooked her arm into mine as we walked towards the door. I caught a reflection of myself in the door as we approached it—I looked anything but cool, calm, and collected. I was hopeful that we would have a good outcome, but I was also realistic in knowing anything could happen today. And that didn't sit right with me. I noticed I was holding my breath as I entered through the door. My temples throbbed beneath my bangs and my stomach tightened, but I felt more at ease once I saw a glimpse of my sisters.

They spotted me right away and ran over as their little shoes clicked against the floor like in Howland-Hughes that day. Like me, they also had on their Christmas dresses but instead of tights, they wore white, ruffled ankle socks. I wondered if the judge would see us in our winter dresses in the middle of July and see us as we were: poor children of an alcoholic father and a depressed mother. I hoped this realization wouldn't change our outcomes, though, and would instead help him see how much we needed one another now more than ever. The girls latched onto me, their little hands wrapped around my bicep and waist at all angles. I grabbed Connie's flushed face in my hands. Her eyes were puffy and small, and I could tell she likely fell asleep while crying last night. It broke my heart to think about how scared they must have been.

We all took our seats in the lobby as we waited for someone to call our case. We weren't our chatty selves this morning. In fact, we simply sat in silence and held hands. Our two youngest sisters' feet dangled in the air since they couldn't quite touch the floor yet from their chairs. A short while later, a woman called our names and we all stood up. We followed our respective foster parents into a room that contained a shiny dark wood table with about a dozen chairs placed around it. I expected to be in a courtroom so I was relieved to be in a private room without everyone in the public watching our sad case. We tried to take seats far away from the head of the table where a cup of water and a notepad were sitting. Our foster parents gestured for us to move closer to the judge's eventual seat. We did as we were told, and they grabbed the chairs over from us. Arnold grabbed a few notebooks and pens to hand out to the other adults.

Just then, the judge walked in the room. He was wearing his black robe and carrying a stack of paperwork, his glasses sliding down his nose. He had white hair and blue eyes under his glasses. He smiled at me and then my sisters, greeting the room with a quick wave before taking his seat at the head of the table.

"Good morning, everyone. Loretta, Frances, Dorothy, and Concetta. Arnold and Annette. Michael and Janet. I am Judge Edward Mason. Thank you for coming today." He took his glasses off his face and placed them on the table in front of him. He stared at us and continued, "I am very sorry about your mother and father. It must be so hard for the four of you. Please know I am doing everything in my power to get you situated in your permanent homes. This has been an unusual case, as you know. Especially since you have no living relatives in this area or any of which we can get in contact with. It truly was just the six of you, huh?" I nodded back at him. "I am sorry again, girls."

My sisters nodded and I muttered a quiet "thank you" while my eyes dropped towards the table in front of me. It was just the six of us. No other family, just us. My heart sunk listening to him say his condolences, because it hasn't quite hit me yet that we were now on our own. The judge put his glasses back on and began reading the paper on top of his stack for what seemed like an hour. My heart fell deeper. Frankie grabbed my hand under the table and I looked at her. Her sweet smile prompted me to sit up straighter in my chair. I was the older sister and I needed to set an example for these girls.

"Okay, let's get started," he stated after a few more moments. "I wanted to thank the four of you for providing much-needed respite care for these children. I have some good news and I have some bad news for you." His gaze moved from the adults back to us. I closed my eyes. "I am going to start with the good news. We found permanent placements for all four of you in a record amount of time. Placing four children isn't an easy feat and your new parents were eager to take you in." He paused. I wondered if the word "parents" was singular, as in one set taking all four of us, or plural, as in multiple sets. "Your new parents are here today and are waiting in the other room so we can talk through some of the details first. Your adoption will take place tomorrow morning. Tonight you will go home with these lovely folks, pack your belongings, and get ready for another day back here. But I expect tomorrow will go by fast, and you'll be in your new homes in no time."

Homes. He said homes. My breathing quickened and my heart stopped this time for a moment. We weren't all getting adopted together.

"So, you heard me say 'homes' as in plural," he continued, looking my way. "This is where the bad news comes in. You are being split, but fortunately, each new set of parents are taking two of you in. Loretta and Frances, you will be adopted by Herman and Anna Taylor. Dorothy and Concetta, you will be adopted by Dominic and Mary Mancini." I felt Frankie squeeze my hand tighter. "They agreed to ensure that you continue your relationships as sisters into adulthood. Let's pause for a moment. Girls, are you understanding what I am saying to you?" He asked as he put down his paperwork.

We all nodded. Dottie looked puzzled. "So, we are getting split up, but we are still sisters and we are going to see each other every day, right?"

The judge couldn't help but smile at Dottie's assumption. "You are partially right, dear. You will be separated, yes. You and your youngest sister will be living in a house separate from your two older sisters. You will not be seeing each other every day, but they have agreed to do their best to support your continued relationship with one another."

Okay, now I was confused. They will do their best? We won't be seeing each other? What did this all mean? My head was spinning as I tried to wrap my head around his words.

"That brings up my next point. This is where your sisterly bond is going to come into play. It will be up to you to not let life's hardships and inconveniences get in the way of staying in touch and maintaining a lifelong relationship with one another. I want you to think about my words and their importance. You four have been inseparable since birth. I don't know you personally, but I know this to be true from looking at you. You've had a painful experience that you have gone through together. You are also lucky that you have found two sets of new parents willing to take you in and love you as their own. But it doesn't mean that life will always be easy." What exactly is he getting to, I asked myself as he started talking again. "I say this because although your new parents currently live in Waterbury, Connecticut, this isn't the case moving forward. Loretta and Frances, you will stay in Waterbury. Dorothy and Concetta, you will be here temporarily while your new parents prepare for their move to Tucson, Arizona."

"Arizona?!" I blurted out instinctively. "What do you mean, Arizona?" I felt like I couldn't get the proper words out. I was being rude to a judge, a person I did not know who was determining the fate of my three sisters and me. Annette cleared her throat and shifted in her chair. Arnold grabbed her arm.

"It's okay to be upset, Loretta. This is why I am highlighting these words that hold so much importance. You might not understand right now, but you will one day. As you get older... as life happens... as distance happens... it might seem harder and harder to keep in touch with your sisters more than halfway across the country. I do not want this to be the case for you four. You are strong girls and you have been through more in your young lives than I wish for someone of even my old age. I can't tell you what to do, but I can tell you that you will forever have a bond and you will forever be family. Prioritize talking to each other and writing to each other. Tell each other your hopes and dreams as you do today. Don't let the distance make you strangers. Hold onto the memories, of course, but always remember to create new ones together. Continue to put each other and your relationships first and you will come out stronger. You will live your lives individually but also as one. Do you understand the significance of what I am saying?"

My sisters nodded, looking at each other first and then back at the judge. Frankie was now squeezing my hand so hard I thought it was going to fall off. I'm sure I was squeezing hard, too. "I understand," I responded. "They are my sisters now and until the end, even if we don't live in the same home." I continued with confidence. His advice only partially sunk in that morning in that room. I only learned later in life the true significance of his words.

Connie was crying, but no sound was coming out. She wiped her tears away and looked at me. She was too little to be going through something like this. Her whole world was being ripped apart, her parents and now her sisters? How could she—or any of us, for that matter—come out unscathed?

Judge Mason motioned for a woman, his clerk, to get the parents. A moment later, they walked into the room in a single file. I wasn't sure who was who yet. The first man and woman that walked in were older and seemed more established than the other two. They sat down at the other end of the table and filled the extra chairs. The judge stood up and walked towards them. "Loretta, Frances, these are your new adopted parents, Anna and Herman." He placed his hands on their shoulders and they smiled at us with soft eyes. We smiled back. "I want you to know that I also have a special connection to Anna. She is my very own younger sister. When she read this case in the newspaper, she wanted to help. She felt confident that she can provide the utmost care for the two of you girls."

"It's nice to meet you, girls. We are sorry about your parents." Anna sounded sincere as she looked our way. Although she was older than our parents, her eyes looked young and soft. The blouse she was wearing looked brand new, like she bought it specifically for this occasion. I noticed how tiny her wrists were under her heavy gold bracelet. Anna was kind and fair like the judge but appeared as if she didn't take much nonsense. Frankie and I would learn that to be true.

"It's nice to meet you, too," Frankie replied. I nodded, still in shock. I don't think the other girls have grasped that we won't be waking up in the same or neighboring bedrooms ever again.

"Dorothy and Concetta, I'd like you to meet Mary and Dominic, your new parents." The girls stared at them, trying to figure them out, presumably. Mary was around our mother's age. She was quite thin and plain, but had a wholesome look to her. She looked like a school teacher I once had. The slight hunch in her back told me she worked on her feet often. Dominic was sturdy—not fat, but built—with deep brown serious eyes and slicked black hair. There was a touch of gray on his temples, indicating he may have been a little older than Mary. He had calluses on his hands. He reminded me of Dad.

"Hello," Dottie whimpered. "Thank you for taking us," she

finished. Mary and Dominic glanced at each other and then smiled at the girls. The girls would later find out that Mary couldn't have children but wanted nothing more than to provide a home for them.

The fourteen of us—my sisters and I, our former foster parents, our new parents, the judge, and his clerk—all sat in the room in silence for the minutes that followed. There wasn't much more to say. The clerk then stood up and broke the silence. She presented paperwork to the adults in the room and they talked amongst themselves. Judge Mason excused himself and mentioned he would see us bright and early tomorrow. My sisters and I stared straight ahead, none of us wanting to look at the other. But, we were still holding hands under the table as we tried to process the events of the day. I internalized the words from the judge. Although I didn't fully understand him, I knew enough to know his advice was worth remembering.

I broke my stare to look down at my wintry dress. It felt silly to me now, especially since my sisters would no longer need heavy dresses or coats in Arizona. Were there Christmas trees there? Or was it barren with cacti being the only green plant in sight? Would we ever be inside our sister snow globe again? Would we remain in each others' thoughts while being over 2,000 miles away from one another? I didn't know the answers to these questions, but I did know that life felt pretty unfair right about now.

4

Teddy Bear Toss

To Whom This May Concern:

I am writing this letter to express an interest in the adoption of the two eldest daughters of the Cipriani family. It is my understanding that their parents passed away recently from tragic events. My husband, Herman, and I read of this case in the local paper. We are in a position to offer a home to the children. However, due to our ages and other various reasons, we are unable to take in all four children.

Herman and I were never able to have children of our own due to medical conditions. After many years in a childless home, we have determined that we can provide many opportunities for these girls. We value education and extracurricular activities that will enrich their teenage years.

We would be very gracious to welcome these children into our home and expand our family through adoption.

Sincerely,
Anna E. Taylor

The adoption proceedings went as expected, and at about 2 p.m., we had two new sets of parents. Frankie and I had Anna and Herman, while Dottie and Connie had Mary and Dominic.

The four of us didn't get to see much of each other all day. We answered questions apart and only came together for a quick lunch that the court brought in for us. But even at lunch, we weren't ourselves. We didn't talk much. We didn't interact. We didn't even laugh. My bones felt heavy in my body whenever I attempted to move.

That morning, various adults whose names I could not remember shuffled me into and out of tiny rooms. Sometimes I would catch glimpses of my sisters as we passed each other in the hall. At one point, I saw Connie throw a fit as a man asked her to follow him and another woman into the boardroom we all sat in yesterday. The same room where Judge Mason broke the harrowing news to us. Knowing she was going into that room must have struck a chord with her, and she refused. The man and woman didn't push the issue and instead left her in the hallway to cool down. She slid her body down the wall to the floor and let out her loudest cry, which echoed as far as the ear could hear. I asked the woman escorting me to my next location if I could go see her for a moment, and she obliged.

As I jogged the long hallway towards Connie, I recalled a memory from our childhoods. Connie was a colicky baby and Mom would sometimes have a hard time soothing her. We tried to help. Frankie made funny faces at her and I tried rocking her cradle to get her to fall asleep. But on this particular day, nothing was working. Mom sobbed all afternoon, wiping Connie's tears with one hand and patting her back with the other as she paced the living room. "Concetta, please, *please* stop," she pleaded. Frankie, Dottie, and I were still young but old enough to feel the stress of the situation. We weren't sure if something was wrong with the baby or when she would ever stop crying. It scared me. Connie's face was almost blue from screaming and her tiny fists trembled as she continued to cry into the night. Mom ran out of options. She told me to run upstairs to ask the neighbor if she could borrow her car to go to the hospital since Dad wasn't home yet.

As I began sprinting up the stairs, the door behind me shot open, and Dad walked through the door. He was drinking, which was an activity I didn't recognize at the time, of course. Now, looking back, I knew exactly what he was doing. His disheveled hair blew in the wind as he slammed the door behind him. I stopped in my tracks and ran back down to hug him. He smelled sour, but I was glad he was home. I took his hand to lead him into the house so he could help Mom, as she was at her wit's end.

Dad walked into the living room. Mom was sobbing, the baby was screaming, and my other sisters were over-tired and on the verge of tears as well. He held his arms out towards Connie and grinned, motioning for her to come into his arms.

In an instant, she stopped crying and caught her breath. In one quick motion, she transferred herself into Dad's arms. She rested her head against his chest as he rocked back and forth, holding the back of her tiny head while starting to hum with his eyes closed. Connie's eyes started to close, as well, and soon she was fast asleep on his chest. My sisters and I watched in awe, wondering if he was a magician. Meanwhile, Mom sat on the arm of the chair, relieved that she could finally hear her thoughts once again.

Meanwhile, I caught up to Connie in the hallway. I crouched down next to her and wiped the tears that fell from her cheek. She looked into my eyes and let out a whimper, but stopped crying, which was a relief. I stared back at her and I knew with certainty that the agony she was feeling was the same pain I was going through. I would wager that Frankie and Dottie felt the same aching heartbreak, too.

Connie sat up and pushed herself off the ground to stand. She leaned against the wall but her gaze didn't leave the floor. Partially because her behavior was embarrassing, but mostly because the life that she grew so accustomed to has changed in a matter of days. I put my arm around her shoulder and we walked to the bathroom so Connie could splash some water on her face. The scratchy brown paper towels she dried her face with made her blotchy and red. I looked at myself in the mirror and was foolish to assume I looked any better. My bangs luckily almost covered my sallow and sunken eyes. My skin looked colorless in the dreadful fluorescent bathroom lighting. Did we somehow skip right by our youth and straight into adulthood, where responsibilities stacked up onto us like books on a shelf? Our eyes met in the dirty mirror and it became clear that our parents' deaths and the aftermath of it all already began to take a toll on us.

After the adoption proceedings wrapped up, our new parents drove us to our respective foster homes to gather our belongings. This was a task we were becoming too accustomed to it seemed. Anna and Herman had to make two stops since Frankie and I hadn't been living together. The first stop was to the house in which I was leaving, and then to Frankie's house where our other sisters were. Our new parents, Anna and Herman, seemed genuine. They looked happy to have us. My first impression of them changed in our first car ride together. At first, I thought them to be super serious and a bit somber, but their conversation made me feel at ease.

Herman started, "Girls, I know it's been a tough few days. Hell, it's been the worst few weeks of your lives. I want you to know that you girls are tough cookies and your strength shines through you. But I also want you to know that we don't expect you to be strong all the time. We know you're going to be upset—with us, with each other, with yourselves, with the world—and we understand. Well, we don't quite understand but we promise to be patient with you and we hope you give us a chance." Frankie continued to stare out the window as I observed Herman and Anna's body language. Her hand rested on his forearm as he drove and she watched his face through her glasses and nodded in agreement as he spoke. They seemed to be married for a long time. I appreciated that he was direct with us versus pretending everything was fine.

Anna waited a few moments and continued. "I think you girls are so brave. You drove off in a car with two people—two strangers—for crying out loud." That made me chuckle, and the two of them laughed in the front seat as well. Not Frankie though; she wasn't ready to laugh, and I can't blame her for that. "I'm serious, though," she pleaded as she shifted in her seat to turn and face us. "Take whatever time you need. We'll be here when you're ready." She turned back around and we sat in silence for a few more minutes until we arrived at Annette and Arnold's home.

They opened the door to greet us when we arrived. They looked doleful to me as they stood in the doorway waving to us. I never asked why Annette and Arnold didn't want to keep me or us; I guess I didn't want to know the answer. Anna and Herman made small talk with Annette and Arnold while I began the familiar process of shoving my belongings into bags. Frankie sat on my bed and watched while I cleaned out yet another room. She grabbed a book off my nightstand and flipped through the pages, seemingly uninterested in the content of the book. She was hoping instead to somehow ease her mix of boredom and anxiety. I leaned backward while I was sliding the items on top of my bureau into a box so I could hear the adults a little better. I vaguely made out Annette telling Anna about me—quiet, good manners, helpful around the house, daydreamer, and nose in a book. I guess that's a good summary of me if you didn't quite know me all too well. I would add protective to a fault, and the most innate ability to know when something is amiss with my family. My mind drifted to our mother and how I knew something was wrong with her over the past few months. I only wish I had the guts to tell her and, most importantly, save her.

I finished packing quickly, seeing as how I never fully settled into Annette and Arnold's house. It wasn't any fault of theirs, but I knew the living situation would be short-lived. We gathered in the parlor for a few minutes after Herman carried my belongings to the car. Annette was kind enough to say that I was welcome in their house whenever, without notice. We spoke for a few more minutes and said our goodbyes. Annette and Arnold hugged me at the same time, and Arnold gave me a quick kiss on the top of my head. I stayed in their embrace for a few seconds longer than I should have, relishing in their touch. It made me recognize that I've been without the hugs and embraces from my actual parents for far too long now.

We got back in the car to head to the Thompsons' house to

collect Frankie's stuff. It was quiet in the car on the ride over until Herman put on some faint music as background noise. Anna cleared her throat once as if she was going to start speaking, but Herman put his hand on hers and shook his head to say 'no' to her. I think the silence did us good after a brutal few days of questions and interviews and hellos and goodbyes.

Soon enough, we arrived at the Thompsons' house. I spotted a few canvas bags packed to the brim and lying on the front porch. Michael swung the screen door open with his foot as he carried a few more piles outside. He was holding some paperwork in his mouth, too. He raised his eyebrows to acknowledge us since he couldn't speak without the risk of dropping the papers. He put down the items and removed the papers from his mouth. "Come on in," he waved. "Frankie, I think your sisters could use your help in there."

I followed Frankie inside and to the bedroom they all shared. Frankie stepped in to help the girls gather their things and calm their nerves. It was eye-opening to see her in what was usually my role as the biggest sister. I was so proud of her and my other sisters for being so resilient. Frankie reminded the girls to get their teddy bears out of the room on the third floor, since she knew they liked to play up there. Dottie and Connie skipped up the stairs in tandem to grab their toys. They then rolled them down to me where I was standing at the bottom, ready to catch whatever they threw my way.

As Connie tossed the first matted bear down the steep staircase, my mind wandered. I realized this would most likely be one of the last childhood memories I had in-person with my sisters. It was hard to think about missing the big milestones of their teenage years. After Connie and Dottie move to Arizona, Frankie and I won't see them whenever we want. We will hear their voices, maybe, and we will see their words, hopefully, but we will only see their faces in our dreams and vice versa. I caught the bear and threw it down the hallway and into the bag Dottie was holding open for me. It was like an assembly line. Connie tossed one bear after the other down the stairs as I caught them and swooshed them into Dottie's bag. They were all different shades of brown, from the lightest tan to the deepest chocolate; there was even one pink bear in the mix that Connie kept beside her at the top of the stairs. Frankie finished cleaning and came to help us with the toys and, soon enough, noticed our assembly-line-turned-game. She wanted in on the fun. Frankie sprinted halfway up the stairs and intercepted the next bear and spiked it to me. She laughed at first, but as the last bear was thrown, she caught it and gripped onto it, holding it against her chest. She stared at Connie and then over her shoulder at me. She wasn't smiling anymore and a wave of confusion washed over me.

"Throw the bear, Frankie!" I playfully yelled, putting my hands around my mouth like a bullhorn.

"No." She snapped. Her words felt like a dagger.

"Come on, Fran, what's going on?" Connie bellowed from

the top stair, her hair falling into her face as she looked down at us.

"I don't want to play anymore. What's the point, anyway? We're not going to be together. We're not friends. We're not even really sisters anymore. Why are we doing this? Are we pretending this isn't the last time we'll all be together?" Her words hit me with the intensity and speed of a shiny bullet moving through the air.

"Frankie, stop," I demanded, as she cut me off and continued.

"Well? It's true, isn't it? Our lives as we know them are over. Connie... Dottie... we probably won't see you guys again, right? I don't even know where Tuuuuu-san Arizona is!" She enunciated the word "Tucson" as if it were a fictional town we made up when we were playing school many years ago.

Dottie placed the bag on the ground and traipsed over to me. She looked up at Frankie and I could see tears forming in her eyes. "Why are you making this harder?" she demanded, trying not to yell. "Judge Mason warned us about this and told us we have to be strong. You're the strongest person I know. You can't give up before the hard part even starts. It's not fair, Frankie."

Dottie started walking up the stairs and extended her arm to Frankie to grab her hand. Frankie hesitated for a moment but then uncrossed her arms and gave Dottie her hand. They walked back down the stairs and Dottie pulled me into their embrace. Connie trotted down the stairs and joined us. We all felt Frankie's frustration and pain. It's like we were the candles on top of a pathetic birthday cake, the wax melting and pooling together on the ground. We were one person in this moment as we embraced and swayed back and forth with tears cascading down our faces and onto each other's shoulders.

After a few moments, a pan crashed to the ground in the kitchen, which jolted us back to reality. We started to loosen our grips on one another. I looked around the room at each other and wiped my sisters' tears away. We hoped to collect ourselves before any one of our foster parents or new adoptive parents walked in on us.

"I'm sorry," Frankie apologized after letting out a loud sigh. We stood there in silence: no more words needed to be spoken. I hoped, for our sakes, that Frankie's concerns weren't valid and that we would continue being each other's best friends and support systems. Even from over 2,000 miles away. I read enough books to know, however, that life wasn't always a fairytale and 2,000 miles might as well have been to Mars and back. We were four penniless kids with no clue how this whole situation could ever possibly work in our favor.

The girls finished packing up their things and straightening up their rooms as I looked on. Our new parents grew anxious as they waited for us, ready to bring us to our new homes to get settled in. Dottie and Connie would remain in Connecticut for another month or so before making the trek to Arizona with their new parents. And Frankie and I would stay in the same town we grew up in with our new parents. It was comforting to know they would be close by for the next few weeks. This would allow us some time to get used to not seeing each other without the large distance between us.

It was dark and cool when we walked out of the Thompsons' house to go our separate ways. With nothing left to say, we each gave one another a kiss on the cheek and then reunited for one more group hug. Although this time, it felt so final. We said our goodbyes and got in the backseats of our new parents' cars: Frankie and I in one car, and Connie and Dottie in the other. Our worlds changed day-by-day after our parents died, but today stung particularly hard. We watched as our two sisters turned around to wave out of the rear window of the car in front of us. Dottie and Connie's tiny pink faces faded into the darkness as their car pulled away from the bright light of our headlights.

5

Wildflowers

Dear Diary,

I am going to start writing more, I promise. I know I always say that but I mean it this time. I need to get used to writing letters. That's how I will stay in touch with Cookie and Frankie. I hope they like my letters. The nice judge told us that we have to make an effort to stay in touch. Maybe I'll write them a letter every week! Is that too many letters?

We are leaving Connecticut in about a month. I hope I have the chance to say goodbye to some of my friends from school. I don't know what Arizona is like, but I heard it's hot, dry heat [whatever that means]. I wonder if it has all the same toy stores as Connecticut. Is the grass as green as it is here? Are there lakes or ponds where we can look for frogs? Will we have to wear cowboy boots to school? I hope the bugs aren't bigger!

I'm going to miss my sisters so much. Dottie and I cried

yesterday but I told her we have to be strong like Cookie.

She's a "Tough Cookie." Get it?
Love,
Connie

Herman put his signal on and turned into a steep driveway. There was a black metal gate at the entrance that was swung open. As we drove up the hill, Anna and Herman's home started to emerge from the horizon. It was a vast white house with stately pillars and black shutters. A pair of rocking chairs sat on the front porch and moved in the breeze. I looked over at Frankie, whose mouth was open as she took it all in. Her eyes widened as she clasped her hands together nervously in her lap, almost like she was trying to contain a pair of mice in a cage. She was in awe of her surroundings, and so was I.

Herman parked the car and we all got out, leaving our bags in the trunk for the meantime. The smell of fresh flowers wafted into my nose the moment I stepped outside. Mom loved flowers and always had them in a clear vase on the counter near the kitchen window. The distinct scent of roses, lilies, and lavender brought her into the moment with me. The smell of hydrangeas—Mom's favorite—lingered in the air. Looking around, there were flowers, bushes, and trees everywhere I turned. The yard was so private that I couldn't see another home. To the left of the house was a wooden fence with a prodigious and brilliant garden peeking through. The wildflowers were vibrant shades of pink, purple, and blue. The textured grass, cornflowers, poppies, and daisies looked wild and untamed as they danced in the summer wind. I found myself excited to see the rest of the home. Frankie and I weren't used to such grandeur, and I had to nudge her to close her mouth as it was open in amazement.

Anna walked us inside as Herman started to gather our belongings. We tiptoed into the foyer as if it was a library, not a home at which we were now living. A gold mirror sat on top of the burgundy striped wallpaper. I caught a glimpse of my reflection, wondering who the outsider was, and how she would ever belong here. I spun around and admired the artwork hung all around. I stopped when I saw the room to my right, filled to the brim with books and mahogany furniture. Resting against the bookshelves was a tall ladder used to reach the highest shelf. There must have been hundreds of books in that room. I hoped that Anna and Herman would allow me to go in there and explore one day.

Anna led us up the stairway so we could see our new bedrooms. Frankie and I used to share a room and I wasn't sure how I felt about not sharing a space with her in our new home. Anna opened the door to Frankie's room first. It looked like it came out of a showroom in a department store. The carpet felt like a soft pillow under my feet. In front of us was a white canopy bed with blue satin bedding, the same shade as the sky in the middle of summer. On either side of the bed sat two nightstands complete with lamps with little fawns painted on them. Next to the lamps were a few trinkets: a pink pony and fresh-cut flowers on one nightstand and a shiny silver block with ABCs etched on the sides on the other.

On the other side of the room, a cozy chair sat near the window overlooking the gardens in the back of the house. There was a giant wooden dollhouse on the floor with all the furnishings inside. Although Frankie was a bit too old for a dollhouse, I knew she'd enjoy it because she loved designing doll clothes. She was always doodling clothing designs and dressing her dolls in clothes that she made herself. A brown leather trunk with a weathered exterior sat next to the dollhouse. Frankie flipped up the lid, and to her amazement, dolls, toys, and games were overflowing inside. There were some never-opened puzzles of a garden and a reflective lake. How did they know that Monopoly and Scrabble were our favorite games? Sturdy furniture lined the other bedroom walls and brand new clothes peeked out from behind the open closet door. A note laid on her bureau that read: "Welcome home, darling. We are thrilled to have you here. XOXO, Anna and Herman".

As Frankie was relishing in her new room, Anna led me next door to see mine. The walls glowed from the sun reflecting on the pale yellow paint, and it immediately gave me energy. I had a canopy bed like Frankie's, but with a yellow and pink floral bedspread and lots of throw pillows. My room didn't have toys but, instead, books lined the walls. They were begging to be read on the welcoming window seat with views of the wildflowers. A small stained-glass kite was suctioned to the window and caught the light. I could hardly believe this was mine. A note was sitting on my window seat as well with similar words: "We hope you are comfortable in your new room, Loretta (A.K.A. Cookie). We can't wait to hear all about these books. XOXO, Anna and Herman".

I sat on the window seat, which was cozy and warm like a daybed. Our parents' faces flashed across my mind. On one hand, they would be happy to see that we ended up in a glamorous home with kind people taking care of us. But I couldn't help but feel ashamed that Frankie and I were feeling joyous despite the fact that this means that our family was broken. Our parents aren't here to play in the dollhouse with Frankie or read novels out loud with me. Our sisters are about to start new lives out west. I would trade the wildflowers, plush carpet, and calming wall colors to be back in our tiny apartment in a multi-family home with my actual family.

Frankie skipped into my room with a new doll in tow, admiring my room and checking out every single detail. She plopped herself on the bed with her arms and legs spread out like a starfish, causing a few pillows to spill onto the floor. Seeing her smile after weeks and weeks of hard moments was all I needed to snap the negative thoughts out of my mind. I hoped that no matter where my sisters were, that they were comfortable and starting to smile again, too.

Dottie and Connie's new home—albeit temporary, as they were soon to move to Arizona—was a stark comparison to ours. They pulled into the short driveway of a three or four-family home on a crowded street. Kids ran and played every which way, and cars were parallel parked on both sides of the street as far as the eye could see. They trekked up the stairs to the third floor, where Mary and Dominic's apartment was. Mary led the way while Dominic followed behind with the belongings.

The air inside of the apartment felt thick and heavy. Mary must've felt it too because she immediately turned on the fan in the family room when they walked inside. Everything appeared dingy and unkempt, and there were moving boxes lining the walls. Mary flipped on some lamps and opened the curtains, which brought some much-needed light into the apartment. She showed the girls their room so they could settle in, as Dominic dropped their bags in the hallway. The bedroom was simple—two twin beds with white quilts and one shared nightstand and bureau. It was like their room at Mom and Dad's house, without the warmth and coziness.

Dottie looked out the window to see another house closely bordering their backyard. A clothesline that held towels and sheets was strung across the yard and swayed in the breeze. She saw a younger boy and girl playing catch in the next yard; they looked like siblings. Connie joined her in the window and they both watched the children for a few minutes as they laughed and played. Dottie wondered if it would be worth it to make friends with their new neighbors since they were leaving town soon. She hoped the kids in Arizona were friendly.

About an hour later, after the girls had unpacked, Mary called them into the kitchen for dinner. Dominic was already sitting at the table, so Dottie and Connie sat on either side of him. Dust particles floated in the air of the dingy room. Mary sat down and started serving a meal of meatloaf, mashed potatoes, and green beans. Judging by her facial expression, Dottie didn't seem thrilled with the meal choice, but she tried to be polite like I taught her before we parted ways. Connie shot her a look and they both took a few bites of food to appease their new parents.

Dominic cleared his throat. "Girls, I want you to know there are a few rules in this house and some things we expect of you," he started. "Dom-" Mary said to try to interrupt, but he kept going. "We are a working family and we expect you to contribute. Mary made up a nice bedroom for you and prepared this fine meal. Helping Mary—um, Mom—clean and keep the house in order is something you girls will do both here and in Arizona when we get there. Understood?" His tone was sharp. He pointed his finger towards them and furrowed his brow until his eyes were barely visible. Mary stared down at the table, embarrassed. Her thin fingers trembled as she tugged on her wedding ring. She pushed her plate away from her before even taking a bite of food.

The girls gulped and the color drained from their faces. They realized they were no longer in the comfort of their own home with their parents and protective older sisters. "Yes," they both nodded in agreement. They locked eyes. Connie wanted so badly to cry, but she knew it would not go over well with Dominic so she remained stoic. They ate the rest of the meal in silence, minus the sound of Dottie pushing around the food with her fork in an attempt to make it look like she made a dent in it. "And don't think you're gonna leave this table without finishing your food," Dom said before standing up and walking out of the room. Mary followed behind him and the girls could hear them whispering in the next room.

There were no warm "welcome" notes left on a cozy new day bed.

There were no new clothes hanging in the closet. No unread books that smelled like fresh paper. No shiny new rooms with canopy beds.

Worst of all, there was no remorse for two young girls who lost their parents, their other sisters, and the lives they left behind.

But this was their new home and Mary and Dominic were their new parents, so complying was their only option. The girls wondered how Frankie and I were faring at our new home. They hoped they would get to hug us again soon.

Frankie was exploring her new dollhouse when I walked by her room. Anna noticed me admiring the flowers outside and asked if I wanted to take a walk with her in the garden so I obliged. We walked through the house to the three-season porch in a screened enclosure, which had a door to the back yard. The warmth of the sun hit my body as I walked outside and I was once again enveloped in floral smells all around me. "Over here is the vegetable garden," Anna said as she pointed towards the lush and leafy area to the right of where we were standing. It was surrounded by wire fencing so animals couldn't get to it. "I tend to the garden. I've watched it grow and grow, and it's where I find I'm most relaxed. Have you ever gardened before?" she asked me.

"No, not at home. But we did have a little garden at school that I helped with a few times," I answered. As we walked closer to the vegetable garden, the faint scent of herbs filled the air. I bent down to get closer to read the little signs in the soil. There were tomatoes, basil, cucumbers, and root vegetables like carrots, beets, and turnips. I followed Anna through the walkways as I brushed my fingertips over the leaves. It was so meticulously maintained.

"Well, you can help me pick some of the vegetables to-morrow morning if you'd like, dear?" she said. I nodded as my face lit up with eager anticipation. I loved spending time outdoors and wanted to embrace my new home, even though everything still stung deep down inside. I looked behind the garden to see a hammock hanging between the trees. "You could read there, you know? It's a great place to unwind." I watched Anna as she glided through the yard. She was a tall, thin woman. Sophisticated. Her hair fell to her shoulders and was gray and beautiful. She had small round glasses over her soft brown eyes. She was wearing a collared shirt with a sweat-er tied around her shoulders. A diamond sparkled on her fin-ger like the ones I've seen in the velvet-lined jewelry cases at G. Fox.

We strolled across the yard towards the flowers. The roses were in full blossom, and the coral geraniums were abundant and bright. Besides the manicured gardens, there were patch-es of wildflowers that looked like they were straight out of a Monet painting. "It's so beautiful here." I blurted out, mean-ing to say it to myself.

"Thank you, dear," Anna said with a gentle smile. Just then, we heard a loud knock on the upstairs window. We looked up and Frankie was waving to us with a toothy grin. Anna put her arm around my shoulder and we both waved back at her.

She seemed happy, which caused a wave of relief to wash over me. I inhaled a big breath of fresh air and let it out as the wildflowers danced around us in the soft summer breeze.

6

Nothing is Forever

Dear Diary,

It's been a few weeks since we moved into our new home. Frankie and I are getting more and more used to our new surroundings every day. She can't seem to get her head out of the dollhouse. When she isn't in the dollhouse, she's next to the dollhouse drawing clothes for her new dolls. Typical Frankie, haha! Herman brought home a huge pad of paper from his office that she's filling up with designs. Meanwhile, I've been reading. Are you surprised? I found some medical books in our library that have been fascinating and a good break from my regular fiction books——Jane Eyre has become a recent favorite of mine. There are about a thousand books in that room, maybe more. I lost track last time I tried to count them.

We are starting school in a few days. We met up with Dottie and Connie at a park last week. They seemed sad and a little out of sorts [aren't we all though?] but seeing us lifted their spirits. Their father didn't even get out of the car to talk to us. Mary, their mother, did sit with us but she's pretty quiet. Compared to us four, everyone is quiet, though. We are seeing the girls one more time tomorrow before they leave. They are coming over for a tea party that Anna organized——I think they'll love it.

Yours,
Cookie

Although I'm typically an early bird, I stayed up late reading last night and fell asleep on the window bench. I woke up to the not-so-quiet sounds of Frankie tiptoeing into my room. She was trying her best not to wake me, but I'm pretty sure everyone on the whole block could've heard her coming! I opened one eye and then the other and saw her climb into my bed that was still made from the day before. I sat up and stretched, and without saying a word, I joined Frankie in my bed.

"I couldn't sleep anymore. Dottie and Connie are coming over today," she whispered. "I spent the morning drawing them a nice picture to hang on their walls in Arizona."

"That's nice, Frankie," I whispered back. "They'll like that." She stared at me for another minute or so without saying a word, but I sat up and continued in my regular voice. "Frankie, do you think Dottie and Connie are happy where they are? Happy in their new home with their new parents? I don't mean happy-happy, because we are missing a huge part of us without our parents. And we miss our sisters more than anything. But Anna and Herman are trying so hard to make us feel at home. They genuinely like us being here, I think. And they give us space but they are there for us when we need them. Do you think Dottie and Connie have that same support?"

Frankie's face looked puzzled. I don't think an early morning philosophical conversation was what she had in mind when she decided to hop into my bed. "Uh, I dunno, Cookie. Now you got me all worried about them," she said.

"No, no. I didn't mean for you to worry," I explained. "We should make sure we ask them how they are today. Like really how they're doing. They're our sisters. Nothing is forever... except us. I truly believe that, Frankie." She shrugged and then nodded her head, pulling the covers up to her chin and letting out a heavy sigh. I worried about how this was going to affect the girls in the future. Heck, I worried how it would affect me, too.

Frankie fell back to sleep for a little while as I laid in bed, staring at the ceiling. Judge Mason's words echoed in my head: Don't let the distance make you strangers. Hold onto the memories, of course, but always remember to create new ones together. How many memories can we make together when we were so far apart? I was looking forward to so many life events: dating and hanging out with our friends in high school, going to college, seeing the world, getting married, and having families. Would so many of our new memories be dampened by the fact that a few key people who completed our souls were missing? Would we have the means and the desire to get together, even when life got hard, as Judge Mason assured us it would?

Anna has been dropping hints that we should begin writing letters. She reiterated how important it would be to stay in touch. As Frankie slept beside me, I pulled a piece of paper and a pen off my nightstand to compose my first long-distance letter. I wanted to somehow repeat Judge Mason's words—but in my own way—to not overwhelm the girls. I needed to tell them how important they are to me, and how I'm always here when they need me. The pen moved fast across the paper as I penned my thoughts and feelings on the matter. Anna tapped on my door before opening it. She looked relieved that Frankie was laying beside me. "Good morning, darlings," she said. "Come down and eat breakfast. We have a fun day ahead of us! Cookie, can you help me gather some tomatoes and cucumbers from the garden after breakfast?"

"Yes, for sure," I replied. We got out of bed and Frankie was more groggy than she even was earlier. We headed downstairs for breakfast and to start getting ready for the day ahead of us.

When we got downstairs, we saw that Herman had picked up some muffins for us. He put the newspaper down when he heard us coming. "Mornin', girls!" he exclaimed. Over the last few weeks, I learned that Herman golfed on the weekend and today was no exception. He ate breakfast with us, which consisted of the warmed-up muffins he got us and fresh fruit, and then he buzzed out the door. But first, he made it a point to wish us well for our tea party later today with our sisters.

After breakfast, Frankie went upstairs to continue her sketch for the girls. I slipped on my rubber boots and went outside, basket in tow, to collect some vegetables for our party. Being in the garden calmed me and awakened my senses—the smells, the vibrant colors, the smooth touch of the vegetables. I picked a few cucumbers and some tomatoes off the vine and wiped them with the bottom of my nightgown for a quick polish before putting them in the basket.

When I went back inside, Anna had cleared the table from breakfast. She was whipping up blueberry scones with the KitchenAid Mixer that was usually tucked away in the corner of the kitchen counter. She asked me to guard the mixer while she cut cucumbers and assembled cute little sandwiches. I later learned these were called 'tea' sandwiches. Dottie was going to love the spread—she had always wanted a KitchenAid mixer of her own to bake with. As Anna cut up tomatoes, cucumbers, sprigs of mint, and red onion for a fresh summer salad, I set the table with her expensive blue Italian china. One by one, I carefully pulled each piece out of the dining room hutch and placed them on the table. Aside from the plates and

bowls, I pulled out a charming pitcher and a few serving plat-
ters. Anna had asked me to also pull out the white dinner napkins since this was a tea party for ladies. She said a lady always
puts out her fanciest dinnerware for her most special guests.

After I finished helping her in the kitchen, she had me go
upstairs to get ready and remind Frankie to do the same. "And
psst," she whispered. "Go in my bathroom and take a spritz
of my favorite perfume before you come down. Only if you
want, of course." She smiled at me and nudged me up the
stairs while removing her apron.

About two hours later, the doorbell rang. After getting
ready and pacing our rooms while we waited, the girls and
Mary were finally here! Frankie and I wore tea-length dresses in floral patterns—fitting for the occasion. Frankie dashed
downstairs, but before I did, I made a quick stop to the bathroom and splashed on Anna's Chanel perfume. This whole
day felt very ladylike, and I wanted the girls to remember our
tea party forever. I made my way downstairs to find Frankie,
Connie, and Dottie already hugging. I joined in and smiled,
taking them all in. When I pulled back from them, I realized
that Connie and Dottie were wearing their winter dresses. I
immediately felt shame in the fact that we had on brand new
summer dresses that were bought specifically for this occa-

sion. I could tell they noticed too, because Dottie crossed her arms, almost as if to try and hide her dress from us. I watched as their eyes widened—Mary's included—and looked around our home in bewilderment. I would guess that this is what Frankie and I both looked like when we first stepped foot into this home, too. Anna motioned for us to take our seats at the dining room table in front of the bountiful spread that Anna prepared with my help.

Frankie already unfolded the napkin covering the scone basket and put one on her plate. Anna giggled at her and told everyone else to dig in. Dottie and Connie seemed nervous at first. They lightened up after they saw Frankie devouring the scone, which left crumbs on her cheeks and nose. The food looked so colorful on the blue and white dinnerware. I was proud that the vegetables were ones that I helped grow and pick in the backyard.

Everyone took some food as we started chatting. I couldn't wait to tell the girls about the gardens in the back and how I saw a few butterflies this morning. Connie wasn't convinced it was a Monarch butterfly—she was the bug expert after all, so I took her word for it. Dottie told us about the neighbors they recently met, James and Bettie. She said James and Bettie would knock on the door right after breakfast and invite them outside to play. They even met a few other kids in the neighborhood. Connie couldn't wait to tell us about the kickball game they had yesterday and how their team won against the team of older kids. I was glad to hear they were making friends and enjoying the rest of their summers before their adventure out west, which was looming. They were set to leave in only a few days. I reminded myself to enjoy the quality time we had with one another today instead of focusing on the future when they were gone.

We ate and talked around the table for about an hour before we were full and ready for a breather. Anna refilled Mary's teacup for the third time. Mary looked slightly uncomfortable throughout the meal and consumed more tea than food. I noticed her glance around the house—her facial expressions resembled Frankie's the first time we drove up to Anna and Herman's house. I could tell this home looked far different than her own.

Anna instructed us girls to go outside and play so they can catch up some more. That's all we needed to hear. "Have fun, girls," Mary said with a sheepish grin before we simultaneously pushed our chairs back and hopped up, my sisters following my lead as we tried so hard not to run to the back door. As soon as I swung it open, though, we ran out onto the fresh-cut emerald green lawn and took each other's hands. We spun around in a circle, laughing and picking up the pace until we all tumbled down like a house of cards. Dottie pointed at Frankie's skirt, which somehow made its way over her head as she fell. She was laughing so hard that tears fell from the corner of her eyes. Frankie looked down and fixed herself, and started cackling so loud as I joined in with her. We all rolled to our backs and squinted up towards the sky, Connie shielding her eyes from the sun with her hands. The sun emerged from behind a cloud and the rays shone down on our faces as we began to calm down from our laughing fit.

Two finches landed on the bush closest to me and I nudged Frankie to look, too. I had a feeling I knew who those birds were. They stood still for a moment before pushing themselves off the branch. Their flapping wings gained momentum as they flew over the four of us and disappeared into the trees.

I turned over to my side, facing the girls. "Are you girls, okay?" I wanted to be blunt. "Tell us anything and everything that's going on."

"We're okay, Cookie. Don't worry about us." Dottie replied, although I didn't quite believe her. "We'll be fine. We just miss you is all."

"Well, you ARE fine or you're going to be fine... which is it?" Frankie asked, pushing herself up off the ground and brushing the grass off her skirt. I noticed some grass stains on the white parts of her floral dress. I hope Anna wasn't going to be mad.

"What Frankie meant to say is: how have you been? How are your parents?" I softened Frankie's question a bit.

"I mean we live in a tiny apartment, which we're used to. But I don't think Dominic likes kids much. Mary's quiet. I don't know. It's not the same—I just don't feel settled. We made some friends, but we're gonna lose them too, Cookie. We're moving soon. I hope things feel more normal when we get to Arizona. I don't think we'll have a house like this," Dottie said while looking up at the vast house behind us. "But we'll have each other. And that's what matters, right?" She grabbed Connie's hand. She had a scared look in her eyes but I could tell she was holding it together for her sister.

Connie chimed in. "Yeah, are you guys, like, rich now?" She smiled to break up the tension a bit. "Anna's so fancy. And, Cookie, you're wearing perfume!" She popped up off the ground and walked around, pushing her nose in the air and mimicking her idea of a wealthy woman. I laughed alongside Connie, but couldn't help but wonder if there was some animosity hiding behind her direct jokes, and how this would play out in the years to come.

"Oh, hush," I muttered. Frankie helped me off the ground and Dottie got up, too. "Let's go see the gardens and my favorite spot."

We walked around the yard as I pointed out the vegetable garden and wildflowers that flooded around us. "There it is," I said, pointing towards the hammock. "That's my spot!" The girls skipped over to it and seemed enthralled. We all somehow maneuvered ourselves onto it at the same time, managing to not flip over onto the ground beneath us. I pushed my foot off of the ground, which caused the hammock to sway back and forth. The tension between us let up and we spent another hour or so swinging in the hammock. We played guessing games, talked about our dreams, and watched the clouds float by. It was a magical afternoon. I closed my eyes as Dottie gushed about James, her neighbor, and how cute he was. I hoped we'd remember this day forever and how the warm summer breeze felt on our cheeks as we swung back and forth for what seemed like an eternity.

"Girls, it's almost time to go! Come inside and get washed up." Mary yelled from the doorway. We all came to our senses. The swinging came to a halt and my eyes refocused on the real world around us instead of the serene world we created for ourselves in the backyard that afternoon. A world that we will never again know to be real once Dottie and Connie leave our home today.

We rolled off the hammock and started walking towards the house. Our pace was snail-like and our attitudes were so low-spirited compared to how we burst into the backyard a few hours before. But, we all knew this perfect day was bound to come to an end and that time was now. We stood around the foyer in an awkward circle while we waited for Anna and Mary to initiate our final goodbyes. Mary looked a bit more relaxed. I wonder what she and Anna talked about while we were outside.

Frankie blurted out "Be right back!" as if a light bulb went off in her mind, prompting her to sprint up the stairs, two at a time. She returned a few seconds later, holding a large rolled-up piece of paper in her hands. "I made this for you!" she said, slightly out of breath. She unrolled the paper and held it in front of her face: one hand gripped the top and the other hand outstretched the bottom. On it was an intricate drawing of four thirty-something year old women. They were all linking arms and wore dazzling jewel toned dresses and high heels. Their coiffed hair and bright makeup looked like it was out of a magazine. Behind the four women was a vivacious cityscape with twinkling lights and lots of action—blurred silhouettes of people passing by on the street and shiny apple red and yellow cars stuck in traffic. The women in the sketch were walking in lock-step and beaming with laughter. It was us—me, Frankie, Dottie, and Connie—in the future enjoying a night out on the town and having the time of our lives.

"It's us when we're grown-ups," Frankie continued. "Look how glamorous we are!" Frankie started rolling it back up and we handed it to Mary as the three of us surrounded her in a bear hug. We squeezed Frankie tight to thank her. I tried to imagine what it would feel like to be thirty-five and hug my sisters after an especially fun night out in Miami or New York City. It felt incredible and although I was sad, I knew deep down that an exciting future was in store for us.

A few minutes later, Dottie and Connie were gone. Mary grabbed their hands as they walked to the car, knowing this was a hard moment in their young lives. They were all leaving for Tucson soon and we didn't know when or how we would see them again in the flesh. What I did know, however, is that we were still sisters and we would always be sisters. Nothing was more critical than keeping each other in our minds as we trudged forward into the unknowns of our new lives apart.

Nothing is forever. Except, hopefully, the four of us.

7

Greetings from Tucson

Dear Frankie and Cookie,

Greetings from sunny [and hot] Tucson!

We're here... we're finally here! It was a long drive to Arizona but we stopped a few times along the way, which made the trip a bit more bearable. Connie's favorite pit stop was in Albuquerque, New Mexico. We got A-1 root beer floats from the coolest drive-in restaurant. The waitresses all wore roller skates and somehow carried trays of food and drinks while skating from one car to another. I don't know how they did it. I joked to Connie that Frankie would have dropped her tray in a second if that was her! Don'tcha agree, Cookie?

We start school right away on Monday and are nervous to meet our new classmates. I wonder if the boys in Tucson are as cute as the ones back home——especially James! Mary and Dominic told us they'd be working a lot and they expected us to pitch in around the house and make supper most nights. Mary taught us how to make homemade pasta before we left so I'm excited to give that a try next week on our own. Connie couldn't be less interested in cooking, but she's a good helper.

When you write back, please let us know how school is for both of you. Did you meet any new friends? Are you liking your classes? Frankie, I hope you're taking an art class at school so you can draw us some more pictures when you get a chance. And Cookie, we're sure you're already halfway done reading a new book for your English class. You must be the teacher's pet by now. Also, we heard you are going to an all-girls school. That is sad because now you can't even tell us who the cutest boys in your classes are! Haha.

It feels strange to be here without you girls. We miss you lots. Please write back as soon as you can. We included our new address on the outside of the envelope.

Love,
Dottie and Connie
Your favorite sisters

Her hands full, Dottie kicked the door open with her foot and held it open for Connie to go inside. Connie dropped her backpack onto the ground of their stucco house, which caused a dust cloud to spread into the stuffy air. Dottie followed behind her and thrust the ten-pound bag she was carrying over her shoulder to walk the last few steps into the kitchen. She dropped it with a thud and took a seat at the table to catch her breath. The girls were sweaty and flushed after stopping at the bakery and making the two-mile trek home from school. They dreaded what they referred to as "flour days" because carrying the extra weight made the heat feel excruciating. The bakery owner recognized them this week, though, and gave them each a free cookie for their walk home.

Dottie and Connie hadn't become used to the dry Arizona heat yet. But November provided some relief from the 90 degree days that felt never-ending when they first started school back in September. Their parents worked many hours, so the girls walked home each day as the sun beat down on their navy blue uniforms and reflected off the streets. Luckily, the walk was flat and straight with not a hill in sight. Connie cried on the walk home on their first day of school after an overwhelming day of meeting their new teachers and classmates. She hadn't eaten much at school that day and felt weak about a mile into their trek home. The 95-degree temperature pierced through her skin, which caused her to fall to her bare knees on the scorching pavement. Dottie watched her cry for a few minutes before helping her up and brushing the tiny pebbles off her knees that stuck to her skin from the sweat. They continued to walk as the heat evaporated off the pavement, making Dottie feel a bit nauseous as they continued on their never-ending trek home. She knew Connie needed that cry more than anything. Heck, Dottie felt like crying a lot these days, but she kept it inside. She knew it wouldn't do any good to let it out and get Connie even more upset.

Dottie and Connie's new home was somehow even smaller than their temporary third-floor apartment. It was a simple four-room house with a white tile floor and a sparse amount of furniture. The light in the kitchen flickered every time they flipped on the switch. The backyard wasn't a yard at all; in fact, it was paved with cracked concrete and had gray pebbles lining the fence. They shared a room, as expected, but this room was tiny with a small window that was stuck shut. The first thing Dottie did was unroll the picture Frankie had drawn for them. She hung it on the wall between their beds, which brought some color into their otherwise dim bedroom. Frankie's signature adorned the lower-right part of the sketch and got a bit smudged on their ride from Connecticut. Fortunately, the rest of the picture stayed intact.

Dottie and Connie changed out of their uniforms and started on their daily chore list. Connie usually swept the floors and scrubbed the bathroom, while Dottie prepared supper and cleaned the kitchen. Dominic and Mary worked at the same factory and didn't usually get home until around 5:30 p.m.. This left the girls about two hours to get everything done. Dominic made it clear that they were to complete the list before they got home and then they could start their homework after supper. There wasn't a lot of family chatter in that house and Dominic didn't seem too concerned with what Dottie and Connie wanted to do in their spare time. He cared that they pitched in, finished their homework, and kept the noise down to a reasonable level. Dottie discovered a radio in the kitchen that she turned on as soon as they got home from school so they could dance and sing as they did their chores. Dottie always remembered to turn off the radio at 5 p.m. so Dominic wouldn't get upset. Blaring the music made their chores bearable—almost enjoyable. Dottie and Connie agreed it would be their little secret.

Dottie was making pasta again tonight with the flour she got from the bakery. She found the art of pasta making to be calming, as it was repetitive and straightforward. She dusted the table with flour first and then added a small pile on top. She carved out a small hole in the middle and cracked an egg into it. She whisked the egg with a fork as she started to form the pasta dough. Dottie worked in small batches to make it more manageable but she tended to make a lot in one sitting so she could use it on other nights. Dottie used the hand crank pasta maker to form her dough into spaghetti and hung it on wooden spokes to dry. She was always proud of her pasta and each strand's unique appearance. Connie loved pasta night, as it was her favorite meal, and she got to reap the benefits of Dottie's hard work.

There was a knock at the door that afternoon. Connie had finished up her chores early and opened the door. Her new friend Josephine stood at the door, which filled Connie with delight. Josephine lived a few houses down and was Connie's age. She had long jet black hair with bangs and tanned olive skin from the Arizona summers. She was wearing shorts and a polo shirt, similar to what Connie wore to clean the house. "Hi, Jo! Come on in," Connie said. She was glad to have made a new friend so soon, especially someone who lived nearby and knew the ropes. Jo also introduced Connie to some other friends, which helped her acclimate easier. She also had an older brother Dottie's age, but he was in the cool crowd and didn't pay any mind to her.

Jo came into the house and yelled "hi" to Dottie when she heard her in the kitchen. "Hey, Jo," Dottie shouted back. Dottie thought Jo was a nice girl and she was glad Connie met her. Jo wanted to show Connie the new game she got for her birthday called "pick-up sticks." She thought they could play for a little while before Dominic and Mary came home. Connie immediately obliged and Jo taught her how the game worked. Jo poured the sticks into a jumble on the ground and they sat down and played. They talked about some of their classmates as they took turns removing sticks from the pile.

As they played their game in the living room, Dottie finished making her pasta and portioning it out. She kept some aside for tonight's supper and took some sauce out of the refrigerator. The fridge was pretty sparse, but they had enough to get through the next few days. Dottie stared at the contents of the fridge before closing the door. She wondered if she had the ingredients needed to bake cupcakes for the school fundraiser in a few days. Money had been tight since they arrived in Tucson, and Dottie's baking days were far and few between. She focused on stretching meals for the family instead of making extra desserts that they didn't need.

After Jo left around 5, Connie switched off the music and helped Dottie set the table. Dominic and Mary came home as scheduled and the four of them ate dinner, mostly in silence. Mary made an effort to ask the girls about their days, but Dominic shut down the conversation. He seemed annoyed with Mary and his mind seemed elsewhere tonight. He wasn't a mean man, but he sometimes seemed like he didn't want to be bothered with small talk. The girls were scared of him at first—I could tell from their letters—but it didn't take long before they realized he was harmless. He expected them to do their chores and have manners, but every once in a while, he would tell a joke at supper or leave them a treat in the fridge for after school. He even watches out the window when Jo leaves the house after dark, just to make sure she gets home okay.

After dinner, Dominic usually sat in a lounge chair in the backyard and smoked cigarettes. Mary helped the girls clean up the kitchen so they could start on their homework. "Mary," Dottie started speaking with hesitation in her voice. "Do you think there's any money leftover this week so I can get some baking supplies? We're having a bake sale at school and I was hoping to make some cupcakes."

"Not this time, dear," she replied with a touch of sadness. She placed the towel on the counter and retreated to her bedroom, shutting the door behind her. Dottie and Connie stayed in the kitchen with their heads down as they continued to clean in the sweltering heat without saying a word to each other.

The next morning, Dottie woke up to a note and a dollar bill on her nightstand. The note read: "Dottie—I heard you needed some money for your cupcakes. It's not much, but I hope it helps. Love, your Dad." Dottie sat up in bed, her eyes teary-eyed. She wondered if life in Arizona with their new parents would be okay after all.

On Wednesdays, Anna picked Frankie and me up from school so we could go to our afterschool activities. Frankie had been taking art classes downtown for about a month, which she seemed to enjoy. I wasn't interested in art, so Anna asked me if I had any interest in helping out at her shop. Anna owned a wedding dress boutique. Once or twice a month, new shipments arrived with dresses that needed tagging and hanging. She asked me to help her last month, and since I did a good job—or so she said—she requested my presence again tonight.

When we pulled up, Frankie hopped out of the car to meet one of her girlfriends outside the art studio. "Wait up!" she said, as she jogged to meet up with her. The two disappeared inside and we pulled away towards the dress shop. Anna filled me in about some of the new gowns and told me about a woman who was coming in tonight for a final dress fitting. She said the bride's wedding was next week at her parents' home in the Litchfield Hills. I was ecstatic to see a real-life bride try on her gown, as I've only seen wedding dresses on mannequins up to this point.

Anna unlocked the door of the dress shop and flipped over the sign to say "open." Marilou, a college-aged girl, worked for Anna during the spring and summer months, but Anna ran the shop alone when the wedding season slowed down. The shop was upscale and refined. Dozens of dresses in thick plastic bags lined the walls while several mannequins showcased some elegant pieces. The heart of the shop was the waiting area, which felt like a cozy living room. Twin tufted couches made of teal velvet flanked a large swirled marble coffee table. Bright pink flowers from our garden sat in the center and bridal magazines fanned out on either side. There were two floral armchairs with round pillows on one end of the coffee table. On the other end was a platform with three-way mirrors and Hollywood lighting. This is where the brides would stand to try on wedding gowns.

I began opening the boxes and used my strength to pull out the beaded gowns. I laid them on the couch one by one and admired their beauty. The style of each dress was unique, but gorgeous nonetheless. I held my favorite one up to my chest. It was silk taffeta with long sleeves, a boat neck, and layers of tulle petticoat underneath. I swung around to face the mirror. I could picture myself getting married one day with my sisters, Anna, and Herman by my side and sharing in my joy. I found the section of long-sleeved dresses and hung it on the rack. I continued until all the new dresses were on hangers and organized.

As I cleaned up the boxes, the bells on the door jingled and a smiling woman flounced through the door. Anna greeted her and welcomed her inside to take a seat on the velvet couch. I nodded at the woman and introduced myself. "Hi, darling. I'm Clara," she returned as she smoothed her skirt to sit down. She wore a navy pencil skirt and matching jacket with nude pantyhose and peep-toe heels. A tan beret covered her curly blonde hair and her cheeks were as pink as the flowers in the vase sitting in front of her.

I poured Clara a glass of water as Anna went into the dressing room to get set up. "Clara, come this way," Anna said, motioning for her to make her way to the fitting room. "A robe is in there for you. I'll be there in a minute to help get your gorgeous dress on!"

I sat on the chair and listened to some muffled chatter for a few minutes until the door opened. Clara emerged, her eyes twinkling and her smile beaming. Her wedding dress was magical. It had long, intricate lace sleeves, a slim darted bodice, and a flowy skirt made of glimmering silk. A long train trailed behind her as she stepped out. Anna bent down to fluff the train before she walked to the platform to face the mirror. She removed her hat and was wearing a floral crown with a veil in its place. Clara's skin glistened under the lights of the shop. It's almost like she stepped off a page of the magazine that I flipped through a mere few minutes before. She stepped up onto the platform to get a better look, and a single tear rolled down her cheek. She caught it and wiped it away before it dropped onto her dress. She admired herself in the mirror for a few moments from every angle and then said, "Anna, you've outdone yourself. It's simply gorgeous." Anna looked pleased. She squeezed her hand as they continued to gaze in the mirror at Clara's perfect dress.

"You look like a princess," I said as Anna and Clara's eyes met mine in the mirror.

"Would you be a dear and fix my veil?" she asked. I hopped up and graciously obliged. I straightened out her veil and admired the fabric-covered buttons that adorned the back of her gown. Anna stepped in to continue with the fitting while I finished straightening up. Frankie's art classes ended for the season in a few weeks and she was also going to help us here, too. I knew she'd swoon over the designs and sparkly accessories in the jewelry case.

Anna carried the gown out to Clara's car and wished her well at her upcoming wedding. It was getting dark, so we packed up our belongings and drove straight home since Herman picked up Frankie from art class as his law firm is also downtown. I found it was valuable to spend time alone with our new parents every once in a while, too. Anna and I gushed about Clara and how lovely she looked. Then she said, "Since you're doing such a great job as my helper in the shop, I'm going to start paying you, Cookie. You can save it for a rainy day." I enjoyed being in the shop and helping Anna, and I'm glad she felt the same way about having me there.

As we arrived home and walked towards the house, I could hear muffled yelling inside followed by a door slam. It was Frankie, I assumed. My eyes grew wide as Anna shot me a glance and grabbed my arm, and we jogged up the front porch steps and into the house. "Hello? What's going on here?" Anna asked out loud to anyone that could hear her. Herman came out of the kitchen and threw a dish towel onto the floor. His face looked flustered and concerned.

"It's Frankie," he said. "*She's* mad at *me* for getting upset with

her for what I saw tonight!" Clearly agitated, he pointed upstairs, indicating that's where Frankie was when she slammed
the door. "I got off work a little early today and waited outside
art class and I saw her smoking with an older kid from her
class—18, 19? Who knows? Maybe he wasn't even from her
art class. How do we know she's even been going to art class?"
Herman pushed his hair back from his face and then took his
glasses off to clean them with the bottom of his shirt.

He continued. "Well, I had to confront her about it. Not
only did she lie, but she yelled at me, and told me I wasn't
her father... I don't need this, Anna." Hearing Herman say
those words worried me. Did he not want me or Frankie anymore? Were we too much for him? He looked my way and I
immediately looked down at the floor. "Hey, I didn't mean
that Cookie. I had a tough day at work and I didn't need the
extra aggravation. I'm not the bad guy and I don't need Frankie telling me I am. We're all in this together." I could tell he
wasn't sure how to handle teenage girls. Especially ones who
were smoking in the alley with boys when they should have
been sketching landscapes in class.

Anna motioned for me to go upstairs to check on Frankie
but also because she didn't want me involved in their adult
conversation. I jogged up the stairs, the whole time feeling
Herman and Anna's eyes on me until they knew I couldn't
hear any further. I knocked on Frankie's door but entered
without hearing from her first. She was lying face down on

her bed—sobbing—and didn't move at all when she heard me come in. Herman was right about her smoking, as the smell of nicotine hit me as soon as I walked into her bedroom. I sat next to her and rubbed her back, all while trying to process the fact that Frankie was keeping secrets from me. I felt so lost in that moment. Had I been too involved in school, the shop, and settling into my new routine that I wasn't paying enough attention to Frankie? I felt like a bad sister.

"He's not our father." Frankie asserted, still lying face-down on the bed and not moving an inch. "How dare he try to tell me what I can and can't do. I'm pissed, Cookie. He embarrassed me."

Still processing Frankie's behavior, I laid down next to her. The room was dark but I could see her face as she looked over at me. "Frankie, what's going on with you?" I asked. "You're smoking? With grown men? And yelling at Herman who was doing you a favor picking you up from the art class that he pays for? And I had to hear this from Herman and not you? Why are you doing this? What the heck, Frankie." I was concerned and a little sad. Of course, smoking wasn't the end of the world. I didn't like it, but I'm sure there were a lot of other 13-year-olds dabbling in it. I didn't like the lying, though. Frankie rarely talked about boys at school, so visualizing her smoking with an older man when she should have been doing art was alarming to me. I worried that my line of questioning came out as patronizing, though. I didn't want to lose her trust and risk her not telling me even more secrets in the future, but I was pissed and she knew it.

"What's going on with me?" she challenged. "I could ask the same of you. Why isn't this hard for you, too? Why are you just pretending nothing happened?" Her watery eyes looked deep into mine and I couldn't believe what I was hearing. She pushed her untamed hair behind her red ears and pursed her lips like she did when she was a kid.

"Of course it's hard for me, Frankie. Our parents are dead. Gone! We'll never see them again. I'm so mad at them for leaving us that I could scream. Dottie and Connie are across the damn country—doing God knows what with God knows who. We had to make new friends. I miss my old friends and I miss everything about our old life. I'm trying though. I'm trying to adjust to this new life and our new parents. They're giving us everything we need and you have the nerve to scream at Herman? Mom and Dad weren't perfect either, Frankie. You know it as well as I do."

"It seems like nothing bothers you. You and Anna are like best friends. Herman adores you. I feel like I don't belong in this perfect home with these perfect people. But you're perfect, Cookie. You belong with them. Maybe I should just leave." I saw the pain in her eyes and I was heartbroken knowing this was how she felt about her and me.

"Perfect? Far from it," I sighed. "Why couldn't I be the one to move across the country and let you three live in this house and all be together? It haunts me every night, Frankie. I'm the big sister and I should have done more to protect you three."

"Don't do that," she countered. "It's not your fault. But it's hard living in your shadow. You're beautiful. Everyone loves you. You're going to be okay in the end. But me? Boys never pay me any mind. But then I met Archie last week after class and he was nice to me and told me I was pretty and I felt alive. I felt like you, Cookie. And then I met up with him again tonight and he offered me a cigarette. Of course, I said yes because I was flattered he wanted to see me again. Herman saw us and humiliated me in front of Archie and I got angry. At him. At me. I thought he was going to get rid of me. Then I wouldn't have him, or Anna, and most importantly, I wouldn't have you." She sounded as if she was disposable, like an old toy that someone threw in the trash.

"You realize no one is leaving you, right? Herman and Anna want you here. And I would die without you. I mean it. They are our real parents, Frankie. They aren't just some foster parents that can give us back to the court if they don't like us. But we have to try, too." I said these words to her, hoping and praying that this was true because frankly, I didn't know. Just then, we heard tapping on the door. It was Anna. "Darlings, can I come in?"

"Yes, come in," I responded, wondering if Herman was with her. Frankie wiped her eyes and sat up, while Anna walked in alone and flipped on the lightswitch.

"Frankie, you okay, honey?" she asked, her voice filled with genuine concern. "We have to talk about what happened. Herman is coming up in a minute but I want to tell you that you two mean everything to me. To us. We're beyond happy that you found your way into our lives. And Frankie, Herman is your Dad and I am your Mom. We're your new parents and you've got to respect this house and our rules. I'd be devastated if something happened to you girls." Herman cautiously rounded the corner and entered the bedroom, too. He folded his arms but his face looked more relaxed than before.

"She's right," he continued. "I was so worried when I saw you with that stranger, Frankie. I lost my head and yelled at him, and I'm sorry if I embarrassed you. But I'm not sorry I did it. You know the rules in this house. We don't need you galavanting with some slick-haired kid when you're supposed to be at art class. You're 13 years old." He paused for a moment. "And it hurt when you told me I wasn't your Dad because I am your Dad, Frankie. And you are my daughter. Both of you are. We need to trust each other and I'll give you girls the world." Herman seemed genuinely concerned about Frankie. His body language softened and the deep lines on his face relaxed once he got his words out. He was far different than our father—kind of straight-laced and far less rough around the edges. He didn't drink often and he was sophisticated. A well-read lawyer, he worked tirelessly at his firm but he was very involved at home too. He adored and respected Anna.

I looked over at Frankie and I could tell she felt bad about what she said; my heart ached for her. This was uncharted territory for the four of us. That became glaringly clear this evening as we sat around and tried to make sense of it all. We talked and listened, as Herman and Anna mostly tried to convince us that the two jaded orphaned girls in front of them were, in fact, wanted... and that they would, in fact, never leave us behind. They were trying. Would we always find it hard to respond to their attempts at loving us? And would it always feel like Anna and Herman were our temporary caregivers as we waited for our "real" parents to come home? Either way, life felt pretty complicated and complex in this big white house on the hill. I was curious if Dottie and Connie were having a challenging time adjusting to their new lives in Tucson. I prayed that they were okay. And although I couldn't be certain, I was cautiously optimistic that we would be okay in the end, too.

8

The Letters,
Part One

December 29, 1946

Hello, sisters!

Merry [late] Christmas and Happy New Year!

We're writing to you from Ridgefield, Connecticut. Anna and Herman have a second home here in the country [we learned of this only last week] so we came here to celebrate New Year's Eve in style. We are surrounded by rolling hills and farmland, but a blanket of snow is covering everything. It's so lovely. We went snowshoeing earlier today and I slipped on my bottom down a hill and tripped Herman on the way down. We laughed and laughed——especially because it's usually Frankie that does the slipping. It's nice not to have an agenda while we are here. I have been cozied up to the fireplace reading, and Frankie's been drawing per usual. She even included a sketch of this house——Anna calls it "The Country Cottage"——on the back of this piece of paper.

We hope you enjoyed your Christmas. Did you get nice presents? What kind of food did you eat for Christmas dinner? Also——and this is a serious question Frankie has been asking me for weeks now——are there Christmas trees in Tucson? And do you wear shorts on Christmas Day because it's still so warm outside? We're dying to hear about your Christmas. Ours was nice. We had a turkey and about ten side dishes! I helped make a sweet potato casserole and we even made fresh bread [it was quite delicious if I do say so myself!]. Anna and Herman had a few relatives over [I guess they are our relatives now, too]. We even met some cousins around our age. They were all so nice and we have plans to see two of the girls again after the New Year.

We all needed this time away. Frankie got in trouble recently for sneaking off with a 17-year-old boy to smoke cigarettes [can you believe it?]. Oh, Frankie——it's become clear that she likes bad boys! Anna and Herman said she's too young to date, though, and shut it down. One positive from Frankie's mischief is that it forced us to communicate more as a "family." Are you both settling into your new home in Tucson? Are Dominic and Mary treating you okay? Do you find it's hard to trust you won't be left behind, again?

We hope to hear from you soon. Happy New Year, sisters. I think you'd agree that we are happy to put this year behind us and try to move forward to better days.

With love and holiday cheer,
Cookie and Frankie

Summer 1947

Hi Cookie and Frankie,

This is our first summer in Tucson and it's as hot as you would imagine. One of our neighbors, Josephine [we call her 'Jo'], has a pool and they invited us over to go swimming the other day. Jo has a brother that Dottie can't get enough of——he's the most popular boy in our school and she swoons over him. I think he's pretty cute, too. You should have seen her strutting around the pool with her bathing suit on like she was a model. He wasn't even home! His name is Scott, by the way. I'm sure Dottie will tell you all about him next time she writes——even though they have yet to have a conversation! Dottie read that part over my shoulder and smacked me for saying that. Ha!

We are happy to be out of school for the summer. It was pretty easy to make friends though and there are a ton of kids in our neighborhood. We met a lot of them because the houses are so close together. Mary and Dominic took us to a desert museum last weekend and we got to see snakes, cacti, and even a strange creature called an armadillo. They work a lot so we usually have to entertain ourselves but they have been surprising us with local trips lately. It's been fun to explore the city of Tucson more.

Oh, and I've mastered cleaning while Dottie cooks supper. We each get a five-cent allowance every week for helping around the house. I'm saving for a doll I saw in the window of a toy shop we walked by recently. Dottie is saving for a hand mixer. She was bringing cupcakes to school before the summer started and everyone always talked about how good her treats were! One day, we will all meet at Dottie's restaurant for a special meal when we are grown-ups. What do you think of that, girls?

I wanted to tell you that we are doing fine here. Good, even. It's been a year since everything happened and I thought we would never smile again. But as the year went on, we did learn to smile again. We fit in better than we thought we would. The kids here seem interested in Connecticut like it's some foreign, far away land. It is fun to tell them what life was like back with you two and Mom and Dad. We sure missed playing in the snow though this last winter. Remember how much fun we had sledding at the park that one time?

We miss you both very much. Tell Frankie to stay out of

trouble, haha. Yeah, right.

With love from hot, hot Tucson!
Connie (and Dottie, too)

September 30, 1947

Dear sisters:

Frankie, here. The air is crisp again and the leaves are vivid
shades of orange, yellow, and red. I can't stop staring out
the window and sketching this scenery. Even the backyard
feels like a real-life painting. It reminds me of that time
Dad and Mom took us to that little farm in Litchfield,
Connecticut. Remember the baby cows and goats? Connie
loved them and 'mooed' the whole way home. And remember when Dad pointed to the hilly landscape and said how
it reminded him of peaceful——but powerful——waves
in the ocean? I don't think I could ever look at the leaves in
the fall without thinking about the ocean. Even though the
ocean now reminds me of something else, too.

   I wanted to tell you that I entered a drawing I did into a
city-wide art contest recently and——would you believe
it?——I won! The drawing was of a bridge Cookie and I

discovered on a walk near "The Country Cottage." I drew
our reflections into the water, too, and the judges said I
captured raw emotion in our faces. There were hundreds
of entries and somehow they thought mine was the best.
Anna and Herman were proud of me and we celebrated
with milkshakes at my favorite diner. Anna also framed
and hung the drawing in the dress shop and she said the
shoppers have been admiring it. One woman even offered
to buy it! Ha! Call me Frankie Van Gogh! Cookie told me
to remind you two to take extra care of the picture I drew of
the four of us in case I get famous one day.

One weird thing happened after I won that art contest,
though. I was driving with Anna to the store and she told
me I was a great artist and all, but that I shouldn't consider
it a career in the future. She said it was more of a hobby.
Winning the contest confirmed my desire to go to art
school one day, so when Anna said that... I will admit, I was
in shock. She told me that art wasn't a practical profession
and any daughter of hers was not going to do something so
whimsical as a career. It's kind of ironic, though, because
Anna owns a dress shop, which feels like a creative job to
me. But she maintains the shop is "all business" and they
were lucky to have the capital to start it. She continued on
that teaching or nursing would be a suitable profession. I'm
kind of bummed about the whole conversation if I'm being
honest. Do you think Mom would have shot down my

dreams? Dad always told us to reach for the stars, but I'm beginning to wonder if he even meant it.

In closing, I hope Tucson is treating you well. Did Dottie K-I-S-S the cute neighbor-boy named Scott yet? I can see her blushing all the way from here. Cookie says hello, too.

Love,
Your sister, Frankie

October 13, 1947

Dear Dottie and Connie,

A quick update for you——I got my driver's license. Frankie is ecstatic that we can drive around town. Herman even bought me a car. I wonder if I can figure out how to drive back and forth to Tucson——wouldn't that be a fun road trip? Ha, ha. Yeah right. I don't think the world is ready for Frankie and I to take on Route 66, but who knows, maybe someday?

P.S. Where have you girls been, anyway? You haven't written in a while. Write to let us know you're okay.

Love,
Cookie XOXO

March 1948

Dear Cookie and Frankie,

We're sorry that Connie and I haven't written lately.
Things have been crazy here in Tucson. I've been trying to
write to you in private for months now to tell you what happened. Please don't share with Anna and Herman——or
anyone for that matter. Anyways, here goes nothing...

Back in the fall when school started up again, Connie
and I were walking home like any other day. It was hotter
than usual that day and Connie begged me to stop to get ice
cream——her treat. She talked the whole walk home about
what ice cream flavor she wanted. All I wanted to do was
to get home, to be honest. We both had chores to do and I
wanted to try a special recipe that night. Anyways, Connie
was so convincing that I obliged. This is not a story about
ice cream, in case you were wondering.

When we walked into the empty ice cream shop,
Dom——yes, our dad——was at the counter holding
hands with the curly-haired waitress! We both stopped
dead in our tracks and watched Dom as he admired this
woman, who was wearing a black skirt and a short-sleeved
button-down shirt. Connie must've gasped because Dom

looked at us as his smile faded from his face. He pulled his hands back from her immediately. He asked what we were doing there and told us the woman was his friend and he was giving her a handshake and nothing more. In an extra-threatening voice, he told us to go home and not speak of this to anyone. We left the ice cream shop sans ice cream, walked home, and started our chores without saying a word to each other. Dom and Mary arrived home later that day, together. Dom shared that he took off work early for a doctor's appointment and picked up Mary from work before heading home. Mary was none the wiser and Dom acted like nothing ever happened.

So, this story gets a little crazier. A few weeks after the incident at the ice cream shop, we heard Mary and Dom yelling. From what we heard, she said she saw red lipstick on his collar when she was doing laundry and found it suspicious because she never wore red lipstick. Dom denied it, blaming us for ruining his collar when we played dress-up with Mary's makeup. She believed him and didn't say another word about it. But later that week when we were at Jo's, Mary went to her girlfriend's house to meet her new baby and we saw the waitress leaving our house when we were walking home! We hid behind a car to watch what was going on and saw Dom chase after her. He was waving his arms and yelling something that we couldn't make out. She slammed the car door and sped off, leaving Dom in the middle of the street watching her drive away. We sat there for what felt like hours until the coast was clear and went home and acted like everything was fine. But we knew it wasn't——something felt extra fiery about their argument and we were dying to know what it was. I should mention that Connie wants to be a detective now.

So, fast forward a few months later to the holidays. We were out shopping with Mary and who do we bump into? THE WAITRESS. Coincidence? She walked by and brushed against Mary's shoulder, hard enough for Mary to tumble backward. Her perfume wafted into the air as she walked and get this: she was wearing red lipstick. She apologized and kept walking, but Mary stopped in her tracks and followed her with her eyes as if she knew something was up. The waitress looked back at us and smiled. She definitely recognized us from the ice cream shop that day with Dom. Then, she smoothed her hand over her stomach, revealing a bump, and turned around and kept walking.

She was having a baby!

It took everything inside of me not to say anything at that moment, about who she was and what I knew. Mary got flustered though and grabbed our hands to leave the store. I think she connected the dots together.

Christmas came and went and Mary didn't say a word. We never heard fighting again. She never accused him of anything. And Dom was back to acting kind of normal. But here we are in March. Mary packed some bags this morning and, while Dom was out somewhere running errands, told us she was going on a trip for a few days with some friends. She kissed us goodbye, put two five-dollar bills in our fists, and left an envelope on the table addressed to Dom. Connie was worried sick since Mary left. I'm hoping she will come back, though. She has to. We can't lose yet another mother.

So I am sitting here trying to get all these words out before Dom comes home and opens the letter. Cookie, what do you think is going to happen to us? Do you think we should have told Mary what we knew? Do you think we are going to have a baby brother or sister soon?

I will write soon once we have more details.

Dottie
P.S. Don't forget that this is a secret.

March 1948

Update!

A lot has happened since I last wrote a few days ago and I couldn't wait to tell you both. Mary came back as promised a few days later. But it turns out, she is leaving Dom after all [we heard them talking through the wall last night]. She left again this morning to go stay with her mother in Phoenix for some time until she figures out what to do next. She offered to bring us along, but said it would probably be best for us if we stayed here instead of changing schools yet again. She said she would come to see us each weekend after she got settled into her new job and living situation. She was calm, all things considered.

So, we also found out that the waitress——her name is Barb——is having a baby in a few months and it is, in fact, Dom's. Barb came over to the house today to see Dom and meet us, officially. It felt weird to be meeting yet another "mother" figure. But, I will say that she was nice and it was refreshing to see Dom so happy. The way he looked at her and adored her was something I hadn't seen yet. He introduced us as his daughters and told us that we'd be seeing a lot more of her now. She is beautiful. She kind of looks like you, Cookie, but with curly hair and makeup.

Connie assured me that she liked Barb, too, but I'm a little worried about her. She's been sad lately, but luckily school and her friends are keeping her busy. I know we will be fine.

Love,
Dottie

April 1948

Dot & Con,

Wow. We are speechless over the events you shared with us in your last few letters. I'm sorry that we were not there to give you both a big hug and tell you everything will be okay. Because everything WILL be okay. We'll make sure of it.

Remember what Judge Mason said? He said to always continue to put each other and our relationships first. Isn't that all that matters in the end, girls? That WE are here to listen to you, and YOU are there for us no matter what? We love you so much and you are both stronger and more resilient than anyone we've ever met. Focus on school and your friendships and on being good people. And remember to speak up if something doesn't seem right.

Not to change the subject, but I want to be sure I share some updates with you about life in Connecticut. Frankie has been bursting at the seams to tell you that she had her first kiss with a kid from school. It was in the library behind the bookshelves! Am I the only one that goes to the library to read anymore? She's so cute when she gushes. She has been sketching beautiful prints of the wedding gowns at Anna's bridal shop and the customers started asking to buy them. I used to think she would love working at the bridal shop with me, but it turns out, she would rather sit on the sofa while I work and draw the dresses instead! I guess we're both making a little extra spending money, so what's the difference?

As for me, I recently attended a winter social at my school——the boys from the all-boys school also came. My friend Martha and I were on the committee for the dance and helped decorate. We hung tons of silver snowflakes from the ceiling and put snow-covered branches and twinkle lights everywhere. It felt like I was inside our favorite snow globe, with shimmering snow every which way I looked. I wore a powder blue tea-length lace dress with peep-toe heels and Anna's shawl. She let me borrow a sparkly necklace from her jewelry box, too! I danced with a boy named Robert who is 17 and rather charming. My friend caught my eye when Robert and I were slow dancing, and I had to excuse myself because I was giggling. Later on, he found me at the punch bowl and asked if I would meet him ice skating the next day at our local park. I went——and Frankie came, too——and we had a ball [well, Frankie and I had more fun than anyone]! I thought of him as a friend though, not a boyfriend, although I hope we stay in touch in the future. Frankie jokes that I won't date just anyone who comes my way. And she's right. I won't settle for anything less than butterflies.

I love you both and please keep us updated if anything
new happens.

With love [and butterflies],
Cookie

Summer 1948

Dear Cookie and Frankie,

It's 100 degrees in Tucson today. So hot that it seems to
take extra momentum to walk from the front door to the
car and the air feels dense when it gets sucked into your
lungs. Hot enough to where the birds won't even bother to
fly and even the shade doesn't provide any reprieve. And
hot enough that the scary furnace room we stumbled upon
that time in the basement would feel like a wintry retreat.
Yes, it is that hot.

The other day when we visited the bakery for flour, the
owner asked Dottie if she was interested in a weekend
job——helping her clean and with odds and ends around
the bakery. Even though she's young, the woman said she
was mature and could start by working a few hours a week.
Dottie jumped at the chance to help out and learn even

more about baking! So that's where Dottie is today. Maybe the baker will let me work there next year, too.

Today I am helping Barb with the new baby. It's a boy named Thomas. Barb moved in with us as soon as she had the baby. I am obsessed with Baby Tommy and Barb isn't so bad. Dottie is still skeptical of the whole situation, but I like how nice Dom is now that Barb is around. Mary moved back to Tucson and has a small apartment downtown. We go visit her every Saturday afternoon and we walk around with her to all the shops. She seems less nervous these days and things are going smoother. We even met her mother and she was so nice——she even bought us presents the last time we saw her! Mary is taking us to Phoenix later this summer so we can stay with her mother and——get this——they are going to take us to the Grand Canyon on the way!

Things are working out for us. Just like you said they would, Cookie. Now, let me get back to Baby Tommy. I love babies and I can't wait to have about ten of them one day! Just call me Mama Connie, ha!

Your sister,
Connie

June 4, 1949

Dear Dottie and Connie,

I woke up to the sound of rain hitting my window and, instead of starting my chores or opening a book, I decided to make the most of a quiet morning with no agenda. I climbed into my window seat and one-by-one, re-read every one of your letters from the past few years. I wanted to relive your most special——and, at times, quite dramatic——moments. As the oldest sister, it's time for me to recognize the remarkable lives we have created despite our challenges.

You've both done so much. You have wonderful friends, Dottie got her first job, Connie has quickly become the most popular girl at school, Dominic and Mary seem to be managing their separation well, and you've seen some new places, like the Grand Canyon, Phoenix, and your most recent trip to Sedona! I am so proud of how you both have handled the hardships thrown your way. And despite how busy your lives are, you ALWAYS take the time to write to us and catch us up on anything and everything. Connie even sent us a joke she heard at school a few weeks ago: a simple letter with three lines that lifted our spirits and got us through our days. You never cease to amaze me and I'm so thankful for how strong and brave you are.

And on this end, I have some updates to share. I am days away from graduating high school [can you believe it?] and heading to nursing school in a few short months at the local college. Frankie continues to win art contests and make money from her prints. It's pretty incredible to see how the ideas in her head make their way onto paper so effortlessly. I could never do what Frankie does! She has gotten pretty close to her new art teacher this year——her name is Millie. You'll love this part——Millie is setting Frankie up on a blind date with her nephew, Ray. Ray is 17 like Frankie and Millie said he's handsome, funny, and as smart as can be. Frankie and I are going on a group date to the diner and bowling alley with Ray and one of his friends next weekend. So we'll see how that goes!

Anna and Herman are throwing me a graduation party. Judge Mason and his wife, Eleanor, will be there, which is exciting because we haven't seen him since Christmas time. He is always so eager to hear how the two of you are doing and asks very pointed questions about your lives. I think it's because he wants to ensure we are following his poignant advice from almost four years ago, which was to share our hopes and dreams and fears with one another and always put each other first. I can't wait to share how well you are doing.

In closing, Frankie and I want to wish a happy birthday

to Connie! I'll never forget how anxious and excited I felt
to meet you. Dad had to yell at us to stop running while we
made our way down the hallway to Mom's hospital room
where we knew you'd be. I remember seeing your little
pink face for the first time as I rounded the corner into
the room. Your eyes were bright blue and curious, and you
stared at each of us with intensity, one-by-one, as we entered the room. You must have known we were destined to
be your protectors and best friends, just as we knew you'd be
the light of our lives from that day on.

Happy 13th Birthday, Connie. Thank you for always
bringing the sunshine.

Love,
Cookie (and Frankie, too)

9

Graduation Day

Dear Cookie,

Happy Graduation Day! We are proud of you! Have fun at your party. Tell Judge Mason we said hello.

Love,
Dottie & Connie

"Hurry up, girls—let's go!" Anna yelled from the foyer as Frankie and I frantically finished getting ready. "Herman is waiting in the car!"

I reached behind my neck to clasp my necklace as I admired the smooth and shiny pearls in the mirror. I pat the necklace against my simple black dress. Anna had given it to me at breakfast this morning and wearing it today felt special. I did a final check to make sure I didn't have lipstick on my teeth before grabbing my purse and making my way downstairs.

Anna was at the bottom of the stairs holding a camera and snapped a photo as I landed on the last step. "Stop," she yelled as I stopped in my tracks. "Don't forget to smile!" I giggled at her excitement and grabbed the railing with one hand, as I smoothed my dress with the other. Frankie followed a few steps behind me and somehow managed to spill the contents of her purse onto the floor while adjusting her hat. Anna's smile turned to a frown, and she sighed. "Oh, Frankie! Get yourself together and let's go! Herman is waiting!" She turned to walk outside and I crouched down to gather her lipstick, which rolled right under my feet. I smirked at Frankie as I popped back up, whispering "Did you hear that, Frankie? Get it together." We both smiled and sped outside to catch up with Anna.

We arrived at the school's parking lot a few minutes later. After a few minutes of cursing under his breath, Herman found a parking spot. He was quiet for the whole ride because he hated being late. He loosened up once he saw many other families standing around the parking lot and mingling instead of heading inside.

Anna wore a yellow pencil skirt with a matching jacket and new peep-toe floral shoes that came into the bridal shop a few weeks ago. She was always meticulous, but today, she was extra radiant. Frankie borrowed a floral dress out of my closet and paired it with a hat that didn't seem to want to stay put on her head. I was having the same trouble with my gradu-

ation cap, but Frankie did a good job of fastening it on the
ride over. I slipped on my graduation gown and the four of us
walked towards the auditorium. Anna, Herman, and Frankie
went inside to get seats, while I caught up with some friends
outside. We all headed into the auditorium once the ceremony
was set to start.

Our principal opened the graduation ceremony with a
speech about our bright futures. I clung to every word. He
spoke about our families and how important they've been in
reaching our goals and making it to this day. Without looking at me, my friend Martha grabbed my hand and squeezed
it tight. She knew that I had lost my parents—not how, of
course—and had been supportive since I met her on my first
day at this new school. The valedictorian's speech motivated
me as much as the principal's did. She said that today would
close the chapter on our previous lives and open the door to
our next adventures. After a troubling start to my teenage
years, I was anxious to start a new chapter, that's for sure.

A short while later, I stood in line near the stage as I waited
to receive my diploma. I scanned the crowd and saw Anna,
Herman, and Frankie. They all looked as proud as can be, and
Frankie caught my eye and made a funny face, which made
me feel at ease. I continued looking around at the crowd filled
with parents, grandparents, and siblings. And for a moment, I
swear I saw them. There they were, my birth parents, sitting in
the middle of the auditorium. They were beaming and laugh-

ing as they got ready to holler as I marched across the stage. They turned to wave at me, and just as I was about to raise my hand to wave back, my eyes welled up with tears. It hit me in that moment that my parents were no longer here. They would never be with me again. They would never be there to celebrate the significant moments, like my graduation. And they would most definitely not be there when my knees wanted to buckle and I wanted to fall apart like I was on the verge of this very second. I looked back at Frankie, who pointed towards the stage, indicating it was almost my turn to walk. I snapped out of it and, with a deep breath, strutted across the glowing stage to accept my diploma. I knew my parents weren't there physically, but wouldn't miss this moment for the world.

We arrived home and Anna took some photos of Frankie and me in my cap and gown. She loved to use the wildflowers as a backdrop and today was no exception. But today, the backyard was transformed for my graduation party that would start in a few short hours. Anna had been prepping for weeks. She created a menu, mailed invitations, and created centerpieces out of fresh flowers from the garden. As soon as we finished taking photos, she was back into party-planning mode. She instructed us to straighten up our rooms and headed into the kitchen to meet the caterers. Anna and Herman invited their families, as well as fellow employees from the shop and law firm. Frankie and I invited some of our friends, too. I never went to a party like this before—let alone had one thrown in my honor—but I couldn't wait to see it all come together. There was only one thing missing—my sisters.

A few short hours later, the guests arrived and the party had begun. I was happy to see Judge Mason and his wife, and couldn't wait to spend some time with him and fill him in on the girls. He had since retired from his job as a judge but he seemed to be enjoying retirement life. Annette and Arnold, my respite foster parents, came which was a shock to me because I haven't seen them in years. Annette gave me the biggest hug and introduced me to their newest addition—their young son, who was standing between them. He looked up at me with his beautiful blue eyes. Annette's eyes were sparkling and she seemed thrilled to be a new mother. I smiled at her and crouched down to greet him. With a gentle touch, he shook my gloved hand and they made their way into the party.

As the night went on, I took a break from mingling to discover the dessert table that Anna laid out. I decided on a slice of almond cake and a few Italian cookies and sat on a bench away from the crowd in the garden. The roaring sounds of laughter was evidence that the guests were enjoying themselves. Anna's jewels twinkled under the stars as she poured drinks for her girlfriends. I watched Frankie as she danced with friends on the far end of the yard and then turned my attention to Herman who was playing cards with a small group. His cigar smoke wafted into the air and disappeared into the charcoal night sky. As my attention turned back to my almond cake, I felt someone slide onto the bench next to me. It was Judge Mason.

"How's it going, Cookie?" he asked, as he stole a cookie off my plate and bit off a piece.

I covered my mouth with my hand as I finished a mouthful of cake. "Oh... hi, Judge Mason. I can't believe all these people came to celebrate my graduation." I pointed towards the party and grinned.

"Well, my dear. Let me fill you in on a little secret. Grown-ups will make any excuse to eat good food, drink a strong cocktail, and socialize under the stars," he said with a chuckle. "But it doesn't hurt that we are celebrating a kind young lady, either."

I blushed, looking down at my feet. It was silly of me to think all these people were here for me and me alone, although I was grateful nonetheless. "It seems like the only people who aren't here are my sisters. Would you believe that the last time I saw them was in this backyard four years ago, almost to the day?" It stung saying those words out loud and thinking about all the time that has passed since I last saw my sister's faces.

"I get it, Cookie. Have you been keeping in touch with the girls?"

"Yes, very often. We write almost every week. I must have hundreds of letters upstairs. Dottie and Connie recently wrote to share their details of their trip to The Grand Canyon and Sedona. And Dottie has a job!" I exclaimed. "And Connie is liking her new friends. She's settled in, for sure." He listened as I told him about the girls and all they've been through. I shared the news of Mary and Dom's separation and Dom and Barb's new baby. It was public knowledge at this point and I'm sure he heard the story from Anna already, but he listened anyway.

"How could four young girls experience so much in their short lives? I ask myself that all the time," he sighed. "But... now that you're an adult, I think I should share something with you. Something that might make it easier to accept your new home and new life here once and for all." He paused and looked at me. I had a pit in my stomach. "I knew your father back when he was alive. I used to see him in and out of the courtroom. His drinking got worse and worse as the years went on. He was a kind guy, Cookie. He loved you kids more than you'll ever know. But he wasn't fit to have you, he simply wasn't." I stared through him as he continued, my mind riddled with anxiety. "Your father almost killed your mother when she was pregnant with you in the car. I was the judge in that case, Cookie. I gave him another chance because I knew your mother needed him, but I always regretted it because he never got better. But then again, your sisters wouldn't be here if I didn't give him another chance. It's something that haunted me forever." Judge Mason had tears in his eyes. So did I. "You don't want to hear this and you might not believe me until you're older, but you're better off here. You're headed for a bright future and I don't think you would have had that in the end."

I wasn't quite sure why he dumped this on me. Dad almost went to jail. He almost killed me and Mom in a car accident. My sisters almost weren't here. I felt like a large brick smacked me in the face and knocked the wind out of me. "Why are you telling me this?" I asked, light-headed and confused.

He stood up and placed both hands on my shoulders. His eyes locked in on my tearful gaze. "Because I don't want you to go through life feeling bad for yourself. You and your sisters are fine. You're growing up as individuals and you'll always have each other, just like I said you would. But you need to move forward, Cookie. You, Frankie, Dottie, and Connie need to focus on what you have versus what you lost." He kissed me on the forehead before vanishing into the crowd.

Dottie woke up early on Saturdays to work at the bakery. She helped mix the dough and sweep the floors. But it wasn't all work—there was some play, too. She learned baking techniques from the owner, Filomena, like how to form perfect meringue peaks or make cherry pie filling. Mary dropped in every week at 7 a.m. on the dot to buy a loaf of bread. On some days, she didn't even need bread. She wanted to spend as much time as possible with Dottie, even though she saw the girls every Saturday night, too.

Mary always chatted with Filomena and they became good friends over the months. A few weeks ago, Dottie overheard them speaking in the front of the bakery. Filomena asked if Mary had an interest in helping her a few mornings a week. Filomena was an older woman and it was hard for her to be at the shop around the clock. Mary jumped at the chance. Since moving back to Tucson, she was unable to find a well-paying job, like at the factory she worked at with Dom. Money was tight since she was living on her own now in a small apartment downtown. And, of course, Mary saw this as an opportunity to further her bond with Dottie who seemed to be struggling from all the changes in her life.

Today was Mary's first official day, so she met Dottie right at 5:30 a.m. to help open the bakery while the rest of Tucson was still asleep under the hazy desert sky. Filomena was there, too. She showed Mary how to use the cash register and walked her through the regular customers that had accounts. There was one gentleman, for instance, that ordered two loaves of sesame bread every Saturday but paid once a month. He mentioned that one loaf was for him and one was for the birds to help them gain energy to fly. Filomena expected Mary to assist customers in the front so Dottie could focus on baking in the back. Although she was the youngest employee Filomena had at the age of 14, she was her best. She took pride in her work and never minded waking up early to start her shift. Dottie liked the peaceful walk to work, too, where she was alone with her thoughts.

The customers slowed down around mid-morning, so Mary joined Dottie in the back to help her clean. Flour always found its way into every crevice, so cleaning the kitchen took hours. Mary took a spot next to Dottie as she dried the dishes. "Hi, baby. I've missed you. How are things at home?"

"It's been a little crazy at home. There are five of us now in that little house. Barb is always home with the baby. Dom's working extra shifts. Luckily, Connie helps a lot with the baby. I don't know…" Her voice trailed off, as she dried a big baking sheet and placed it down on a towel.

"Well, Dottie, you can come and stay with me. I know my place isn't big, but it's close by and you'd be able to see your friends still." Mary had brought up the idea of coming to live with her in the past, but Dottie brushed it off. She didn't want to leave Connie again and there was not enough room for both of them at Mary's apartment. Plus, Connie got along well with Barb and was a natural with the baby. She wakes up with him at night and even watches him alone if Barb and Dom need to go out.

But for Dottie, the cramped living quarters, tight money, and baby's nightly cries led to many worrisome, restless nights. The house was a constant reminder that she was part of yet another broken family. Her and Connie's bedroom fan broke a week ago—in the middle of an Arizona heatwave—and Dom couldn't afford to get it fixed. They would each wake up drenched in sweat on top of sheets that were twisted from tossing and turning each night. Dottie saved every penny for a new fan, so they didn't have to sleep on the cool, hard family room floor. Instead of the luxuries her Connecticut sisters got to enjoy with their spending money, Dottie often spent her paychecks on necessities. She began to resent it.

Dottie began to consider the move more and more. She'd still be close enough to see Connie whenever she wanted, but far enough to have some reprieve from the chaos. And she wouldn't have to switch school districts in the fall. "Well, maybe I can start spending a few more nights a week with you. Would that be okay?" Dottie asked. She focused on the dishes and didn't look in Mary's direction. She was vulnerable and didn't want to cry.

"I think we can arrange that," Mary said with a smirk. She grabbed Dottie and pulled her into her chest for a hug. Dottie hugged her back as a single tear fell from her eye and landed on her apron. She hoped this was the change she needed.

10

Ray

Dear Dottie and Connie,

Oh, what a week. My graduation day came and went, and
it was memorable, to say the least. I felt like such an adult
walking across the stage and I can't wait for you guys to
experience this feeling. It feels like a whole new chapter is
about to start. I wish you girls were there to celebrate with
me.

And then there was my graduation party. It was great——
lots of food and dancing! But Judge Mason was there and
caused quite the stir. We had our usual chat session but
something was different this time. I don't want to go into
detail about what he said——we'll save that for when we're
old enough to have cocktails together. Plus, it's not like he
was mean or out of line. But he did say something that I
wanted to share with you both. He said we must continue
to move forward and focus on what we have versus what we
lost. I've been thinking about that advice a lot since he said

it. It's been four years since I've seen your faces. It's so hard not to dwell, but you girls are doing great now and so are we and that's what we have to remember.

After my talk with Judge Mason though, he and Anna had an explosive fight and they haven't spoken since. I felt bad for telling her, but I thought she should know. Anna thinks he overstepped his boundaries by always bringing up the past and for speaking to me like I'm an adult. She said there's enough negativity in the world and I don't need him bringing me down. I overheard their conversation and Anna was ruthless——she doesn't take anything from anyone, that's for sure. I hope they make up soon, though. I'd feel bad if they didn't.

Anyway, that's a lot to digest. I hope summer is going well for you both!

Love,
Cookie

I glanced over at Frankie who was rummaging through her purse. She pulled out her compact and applied yet another layer of lipstick. Then she began patting her face with powder, causing a small cloud to puff into the air.

"Frankie! Would you stop? You look perfect!" I asserted, waving the powder out of the air and turning my attention back to the road as the light turned green. We were driving to the local diner for her first date with Ray and, to put it lightly, Frankie was nervous.

A few months ago, Frankie's art teacher, Millie, started mentioning Ray in conversation. She told Frankie he was the intellectual type, but also quick-witted and kind. He was heading into his senior year of high school at the top of his class—he was ready to make a name for himself after graduation. She later learned that Ray's parents were well-off and his father, an inventor, recently passed away. Like Frankie, he also had three siblings; but he had one brother and two sisters. Millie mentioned he had his heart set on MIT in Cambridge. She thought he had a good chance of getting in because he was such a math wizard.

At first, Frankie would casually mention Ray in conversation over dinner with our family. Soon enough, talks of Ray became more prevalent and we started to feel like we knew him ourselves, even though the two of them hadn't met. But then one day, when Frankie and I were cleaning up the kitchen, the telephone rang. I answered.

"Hi, miss. Is Frankie around? I'd like to speak with her if I could." A young, smooth voice came through on the other end. I held the phone up to my chest, covering the mouthpiece, and mouthed to Frankie: "It's Ray!" She jumped up and down as if she saw her favorite celebrity walking down the street but collected herself once she picked up the receiver.

After speaking for a few minutes, the two hung up and Frankie was so excited she could barely get the words out. He asked her out on an official first date and he was bringing his buddy so I could tag along, too. It was payback for making Frankie go along on my date with Robert last year. But neither of us ever minded helping the other one out.

Just as Frankie finished gushing, Anna walked in to get something from the kitchen. Her ears perked up and I knew she was trying to overhear. "Who was that on the phone?" she asked while pretending to rustle through the drawer.

Frankie rolled her eyes and muttered, "Oh, it was a friend."

Anna looked up and shot Frankie a knowing smile before walking out of the kitchen. "Okay, dear. Whatever you say." Ever since I decided on nursing school, Anna has been on top of Frankie about her post-high school plans. This caused Frankie to be a little more closed off to Anna. She means well, but Frankie was dead set on art school after graduation and now she feels like she can't be herself. She tends to be short with Anna lately.

As soon as Anna was in the other room, Frankie's grin returned to her face. "What am I going to wear?"

We pulled into the parking lot of the diner. Frankie fidgeted with her nails and glanced around to see if she spotted Ray.

She had a good idea of what he looked like from the description Millie gave. A small crowd of people buzzed around the entrance—but there were no signs of Ray. This was Frankie's first date and her expectations were high. I hoped for her sake that he lived up to what she was anticipating.

"You ready?" I asked.

"Yeah, let's go. Maybe he's inside. Do I look okay?" Frankie glared into the mirror as she rubbed the mole on her cheek, almost as if she was trying to erase it with her finger. Her sleeveless pale yellow blouse had a bow tied at the collar. She tucked it into a knee-length flowy skirt and wrapped a navy cardigan around her shoulders. Frankie's jet black hair had a ribbon tied around it to keep it pulled back. Her profile reminded me how much she looked like our mother. She had grown up over the last few years, that's for sure.

"You're lovely, Frankie." I grabbed her hand. "He'd be crazy not to like you!" She brushed me off and chuckled, and we stepped out of the car to make our way inside.

The crowd near the door started to thin. Sitting behind them were two boys around our age—it was them. From Frankie's description, Ray was on the left. He was attractive— that was undeniable—but was approachable, which immediately put me at ease. He was facing his friend—who was cute, but nothing like Ray—and they were both laughing. He must have sensed us walking towards them, because a few seconds later Ray popped up. He brushed himself off and jogged towards us, his friend following behind. Ray's deep blue eyes narrowed in on mine for a considerable amount of time and he smiled wide, causing my body to feel flush. I broke his gaze as they caught up to us.

"You must be Frankie?" he said as he extended his hand out to meet her. "It's nice to meet you, finally." Frankie's dainty hand met his and she shook it gingerly. "And you must be the infamous sister."

His gaze turned to me. His chestnut hair was parted on the side with gel keeping it slicked in place. I put out my hand to meet his, my fingers meeting his palm and sliding into his grip. I yanked my arm back, reeling from the electricity, and focused my eyes on the ground to snap myself out of whatever I was feeling. "And this is my friend, Greg," he stated, and we both smiled to greet him.

We followed Ray and Greg inside and Frankie intertwined her arm into mine. She let out a deep sigh, relieved we had gotten the initial meeting out of the way. I slid into the booth across from Greg. Just as Frankie was about to sit next to me, Ray motioned for her to take the seat nearest Greg instead. He sat down and his leg grazed mine.

Over dinner, we learned that Greg was Ray's neighbor and that they grew up together. Greg was reserved, but Ray's story-telling was so boisterous and infectious that he couldn't help but open up. He told stories about playing football together in their neighborhood. We got a sense of his home life when he talked about his relationship with his sisters. He mentioned that he got in trouble for covering for them when they snuck out of the house to meet some boys. I hadn't laughed that hard in a long time; Frankie, either.

"So, Aunt Millie told me you're quite the artist, Frankie," Ray said. "I'm not much of an artist myself."

"Oh, yeah. I guess. I like to draw and paint, but it's more of a hobby."

"She's being humble," I chimed in. "She's the best in town."

"Is that so?" Greg asked. "I like to dabble in the arts myself. I'm not the best in town, though, that's for sure. Ain't that right, Ray?"

"Well, he's no Michelangelo but he's planning to go to art school in Boston down the street from where I'll hopefully be in Cambridge. The guy just won't leave me alone." We all laughed and Greg nodded his head in agreement. "Hey, should we get out of here? The bowling alley is calling our name."

A few minutes later, Frankie and I hustled through the parking lot to the car and got inside. As soon as the doors shut, we erupted into laughter. Tears were streaming down my face and Frankie leaned over and put her head on my shoulder. The world stood still as we savored the moment. "That was fun," she declared.

"Oh, goodness, Frankie. We haven't had a night like that in so long. And I'm dying to know what you think of Ray..." I wiped the tear from my face and wondered what her answer would be. I braced for the inevitable.

"Well, if I'm being honest. He's not my type." She went on, "Greg, though. He's artsy and reserved and funny, but quiet—kind of like me. And you realize, Cookie, that Ray has it bad for you? He didn't stop staring at you all night!"

My heart sunk low into my chest and my body tingled. "What? You think Ray likes me?" I was genuinely curious. Hell, I know how I felt, but I wasn't quite sure where his mind was. I mean the chemistry was electrifying; that was undeniable. But, Ray wasn't even my date and I didn't know if I wanted to get involved with school starting up in a few weeks.

"It couldn't be more obvious—Cookie, this. Cookie, that. He was vying for your attention all night, Cook!" I thought back to the moment we first touched hands and the only way I could describe it was an actual spark.

"Oh, quit it, Frankie! You're too much." I put the car in reverse and pulled out of the spot to head to the bowling alley. I was happy to continue the night with Ray and Greg.

We walked in and were greeted by Ray holding up two pairs of women's bowling shoes. "Hope we guessed the sizes right!" he shouted over the noise from the radio. We followed Ray over to the lane while Greg got us some sodas from the snack bar.

"Boys against girls," I said. "You guys are going down!" I tied my hair back and did some fake stretches, which made Ray laugh. As expected, the rest of the night flew by and was full of fun but embarrassing moments, which had us in stitches. I was glad I wore cigarette pants because Frankie almost flashed everyone around us when she slipped on the wooden floor! She was a good sport, though and we all had a chuckle.

After a few competitive matches, we were tied—one to one. Ray walked over to me and without hesitation, brushed a piece of hair from my sticky face. "You're going to need all the help you can get winning this tie-breaker, Cookie." His intense stare burned into my eyes and my cheeks grew flushed. I tucked my loose hair behind my ears.

Through a twisted mixture of adrenaline and soda pop, Frankie and I gave the last match every last drop of energy we had and we beat the boys. We lost all control and sprung up and down when Frankie got the final strike needed to win. I felt like we were the Yankees winning the World Series. It was the most spirited match of our lives.

"Okay, girls. You win. Good game, but this means we need a rematch one day." Ray said while looking in my direction.

"I think we can arrange that," I answered. "Good game, guys. That was too much fun."

After changing out of our bowling shoes, we all headed outside. It was dark at this point, and the moon illuminated the sky. Ray and I trailed behind Frankie and Greg, who were deep in conversation. "Cookie, I'm glad you came along tonight," he asserted, his voice was weighty and sincere. "The stars aligned, didn't they?"

"I guess we'll have to see what happens," I flirted back, nudging him with my shoulder as we strolled through the parking lot. They walked us to our car and we said goodbye. When Ray hugged me, he lingered for a few extra moments. His musky aftershave filled my nose with a smell I might never forget—burnished leather mixed with the antiseptic smell of alcohol. "It was nice meeting you," I whispered as I pulled away from him.

It was one of those kinds of nights I wished would never end. The kind you replay over and over in your head. As I laid in bed that night, I pondered what the future might have in store for us. For Ray and me.

Connie didn't take the news of Dottie leaving her to go stay with Mary more very well. She started spending more and more time out of the house. When she wasn't doing homework or watching the baby, Connie was at Jo's house. She felt abandoned, even though Dottie only stayed at Mary's house one or two extra nights per week. On the weekends, Connie stayed at Mary's apartment as well, but as time went on, she started to feel a little uncomfortable. Mary and Dottie grew closer with time, since Connie preferred spending time with Dom, Barb, and the baby, Tommy.

One Saturday after work, Mary and Dottie left the bakery

and picked up Connie on the way home. Mary beeped as she always did, but Connie didn't come out. "I'll go get her," Dottie said and jumped out of the car to the front door. "Hello?" she said, as she pushed open the door. "Anyone here?" She heard music and muffled conversation coming from the kitchen, so she made her way inside. Dom, Barb, and Connie—who was holding the baby on her lap—were sitting around the kitchen table and talking amongst themselves. They looked like a real-life family.

Dottie stopped in the doorway and watched for a moment. The scene in front of her confused her because it felt so different for her when she was living it day-to-day. Where Dottie felt the weight of a broken family dynamic, Connie was thriving as a daughter and big sister. And then there were Dom and Barb, who seemed happy in love. "Hey! Dottie!" Dom shouted. "We didn't hear you come in. Pull up a seat." Dom never seemed upset by Dottie splitting her time between the two homes, but Barb didn't agree with the living situation. Dottie and Barb didn't quite get along because Barb thought she was taking sides.

"Hi, everyone. Hi, Con." Dottie said as she sat down. "What's everyone talking about?"

"Well, Dottie. Good timing. The four of us are celebrating some big news." Dom said. Beads of sweat filled his ruddy round face and pooled into the divot above his lip before he wiped it away with the top of his shirt.

"Oh? What news?..."

"We're getting married!" Barb exclaimed, holding up her left hand that held a shiny new gold ring. Her eyes squinted as she saw Dottie's face drop. "Don't look so shocked, Dottie." She was right. Dottie was in shock, although she should have been expecting this.

Dottie cleared her throat. "I'm just surprised, that's all! But, congratulations. That is big news." Dottie wondered how Mary would feel about this. Dom and Mary separated a while ago, but their divorce only finalized last month. Sometimes Mary confided in Dottie about how loveless their marriage was. But there was a part of Dottie that thought Mary was sad he moved on to someone else. Dom needed a woman to take care of him, so the news of this impending marriage seemed inevitable. Dottie turned to Connie, who hasn't said a word since she walked in. "Mary's outside waiting. Let's go, Connie."

"I don't think I want to go tonight. Barb wanted to take a ride over to the department store to look at wedding dresses and she invited me. I want to go."

Dom must've seen the look on Dottie's face because he stepped in. "No, honey. You gals can do that another day. You've got to go with Dottie to Mary's house. Now, hurry up. She's waiting for you. You don't want to keep her." He patted the top of her hand and grabbed the baby from her. Connie glared at Dottie. "Fine," she said.

"Bye, everyone. I'll be back on Monday." Dottie said as she exited the kitchen. "Congratulations, again." She sounded sincere but was uneasy about the whole situation. Connie sighed and followed behind.

Before they opened the front door to head outside, Dottie turned around to face Connie. "Hey, a letter came from Cookie that I want you to see. She had a talk with Judge Mason." Connie's face softened a bit as they opened the door and walked to the car.

Dottie and Connie didn't share Dom and Barb's engagement news with Mary quite yet, as they didn't want to sour the day. Mary was treating them to ice cream and roller skating, using some of the tip money she earned at her new job. "Connie, dear. What's new?" Mary asked her while looking in the rearview mirror. Connie shrugged her shoulders, still miffed that she had to leave the rest of the family at home to stay with Mary and Dottie for the night. She stared out the window as Mary drove and thought about how different the houses back in Connecticut looked compared to the Spanish style of homes in Tucson. That was one of the things they missed the most about their neighborhood—the character of the homes. Every house looked unique and charming. In Tucson, every row of stucco homes seem to blend together.

Mary turned her attention back to the road, while Dottie reached into her pocket and pulled out the latest letter from Connecticut. She unfolded it and slid it across the backseat to Connie. Connie glanced at Dottie, rolled her eyes, but snatched the note to read it. A few minutes later, she placed the note back on the seat and reached out to grab Dottie's hand without looking over. Dottie grabbed Connie's hand and held it tight. The two internalized the words from the letter—to focus on what they had versus everything that they lost along the way.

Once Dottie and Connie laced up their skates, the heaviness of their lives floated away. They stumbled and gripped onto each other as they made their way to the rink, while Mary looked on. Soon they were doing laps, and with each loop around the rink, they became more and more confident. A few kids from school happened to be there, notably Jo's brother, Scott, who was in Dottie's class. Connie searched for a sign of Jo but didn't see her.

Even though it was Dottie who initially had a crush on Scott, Connie was over Jo's house so often that she was the one who became chummy with him.  And plus, Dottie moved on— there were plenty of other boys at school. Connie caught his eye and gave him a quick wave as she passed—nearly losing her balance when she raised her hand. He called out "Don't fall, Connie," mimicking her arms flailing in the air, while his friends doubled over in laughter. But Connie didn't pay any mind to it, though, because she knew Scott wasn't making fun of her. In fact, Jo recently told Connie that her brother had a crush on her.

One sweaty hour later, the girls stumbled off the rink and headed over to Mary, who was chatting with another mother she knew from the neighborhood. The girls were in their element, giggling and breathless, as they unlaced their shoes and whispered about the boys sitting a few benches away. Mary held up two nickels, beckoning them to go get some ice cream from the snack bar to finish the day.

The ride back to Mary's house was less quiet. Connie and Dottie joked about the number of times they each fell and brought the other down with them. Mary talked about how much they improved by the end—she was so pleased they had a great day. A light-hearted Saturday allowed the three of them to settle into their new family dynamic, which they haven't felt since Dom's affair shook things up.

Mary, who was usually reserved, opened up while cooking supper for the girls. "There's something I want you to know," she said, her voice sounding low and serious. She was chopping vegetables and her back was to Dottie and Connie, but she continued. "I knew about Dom and Barb for a while before he had the guts to tell me. It wasn't easy living under the same roof as him, knowing he was seeing someone else. But I wanted so badly to have a family and to be with you girls that

I stayed far longer than I should have." Dottie and Connie put their cards down and looked at each other. Although they were young, they realized this conversation was too important to ignore. Mary spun around to face them.

"When we saw her in the store that day, I knew it wouldn't be much longer before we were all broken apart, and it tore me up inside. I cried every night wondering how this would affect you both. You've been through so much already. I adopted you, knowing my relationship with Dom was rocky, but all I wanted was children. I thought things would be different once we moved to Arizona, but Dom met Barb and things got worse. Your father is a good man and he does love you girls, but he didn't love me any longer. And when you're old enough to start dating, I want you to know that I want more for you. I want you to be with someone who will love and respect you. And I want you to be happy. Learn from my mistakes and don't settle." She looked down at the floor, embarrassed.

Dottie and Connie rose from the table and walked towards Mary. They hugged her as she sobbed in her tiny apartment, while the emotions of the last few years escaped through her tears. Connie's eyes welled up, too. She finally understood that life had been hard on Mary, and she hasn't made it easier by any means.

And Dottie cried for a different reason as she realized every man in her life thus far taught her the wrong way to love. She hoped and prayed right then and there that she'd be able to love someone the right way someday, and that they would love her back.

11

❦

Weekend at
Country Cottage

November 1949

Cookie and Ray sitting in a tree:
   K——I——S——S——I——N——G!
First comes love,
Then comes marriage,
Then comes a baby in the baby carriage. [Well, maybe not yet, but we can hope right?]
   Frankie told us all about Ray, Cookie. We can't wait to hear more!

Love,
Dottie and *Connie*

The crisp air and fallen leaves indicated that time was always moving forward. November seemed to be here in a flash. After a bustling wedding season and heavy workload at the firm,

Anna and Herman headed north for a weekend getaway. They left on a Thursday, leaving Frankie and me on our own for the first time. We decided there was no better time to escape to The Country Cottage for a few nights for a change of scenery. After all, fall was somehow coming to an end. Frankie and I headed to Ridgefield after school on Friday to soak in the last bits of fall and spend some quality time together.

Life felt extra busy to us, too, lately. Frankie began her senior year of high school and daydreamed about what life looked like after graduation. I transitioned into college life while still helping Anna with her fall brides at the shop. And to top it off, Ray and I started seeing each other more and more, and things between us were starting to get serious.

Looking back on the last few months since I met Ray, I realized why I'd been so attracted to him the instant I laid eyes on him. Aside from being handsome and cool, he was well-read and intelligent—it was an enchanting combination. Even Anna and Herman were smitten by his attentiveness and how kind he was to both me and Frankie. Every time he came over to visit, he would make small talk with Herman about golf and would compliment Anna's cooking. I even looked out the window once to find him helping Anna with the garden one day. He wore her pink floral gardening gloves and had his slacks rolled up off the ground. The two of them were cracking up, like they were old friends from school who knew each other for years. He had this way of making everyone feel at ease and listened with such intensity. When I was with him, it felt like no one existed except the two of us. He made me feel like a princess and everything felt right.

Two months ago, I was zipping up a bride-to-be's wedding gown when I heard the bells on the front door jingle at the shop. There he was—hiding a lush bouquet behind his back as he grinned from ear-to-ear once our eyes met in the mirror. His hair was a bit disheveled and his uniform wrinkled from the school day, but he looked perfect in the afternoon light. I straightened the bride's veil as he leaned against the counter and watched my every move. Anna moseyed out of the backroom and knew right away that the young man standing in front of her was Ray. This was their first meeting, so Ray extended his hand and introduced himself. She gave me a wink and I knew she approved.

It didn't hurt that Ray's prominent family was known around town. The local newspaper featured his father dozens of times for work he had done while he was alive. Ray's mother was somewhat of a socialite and Anna saw her at various events. Although, after Ray's father died, his mother tended to stay out of the spotlight. They were well-off, but Ray was so down-to-earth that no one would know that they had means unless you knew his parents and their accomplishments.

Soon after Anna met Ray, he asked me to meet his family, too. Ray had three siblings: Marty, Peggy, and Rita. The two sisters resembled each other so closely, right down to the dark-rimmed cat eye glasses and auburn hair. They both talked with their hands and tilted their heads back when they laughed—it was endearing and made me wonder if Frankie and I had similar mannerisms to each other. I hit it off with his sisters right away, which was a relief. We stood around in the kitchen and chatted about the boys they were dating. They even showed me a photo of Ray in a sailor outfit when he was little, his small face beaming with pride as he sat on top of his father's lap. His brother was tougher, though. Marty, with his icy blue eyes, was stoic and intense as he questioned me about my life and my plans, but warmed up to me as the evening went on. He was impressive, and he didn't let you forget it. Ray, as wonderful as he was, was oftentimes overshadowed by his brother's drive and perfection. There was nothing Marty couldn't do, and Ray always felt like he had to keep up. This included his decision to pursue his top-school, MIT, in the fall. It was always Ray's dream to go to Cambridge, but then Marty got in with a full scholarship. He hustled to stay at the top of his class, turning Ray's dream of MIT into Marty's reality.

Fast forward to a few weeks ago: Ray shared that he submitted his paperwork for an early decision at MIT, along with other back-up schools. Nervous, but excited, he took me into his arms and hugged me deeply, almost as if he was trying to transfer all my positive energy to him. He held me and we swayed back and forth. I was happy for him, but my mind wandered to what it meant for us. I wanted Ray to have the full college experience at MIT without the worry of a long-distance girlfriend. I let those thoughts escape my mind, pulled back, and smiled up at him. "I don't want to get your hopes up," I said, "but I am pretty sure I'm in the arms of MIT's next brightest star."

The thought of Ray leaving weighed on me, which is part of the reason I suggested getting away for the weekend. Frankie always grounded me and I needed her perspective. After a quick drive to Ridgefield, we set our bags down and changed into hiking boots and sweatshirts to take a walk on the property.

"How's school?" I asked as we walked down the hill towards the shallow brook.

Frankie rolled her eyes. "It's going. My classes are hard this year. Oh, and Anna slipped a brochure under my door the other day. It was for the same X-ray program you're in now. She acts like it never crossed my mind that you're in nursing school. I don't know what it is, but she can't seem to let me enjoy my senior year without the constant reminder that I have to decide what's in store for me afterward. How come she was never on top of you like this?"

"Good question. I think it's because I kind of knew that's the path I wanted to take. With you though, she's so worried you're going to go rogue and move to California for art school." We both let out a chuckle. "But she also has to know that she can't force you to follow in my footsteps if that's not what you want to do. It can't end well." My thoughts went straight to Ray and his brother, Marty.

"Well, what if I do want to go to art school, Cookie? I mean, it's not the end of the world. At least I want to go to school. She makes it seem like I'm going to prison or something."

"You know those two. They want to set you up for success. And I wonder if Anna kind of regrets not going into something more stable like nursing. I mean her shop does well, but Herman's a lawyer, so she has something to fall back on if she needs to. Maybe she doesn't want you to worry?" Without question, I knew this was why Anna was so set against Frankie being an artist. She wanted us to have our own careers and not depend on anyone in the future. Anna was a strong woman who valued independence and making a name for herself, and she wanted that for us, too.

We walked in silence for a few minutes, stepping on the rocks as we waded through the shallow stream of water. We spent the next hour strolling along the brook, watching as the cardinals and squirrels buzzed around their playground. The large leaves that fell off the trees crunched under our feet as we moved in slow motion. There was a recognizable chill in the air that told us winter was coming. When the sun started to set and cast shadows over the property, Frankie and I decided it was time to make the trek back up the hill to the house and start supper.

The Country Cottage was a place where we made memories

and all stress melted away. It was a home you would see on a star-studded movie set. It was full of warmth and decorated in muted blue and cozy yellow florals. Everything in the main room centered around the floor-to-ceiling stone fireplace and its heavy barn wood mantle. On it were photos of Anna and Herman and, of course, Frankie and me. Knit blankets draped over the couches to keep us warm from the snow-filled nights. Herman's worn-in mahogany leather chair glowed from the light of the fireplace. His reading glasses sat on the side table atop a birdwatching book he often skimmed through.

After supper, Frankie and I spent the evening alternating between doing school work and dozing off in the dimly lit room only illuminated by flames. At some point, Frankie pulled out her sketchbook and started to draw the intricacies of the fire: ash and all. She said the charcoal scene would make a perfect Christmas gift for Herman and Anna. I tried to focus on my chemistry textbook but found my thoughts drifting to Ray. When I told him I was going to The Country Cottage this weekend to take a break, he got worried. He thought a break from life meant I was unhappy with him, but it was quite the contrary. I was too happy with Ray, which made me worried. I was too used to being left behind by the people I loved the most, and the last thing I needed was Ray—someone I could see a future with—leaving me, too. As the fire started to flicker and die, my eyes closed and I drifted to sleep.

The hazy morning rays filtered in through the blinds, warming my eyelids and drawing me awake. It was early morning, and Frankie had fallen asleep next to me, her legs intertwined with mine on the couch. She looked so peaceful and I wondered what Frankie dreamt about—was it our birth parents, our new parents, her sisters, school, or art? Most likely, her dreams were like mine, nonsensical and seemingly unrelated to the real-world, for better or worse. I wished Mom and Dad made their way into my dreams more—mostly to show me they were at peace, but also to give me hints about why their lives were cut short, leaving the four of us to discover our new destinies.

A light knock at the picture window startled me and I popped up out of my seat. Frankie, none the wiser, rolled over and buried her head deeper into the cushions. I peered through the blinds and was shocked to see Ray standing there

on our front steps. I slipped my feet into slippers, wrapped a wool blanket around me, and crept over to the door to pull it open. This caused a cool burst of November air to hit me in the face. Instead of inviting him in, I joined Ray on the porch. I hugged him and took in his warmth.

"What are you doing here?" I asked as I looked up at his sculpted, grinning face. I was happy he was here but also so confused. Why did he drive all the way out here when I would be back in town tomorrow?

"I forgot to tell you something the other day when I saw you."

"Oh? And what's that?"

"I love you, Cookie," he replied.

The world melted into the picturesque landscape around us. He kissed my forehead and walked back to his car to drive away, making me wonder if Ray was even here at all or if I was still dreaming.

Or maybe—just maybe—it was both.

On a chilly spring morning in Tucson, Dom and Barb eloped at the local courthouse. It was different from the only other courthouse they knew of back home in Connecticut. This one was brighter and hollow, every noise echoed off the tiled floor; whereas the courthouse in Connecticut seemed so dark and forlorn. It had Native American tapestries adorning the walls in shades of orange, brown, and yellow. Aside from Dottie, Connie, and little Tommy, Barb's mother and father came to witness their vows. The ceremony was brief, but Dom and Barb looked happy as they kissed for the first time as husband and wife. Afterward, everyone retreated to the diner where Barb worked to celebrate a fresh start.

Barb wore a knee-length ivory skirt with a matching jacket and peep-toe heels. Her hair was tied in an updo, with tendrils cascading down her face. On her lips was the same shade of lipstick she wore that day in the department store, the same day the girls and Mary first saw she was pregnant with Tommy. Barb was unusual looking, but stunning. She had full lips, a distinctive mole on her cheek, and a curvy figure that she flaunted—in other words, she couldn't look more different than Mary.

Dottie donned an oversized dress that she picked up from the thrift store with Mary. Unlike Barb, there was not a curve in sight on Dottie. Connie opted to wear a suit like Barb's but gray instead of ivory. She even wore her first pair of heeled shoes. After Mary poured her heart out to the girls, Dottie and Connie made every effort to not let the intensity of their worlds get between them. Although they split their time between the two homes, they were closer than ever these days. Dottie and Connie appreciated the fact that they were each other's constants in a place that seemed to be ever-changing.

Life didn't break them and they had each other.

Barb's coworkers draped the corner table with streamers and confetti for the occasion. Connie and Dottie slid into the booth and Barb's parents sat across from them. They were pleasant people, younger than expected. They talked to Dottie and Connie about school and told them about where they lived in New Mexico. The cities out west were far different than the quaint New England towns they grew used to while growing up in Connecticut. Sure, Dottie and Connie were used to the cacti and rocky terrain. They even grew to love the painted desert skies, in hues of purple and orange. But they missed the winding hilly roads with green grass as far as the eye could see. And the white picket fences lining the roads with cheerful pink and yellow blossoms. And nothing compared to the first fluffy snowfall of winter, where their eyes lit up as they watched each unique snowflake fall to the ground out of the picture window of their bedroom.

While Barb's parents chatted with Connie, a memory from a family trip to Cape Cod, Massachusetts crept into Dottie's head. Against Mom's wishes, Dad convinced the family to go on a fishing boat out of Provincetown. Dottie remembered looking out into the sea as a whale emerged and rolled onto its side. It raised its fin into the air and flopped it against the waves—like it was waving to her—before sinking into the deep blue ocean. Somehow, her sisters missed that enormous whale. Meanwhile, Mom spent the entire boat trip curled up on a bench. Her gaze fixated on the horizon, making every effort to not throw up, although her efforts eventually failed her. Dottie named the whale "Blue." She hadn't thought of that memory in several years, most likely because she hasn't seen the ocean since living in Arizona. Blue and the memory of that trip made her nostalgic for simpler times.

After lunch, Dom clinked his fork on his glass to alert the table's attention to him. He started speaking. "I wanted to say a few words to everyone. To Paul and Cindy, thanks for coming in from New Mexico. I know we did things a little backward here, but I'm grateful you didn't write me off. I think it's clear how happy this pretty little woman over here makes me, and I know she feels the same. And to my children, you stood by me as I figured things out and helped me see the true meaning of life, which is love. Love for your children and love for your other half. Which brings me to Barb, you came into my life and turned it upside down, but we made it to the other side. You brought me a son and a brother for the girls, and you brought back the twinkle in my eye. I love you, Barb."

Dottie squeezed Connie's leg and shot her a smirk, as they all clinked their glasses together in unison. And there the girls sat—cozied into a booth with their imperfect, expanded family, consisting of a dad, stepmom, half-brother, and even step-grandparents. They finished off the last bits of wedding cake and laughed. To the world, they looked like a real family, because that's what they were.

Life was good for Dottie and Connie on that Tuesday afternoon in Tucson.

12

The Storm

Spring 1950

Dottie and Connie,

How are things in Arizona? I hope we can visit you someday. How have things been since Dom and Barb got married? You said he was happier, so that must be a relief. Wish
them well for us, would you girls? Maybe Mary will find
love again, too. She's a nice lady.

So, I've made a decision. I decided to go to nursing
school in the fall like Cookie. However, Cookie is going to
be an X-ray technician and I'm not sure what path I want
to take yet. I will still do art on the side, though. I'll never
give that up. Actually, a few of us from art class are taking
a ride this weekend to a garden that has rows and rows of
lavender fields. We are going to practice oil painting for the
first time. Wish me luck!

With love,
Frankie

I placed my book on my lap and peered out the window into the garden. After a cold Connecticut winter, the days were lighter and the temperatures started to rise. Any evidence of snow had finally disappeared and subtle signs of spring were all around. I watched as a goldfinch landed on an empty birdhouse, reminding me to fill it when I had the chance. A budding pink rose stood out amongst the dreary gray and brown palette. Spring was my usual annual cue that change was near; however, I wasn't quite sure if I was quite ready for a change this year.

I spent the winter with Ray. He was finishing up his senior year of high school, and I spent my days in class and nights studying. I spent time with my friends, and he saw his friends, too, but we spent every other moment together. We went ice skating, took long drives around the state, and we even walked along the shore when the weather was decent. He was the type of person you could spend all day with and never tire of. Ray and I talked about everything and anything. He knew how close I was to my sisters and began talking about them in conversation, almost as if he knew them himself. He knew of my birth parents, too; however, he didn't know how they died and I never planned on telling him the full details of that day.

Anna and Herman adored him, and he and Frankie became close friends, too. All in all, we were two peas in a pod. But one thing was looming over us. One by one, his college acceptance letters started to trickle in. All but one: MIT. Until today.

The doorbell rang and I heard Frankie scurry to answer. It was Ray. I wasn't expecting him today, but I made my way downstairs to greet him. Ray was holding a sealed envelope in his hands with the familiar MIT logo in the corner. He held it up, saying "I got this in the mail today. I wanted to open it with you." He looked nervous. By then, Anna and Herman had also gathered in the foyer to see Ray. They soon retreated to the kitchen once they learned why Ray was here to give us some privacy.

"Here goes nothing." His usual confident tone was absent from his voice. He dug his finger under the flap of the envelope and tore it open in one swift motion. Frankie glanced at me as I watched his eyes as he scanned the unfolded letter. "Well, that's that," he chided, as he clumsily shoved the letter in the envelope, not bothering to read the rest. "MIT doesn't want me, after all."

My heart sank into my stomach. "Let's go outside," I suggested as I pulled him towards the door before he had the chance to respond. I wanted to spare him the sympathy pep talks from my family. He followed me into the garden. Although the plants and flowers were still thawing from winter, the grounds were a welcome and silent reprieve. I led him deeper and deeper into the yard until no one could see us from the windows.

"Are you okay?" I asked as I held his shoulders.

"Yeah. I'm okay. Don't worry about me, Cookie," he replied. He locked his eyes on mine, but I could tell his mind was elsewhere. "It wasn't meant to be."

"What do they know, anyway?" I questioned, knowing the thought sounded silly coming out of my mouth. They are MIT, after all. "Well, it's their loss." He let out a chuckle as he pulled me towards him.

"I think it might be a good thing, Cookie. Maybe I shouldn't be following in my brother's footsteps. And, maybe I should stick around here so I can be closer to you..." His voice trailed off. It's the first time he's addressed what moving away from here meant for us.

"You can't stick around here, Ray. You know that. Where are you going to go to school around here? All the other schools you applied to are down south."

"I mean, Georgetown was my second choice and I got in there. But it's so far from you. I don't think I can do it."

"Listen to me, Ray. You're not going to jeopardize your future and stay here just because of me. I won't let you do that."

"Well, there's no other option."

For some reason, I've had this heavy feeling weighing on me all week, almost as if I knew this moment was coming. "I think we should take a break from each other then. You need a clear head going into the last few months of school while you figure this all out. And I need to get through some big Chemistry and Physics exams. The timing isn't right for us." My voice was stern as I pulled back from him and I couldn't look into his eyes for even a second longer. Saying those words out loud broke my heart as much as I knew they would break his.

"Cookie, don't do this. I know you don't mean it." He sat down on the bench nearest to us and put his head in his hands.

"I'm not breaking up with you, Ray. I just think we need a breather." But deep down, I knew that taking a break from each other was only the beginning and, in due time, it would lead to a more permanent ending. I sensed that MIT would be hard on our relationship since we wouldn't see each other as often, but I knew we'd be able to make a few hour distance work. But, with Ray now planning to move to Washington, D.C. in the fall, it would be selfish for me to hang onto him instead of letting him focus on his studies. He deserved the full college experience without running back and forth to Connecticut every weekend.

"If that's what you want, Cookie. So be it." Ray stood up and walked towards me. "I'll be here when you change your mind."

He kissed me on the forehead and marched the other way, leaving me to collect my thoughts in the garden.

"Connie? Are you awake?" Dottie whispered in case she was still sleeping.

"Yeah, Dottie? What's going on?"

It was 5 a.m. and Dottie was getting ready for work in their bedroom. It was getting hot in Tucson and Dottie tossed and turned all night. "I had a dream about Mom and Dad last night," she said.

"What happened?" Her eyes were groggy as she turned towards Dottie.

Dottie started, "We were all on a huge ship with Mom and Dad. Frankie and Cookie were there, too. We were heading into a storm that was brewing overhead. The seas were rocky and the ship tilted from side to side. I remember almost being able to reach out and touch the ocean as the boat rocked so far that it felt it was going to tip over. And the black sky swirled as lightning lit up the sky. We couldn't even walk around the boat. As we braced for the heavy rains, I looked over to the steering wheel and Dad wasn't there anymore. I yelled for him but I couldn't even hear myself over the intense sounds of thunder and the waves crashing against the boat. So I kept looking and I discovered him downstairs in a cabin, drinking by himself. And then I heard Mom scream from the deck that the ship was headed towards another ship, but Dad didn't get up. He just kept pouring brown liquor into his cup as chaos ensued around him. And then, there was a deafening crash and everything around me went dark. That's when I woke up. I couldn't sleep for the rest of the night."

"Geesh, Dot. That's intense for a Saturday morning. It was just a dream though. You must have been thinking about the storm we had the other night and all that lightning."

"It's weird, that's all. Even in my dream, Dad couldn't save us." Dottie finished tying her shoes and grabbed her bag. "I'll see ya later, Connie. Go back to bed."

"Oh, thanks for nothing, Dottie. Easy to say now after you told me that story!" Connie laughed and rolled over, pulling the pillow over her head.

As Dottie mixed the dough in the bakery, she thought about Mom, Dad, and her sisters. She realized that in her dream, no one had aged. Every time she thought about me and Frankie, she envisioned us at 14 and 13, the same ages we were when she last saw us. This thought infuriated Dottie. She didn't even know what her sisters looked like now. Yes, we spoke all the time through letters and an occasional phone call but it's been years since she's seen and touched us. A lot has happened in almost five years.

Mary interrupted her thoughts. "Hey, Dottie! What's shakin', honey?" She threw her purse onto the counter and washed her hands to get started for the day.

Dottie smiled at Mary. "Hi... Can you check on those cookies in the oven for me?" Her mind was blank as she continued to knead the dough, and thoughts of her family crept back into her head. Her dream was nagging her. Why couldn't Dad save them? He had the strength and power to do so, but he chose to hide below deck and lean into alcohol as if that would solve his problems.

The day went on and Dottie was on auto-pilot as she baked cookies and loaves of bread for the customers. Mary hustled around the shop, too, as she helped customers and filled orders. At the end of the day, Mary asked Dottie if she could lock up so she could run to the bank and deposit money for Filomena who was out of town. Dottie used the extra time alone to deep clean the kitchen and prep her space for tomorrow morning, which meant organizing the ingredients in the cabinets. She lifted heavy bags of flour and sugar out and onto the counter to wipe the spilled bottle of vanilla. That's when she noticed it: a bottle of light rum that Filomena used for her famous Italian rum cake. She's seen it before but never thought about drinking it until now. She pulled it out by the handle and poured some into a mug, staring at it for a few moments. She closed her eyes and gulped it down, cringing at the taste of it, but not stopping.

"This one's for you, Dad," Dottie said out loud, alone in that dark steel kitchen. At almost 15, she was too young to comprehend the gravity of the decision she made. Dottie slumped down on the floor and continued sipping the dark liquor. But although she knew she shouldn't be doing this, it felt a little too natural. Soon enough, it would become a habit.

13

New York, New York

Fall 1950

Dear girls: "Greetings from New York!"

We've arrived in New York City! Since Frankie didn't want a graduation party, Anna and Herman treated us to a weekend getaway in the city instead. This was the first weekend we have been able to get away since school started up again in the fall. Our hotel overlooks Central Park and we've seen several horse and carriage rides right from our room.

This is the first time we've been to the city, and there's a list of sites we want to see. Well, Frankie's list consists of art museums and galleries, while I want to see where the days take me! We will tell you all about it.

Maybe one day, we can meet here for a sisters' weekend!

Missing you both,
Cookie

Frankie and I peered out the window in awe of the cityscape. My senses were overloaded. Horns honked in every direction, the siren lights illuminated the smoky sky, and the smell of clean linen sheets from our luxurious hotel room filled the air around me. I looked up at the skyscrapers that lined the block, each one with hundreds of shiny windows reflecting the light from the sun overhead. I wondered about the people who lived inside those buildings and thought about how their lives were probably so different than mine. We were in New York City and, so far, it was everything I thought it would be.

Frankie begged Anna and Herman to forgo her graduation party and come here for the weekend instead. Frankie didn't love the attention on her to begin with, and she has been reading about the plethora of New York museums in her art classes. This disappointed Anna at first—she loves planning parties—but she caved in. She decided it would be good for us to spend some time away from Connecticut as a family. The four of us had different agendas while we were here, but Herman was adamant about getting together for dinner and a show on Saturday evening. Otherwise, we were left to our own devices in the hustle and bustle of the city.

Anna's wedding gown distributors were located in the city, so she scheduled meetings with the men and women she worked with while she was here. And since I was so involved with day-to-day business at the shop, she asked me to join her to get some inspiration. The community admired Anna's bridal shop, but it was quite traditional. Anna hoped to bring more avant-garde inspired looks into the shop, and what better place to spark our imaginations than New York City.

On the other hand, Herman revered history and architecture, so he opted to explore the city on foot at his own pace. His idea of a perfect day was to walk the streets with a map in hand only stopping to pop into The American Museum of Natural History to take in the exhibits. He would later describe what he learned to us and hope it would drum up some interest in the topics he loved most.

Frankie, of course, desired spending time in art museums and galleries. She also wanted to walk past the creative window displays lining the storefronts on Fifth Avenue. She lugged her sketchbook along and planned to spend her downtime sitting in the park and drawing—that's what she loved to do best.

And then there was me. I would most likely shadow Anna on Saturday morning as we visited bridal shops around the city. Part of the intrigue of being in a new place was to discover where the day would take you without an agenda. The thrill of slinking into a cafe and sipping hot coffee while watching people go about their days, or disappearing into a movie theatre and shutting the world out—those are the types of indulgences that appealed to me. And this afternoon was no different. I excused myself from the hotel room and trotted towards the park to take in the last bits of sunshine before it got dark. People lined the sidewalks but were sparse once I entered the park. The smoggy air smelled of hot dogs and sweet roasted nuts and the green grass reminded me of home, but the sirens and horns didn't let up for a second. I purchased a few postcards from a street vendor and took a seat on a metal park bench. A young boy and his mother walked by and I grinned at him. He stuck his tongue out at me and was so distracted that he dropped his ice cream cone onto the pavement. I looked away and heard the trailing sounds of his mother scolding them as they continued on their way. Being alone was no longer frightening in the way it had been before.

For the months following my parents' death, there were times where I thought I'd be alone forever. Then Anna and Herman came along and welcomed Frankie and me into their home and loved us without question. My sisters and I fell into a new normal—although we were apart and missed each other, we all felt connected. Well, I think we did, anyway. I know Frankie would stop everything to read a letter that came in from the girls. And as crazy as it sounds, when Ray came along, he seemed to love me from the moment we first touched hands. I no longer felt alone in this world, and that's when I learned to love my own company. Even when Ray and

I broke up, spending time alone felt welcomed because it was on my terms.

I broke up with Ray for two reasons. First, I wondered if it was possible to find the love of my life within my first-ever boyfriend. Sure, I've dated before Ray and I've dated here and there since, but no one else had electrified me the way he did. His touch. His mind. His soul. When we talked, he shut out the rest of the room and his blue eyes pierced through me. We could be talking about the weather and even that was exciting. When we walked down the road, he would sometimes tuck his hand into my back pocket with a wink, which always made the hair on my arm stand up. And he would get into intellectual—not heated—debates with Herman in his office about President Truman. He was able to connect to people in a way that felt natural. Everything about Ray was magic. But I questioned our relationship because I didn't want it getting ripped away—much like the lost relationships of my loved ones who came before him. Second, I didn't want Ray to be the type of guy who stayed behind instead of pursuing his dreams. He was far from mediocre, and I knew life had big plans for him that weren't in our hometown.

We met up a few times after our break-up and each time got harder. The last time I saw him was at Frankie's graduation in June. After her ceremony, Frankie, me, and a few of her friends went out for a bite to eat and Ray was there as well. I slipped into the booth and noticed him immediately across the room. A woman around his age—a friend, I assume—was fixated on Ray. She touched his arm as he boisterously told a story to a table full of friends. I looked away and wondered if he had already moved on from me. By the time I looked back up, he was standing at the end of our table looking down at me.

"Hi, Cook," he said, as he raised his eyebrows and waved to all the girls at the table. "I thought I'd see you here."

"Hi, Ray," I replied, trying to sound confident when I felt anything but at that moment. "Congratulations. It's a big day for you!"

The waiter had come over and was standing behind Ray in annoyance. "Sorry, man, just one more second." He reached into his pocket and pulled out a folded up piece of paper and shoved it into my purse. "This is for you. It was nice seeing you, Cook." My face was hot and I couldn't help but feel embarrassed.

Somehow, Ray's note fell into the back of my mind, until today. As I sat on the park bench in the middle of the city, I opened my purse and pulled it out. The note read, "I know you don't want to believe me, but I'm yours forever, Cook. You'll come around."

I held it up to my chest and looked up towards the sky, giggling as a single tear streamed down my face. There I sat, alone in one of the largest cities in the world, as I came to the realization that no one would ever come along who made me feel the way Ray made me feel. I vowed to call him on Sunday when I got home to see if we could work things out, if it wasn't too late, of course.

As I crossed the busy street back to the hotel, I spotted Frankie standing in front of the doors. She saw me right away and smiled big, waving for me to come over. "I know you were planning to explore on your own tonight, but I was wondering if you want to catch a movie with me?"

"What happened to the gallery you wanted to see?"

"Eh, the gallery will be there tomorrow. I'd rather spend tonight with my best friend." She linked arms with me and we strolled down the crowded sidewalk. I concluded that being alone was fine and all, but nothing beat the way I felt when I was with the people I loved the most.

I couldn't help but think about Dottie and Connie in that moment. I wished they were linked on either side of us while we laughed and walked around the vibrant city, recreating Frankie's drawing from years ago. Four girls in the big city; four girls who have it all...

Sunday afternoon, Anna, Herman, Frankie, and I arrived home. We were gritty and exhausted from the city and our wonderful adventures. After washing up, I snuck down to the kitchen to call Ray's mother to get his new phone number in

Washington D.C. I couldn't wait to tell him that I found the note and he was right—I finally came around.

I felt anxious as she answered the phone, pouring my heart out about why I needed to speak to him so urgently. His mother paused before responding. "...oh, I'm sorry Cookie, I thought you knew. Ray didn't go to Georgetown. He's not in D.C. after all. He got drafted."

I gasped.

"Ray's in the Army now."

Dottie sat on the edge of her bed and stared up at the drawing Frankie had made of her and her sisters. She remembered rolling it up and tucking it into her suitcase for the voyage to Arizona almost seven years ago. On the cross-country drive, she would stare out the window into the wide-open rolling fields in the middle of nowhere. She'd imagine what it would feel like to be an adult woman roaming the streets of the big city with her sisters by her side. She suspected life would feel whole again once they were old enough to recreate the four cosmopolitan women from the drawing. The same drawing that would soon hang on their bedroom wall in Tucson.

The funny thing, though, is that Dottie hadn't looked at the drawing in years. The heat had aged it—the corners curled up and the paper turned yellow and brittle. But the four women remained. They skipped down the street like all was okay in the world. Dottie continued to stare at it. She noticed the intricacies of the drawing that Frankie added, down to the litter on the ground and the license plate on the red car parked on the road. The longer she stared, the more it seemed like the drawing came to life. Her imagination took over as the four women leapt off the page and slipped into a speakeasy for an after-dinner cocktail. She visualized the passers-by staring in awe of their beauty and friendship, but they ignored everyone else. The four women floated in their own little snow globe in the big city as the world spun around them.

Dottie rested her chin into her hands and thought about her sisters. In almost every letter, the writer mentioned how much they missed each other. It was hard to believe so much time had gone by, and she hoped something would bring them together soon.

It was Friday night and Dottie was waiting for some friends to pick her up from Dom's house. Connie was at Jo's, and Dom and Barb had taken the baby to see her parents for the weekend. She was alone for the first time in years. Dottie grew surprised at how deafening the silence was—she was so used to having people around. If she wasn't at Dom's house with Connie and her family, she was at Mary's downtown apartment where she could hear the neighbors through the walls. When she wasn't home, she was at work or school. And when she wasn't there, she would be with her friends. Dottie never had the opportunity to sit still. She wasn't sure she liked it.

Being alone led her mind to wander. She noticed this was when she would sneak alcohol from Dom's liquor cabinet. She wasn't home alone often enough for it to become a problem but it was her first instinct every time she was alone—which was the issue. Although she was alone, she tiptoed to the dining room to see what she could drink before her friends arrived. On the bottom shelf was a glass decanter filled with an unknown dark brown liquor that Dom sipped after work from time-to-time. She pulled it out and brought it to her lips, sucking down a few mouthfuls before wiping her chin and closing the lid.

Her friends knocked on the door, startling Dottie as she put the bottle back onto the shelf. Dottie's friends were more like acquaintances—they weren't the studious types like Connie's friends. They got in trouble for smoking cigarettes in the boys' bathroom at school. They wore tight jeans and had long flowing hair but harsh faces that didn't look youthful. They stole each others' boyfriends when the other wasn't looking. They were "those" types of friends.

Dottie hid these friends from Dom, Mary, and Barb and they were none the wiser about the crew she associated with. Connie warned Dottie about them after hearing stories from Jo's brother, Scott, but Dottie didn't listen. Dottie had fun with them and she wasn't going to let a few stories ruin her good time. The girls drank, too, so she didn't bother to conceal the alcohol on her breath before heading outside to the car.

Dottie and her friends headed to a party on the local college campus. Some of her friends were older and hung around college-aged kids instead of with their high school classmates. The idea of attending a college party intrigued Dottie. The thrill of remaining anonymous amongst the sea of others intrigued her. She also wanted to find her place in the world—she didn't seem to fit in anywhere. When they arrived, her friends scattered, leaving her alone to discover what the night would hold.

Dottie was generally a quiet observer. She enjoyed being in the kitchen or at the bakery and getting lost in baking. At school, she stayed under the radar. She met a few friends over the years in Tucson but hadn't had the same popularity as Connie. She liked to keep to herself until, of course, her new friends came into the picture. They started giving her more attention, which caused Dottie to break out of her shell. So there she sat on a crowded couch in a smoke-filled room while eavesdropping on others' conversations. She overheard them talking about their classes and a hot new spot that opened up downtown where the music was loud and the bartender had a heavy hand when pouring drinks. College boys and girls flirted and danced next to her as their drinks spilled onto the carpet. She looked stiff as she tried to fit in, shifting in her seat and straightening her back as she watched people move in and out of the room. That is until someone noticed her. "Hey, dolly. Where are you from?" asked a nice-looking man a few years older than her. He had dark eyes, jet black hair, and a mole on his cheek that made him look unique from the rest.

"Oh, hi," Dottie replied while fidgeting with her folded hands over her crossed leg. "I don't live too far from here. I go to the local community college." She lied because she wasn't sure if she should be truthful about her real age. "I commute, though."

He smiled and nodded back, seemingly believing her story. "Well, can I get you a drink?"

"That would be nice," she said. "Thank you. I'm Dottie, by the way."

"George," he responded, extending his hand. "Nice to meet you. I'll be right back, okay?"

"I'll be here."

A few minutes later, George returned with her drink, this time inching closer to her on the couch. It was hard liquor— rum, she thought, mixed with soda—and it went down smooth. Dottie wasn't used to attention from men; in fact, she perceived herself as average looking. She paid more mind to how her stainless steel kitchen looked at the bakery instead of her own appearance. But, she liked how this felt.

As the night went on, George told Dottie of trips he's taken and subjects he excelled in. He went on about Barcelona, where he visited the Sagrada Familia and became interested in architecture. He didn't stop to ask Dottie about her personal life, which was fine with her since there wasn't much to tell. She sat and listened as he spoke—he only stopped talking to make more and more cocktails for Dottie. He lit up a cigarette and she asked if she could have one, too. The smell reminded her of Mom and how the smoke would make its way into their bedroom window from outside.

He leaned over and gave her a soft kiss on her lips. He tasted like strong alcohol mixed with nicotine. She lingered for a few seconds before pulling back, putting her finger to her lip to savor her first kiss. She always thought her first kiss would be with someone who loved her—not a stranger on a couch soiled with liquor and smoke. "We can get out of here if you want," he said while pointing his thumb towards the door. "How about a walk?"

Dottie thought about it for a moment but declined. "I have to find my friends." She stood up but was wobbly from the alcohol. "Thank you for a fun evening. It was nice meeting you, George." Before he could retort, she turned and moved towards the kitchen, where she saw one of her friends hanging out a few minutes earlier. She was ready to go and was happy to learn they were ready, too. All but one, Florence, who she learned had a habit of staying behind at parties like this with men she barely knew. She had these emerald doe eyes that were mesmerizing, almost spell-like. The other girls would often talk about what a flirt she was and how messy Florence always got, but never said those things to her face. Dottie thought they were jealous of her because she always got so much attention. Dottie stumbled to the car—the night sky was spinning around her, but she felt alive. She conversed with a nice guy, socialized at a college party, and got her first kiss.

When she got home, she crept into the dark house, tripping on the rug near the front door. Connie sat up straight on the couch while watching Dottie fumble through the room, wondering when she would notice her presence. "Oh! You scared me! Don't do that, Connie," she yelled, grabbing her chest out of fright.

"Save it, Dot. Where the heck were you? You smell like a bottle of cheap booze."

"I went to a party with my friends." She grew upset by the fact that her younger sister was quizzing her about her whereabouts. "Don't worry about it, Connie. I'm fine."

Connie stood up and placed her hands on her hips. "Oh, you're always fine. That's all you say! You're going to turn out like him if you don't stop this, ya know?"

"Like who?" Dottie gave up on trying to collect her belongings that had fallen out of her purse. "Are you saying I'm going to end up like Dad?"

"Yes, that's exactly what I'm saying, Dot. Either stop this nonsense or I'm telling Dom."

"Go ahead, Connie. It's like you forgot all about Mom and Dad. Dom, this. Barb, that."

"For Christ's sake, Dottie, I found my way out here. I can't say the same for you. Do you remember what Judge Mason said? He said to not let the distance make us strangers. I thought those words applied to our relationship with Cookie and Frankie. I didn't think that you and I would become strangers under the same roof."

Connie turned and walked towards the bedroom. She slid into bed and faced the wall, leaving Dottie crouched down on the floor. Connie's words overwhelmed her and the alcohol made her nauseous. She lost her balance and closed her eyes, finding comfort against the stucco wall. In the moments before drifting to sleep, the image of her and her sisters rushing down a crowded city street in tandem swirled in her mind.

She smiled as she fell asleep, dreaming of how lovely life would be if they could live inside that picture. Together forever.

14

❦

Bonjour from Paris

Christmas 1951

My sweetheart:

"Bonjour de Paris," Cookie. Look at me——I'm even speaking French now. Thank you for your last letter. It arrived at a time when I needed to hear from you the most. As picturesque as this city is——and it's beautiful, I mean BEAUTIFUL——I miss home more than ever. I think it's the holiday season. Watching families buzz by in excitement and kids' faces beam when they see the Paris lights. Seeing couples stroll along the streets while the world move arounds them. There's even a Bing Crosby song playing softly on the radio right now over the loudspeaker. Every song and every single thing reminds me of you, Cookie.

When I close my eyes, I can imagine you curled up in my arms on a snowy Christmas morning in the future. Our four children are running around the tree and playing with the toys we spent all night wrapping for them. I can see the silver tinsel you strung on the Christmas tree and the stockings hanging from the mantle. I can see the twinkle in your beautiful brown eyes as you watch the children's faces light up with joy. I can see a little scruffy dog laying in front of the fireplace, sighing in comfort at the home you created for us. I pull out a tiny box with something sparkly inside from my pocket to surprise you because you deserve the world.

You are my world, Cookie, and I'm so glad you found your way back to me.

As lonely as it is, Christmas in Paris is bewitching. A few buddies and I from my bunk had some free time and made our way out last night. We strolled down Avenue De L'Opera and saw the most perfect Christmas tree——it reminded me of the one you helped decorate at Anna's shop. My buddies and I spent the night causing trouble around the streets of Paris, only stopping to get some warm spiked drinks. We ended the night at a speakeasy near The Arc de Triomphe at the end of The Champs Elysees. Lining the avenue are trees with twinkling lights that brighten the sky. The guys gave me hell because all I could talk about is you. But I know they're missing their girls, too.

I've been thinking about what life looks like for me after I come back home. For starters, I want to take you to New York City. When you wrote to me about the trip you took before you found out I was in the Army, I could tell how much you loved the sights and sounds of the city. Let me walk you through my idea of a perfect date night with you. I check us into the best hotel money can buy right in the middle of the action. You'll get dolled up in a gown that will make it hard for me to keep my hands off you. I'll even put on a tuxedo. We'll hop in a cab and I'll take you to a fancy dinner theatre, where I would have called ahead and reserved a table right in front of the stage. The spotlight will reflect off the beading of your dress. All eyes will be on you, Cookie, including mine.

But the night won't end after the show. I'd want to show you off to the world, so I'd then take you downtown to a jazz club. It will be full of smoky elegance and packed to the brim, where we'll hoot and holler and dance the night away. We'll be the best-dressed couple in the place compared to all the other sweaty people.

We'll end the night around 3 a.m. and stroll uptown to our glamorous hotel. You'll be cold so I'll wrap my tuxedo jacket around your shoulders as we walk. We'll laugh about our night and talk about our past in a way that makes me look forward to our future. We'll end the night in our room as I unzip your gown, and I'll let your imagination visualize what comes next.

Oh, and let's not forget the next morning. I'll bring you coffee in bed that I gathered from a Parisian cafe around the corner [Paris has the best coffee]. I'll have you get dressed in comfortable, warm clothing. Next, we'll head to Rockefeller Center where we'll go ice skating at the "Rink." You'll stumble at first as we glide along the ice but I'll keep you from falling.

I'll always keep you from falling, Cookie. And you'll do the same for me——I know it.

I want nothing more than to be back in Connecticut and hold you in my arms. But I have a job to do here. I pray the time goes by fast. Until then, keep writing me letters. Heck, tell Frankie to write to me, too. It keeps me going. Oh, and send my best to Judge Mason. In your last letter, you mentioned he fell sick.

Merry Christmas, Cookie. I'll love you forever and I'm so glad you came around.

With love,
Ray

15

Saying Goodbye

Summer of 1952

Dear Connie and Dottie,

We are writing to share some sad news: Judge Mason has died. When we first told you he fell ill, we didn't realize how serious it was. Anna was hopeful he would be able to recover, but unfortunately, he was too weak. He passed away late yesterday evening at home. We stood by Anna, Herman, and his wife, and stayed until he took his last breath. His funeral will take place in a few days.

   He and Anna made up last year after not speaking to each other for years after my graduation party. They were close all their lives, and I felt extreme guilt for being the reason the two were in an argument. I find comfort in the fact that he loved us all so deeply.

   I hope the thought of him brings you fond memories. He was the catapult in ensuring we remained close through the years. I think I can speak for all of us when I say his words helped me get through some tough times.

He was an extraordinary man who will be missed.

Please say a prayer for him,
Cookie

Frankie and I sat in the backseat of the black town car in silence. It was a dreary day in the middle of a hot New England summer. The weather was suitable for Judge Mason's funeral, as it reminded us that we lost a decent man. When the car pulled up to the cemetery, Frankie squeezed my hand before we both stepped out of the car. Rain threatened overhead as the humidity instantaneously cast a layer of moisture onto my skin.

Aside from being a well-known and respected judge, he was a war veteran with an ivy league education. People near and far came to pay their respects—hundreds of cars lined the cracked winding roads within the cemetery. I spotted a group I suspected he knew from law school. They were similar in age to Judge Mason with white hair and wrinkled foreheads. The deep type of wrinkles one could only get from studying day and night for the bar exam. One gentleman sported a maroon Harvard cap atop his head.

Frankie and I joined Anna, Herman, and Eleanor in front of

a large portrait of Judge Mason. A plethora of red and white floral arrangements sat on and around his closed mahogany casket. Decorated soldiers in pressed uniforms stood tall next to the priest as the service began. The crowd watched as the soldiers folded an American flag and presented it to Eleanor before firing honorary shots into the air.

This was the first real funeral that Frankie and I attended. We were young when our parents died. There was no official funeral for them; only a short mass in the chapel at the hospital. No fanfare. No hugs from family or friends that knew our parents. No headstone with a brief phrase describing the legacies of their lives. Simply a prayer from the priest as we hung our heads in a pew alongside some nice police officers while we held hands and cried.

Eleanor centered herself in front of the crowd to say a few words before the priest said his final prayer. She began. "Thank you all for coming here today to celebrate the life of a remarkable man—my beloved husband, Edward Mason. Some of you may have worked with him during his long career as a respected judge. His Harvard law classmates and friends stand alongside us today, as well as men and women who donated their time to serve our homeless community. We have some members from our armed forces, whom we respect and honor always. And of course, his loving family and friends who he was proud to know. I also recognize some of his favorite people, those of you who may have at one time been on the wrong side of the law. My husband may have put you behind bars, which—as you told us over the years—changed the course of your lives for the better. He spoke so highly of you and respected you more than you'll ever know."

She turned her attention to Frankie and me. "To Loretta and Frances and their sisters Dorothy and Concetta who could not be here today: I want you to know he cherished you like you were his own and always wanted the best for you. Lastly, to my husband's sister, Anna, and her husband, Herman. You were everything to him and more. He loved hard and was a fair and decent man. Edward, my sweetheart, you will forever be my hero. I know one day, you will be waiting for me as I enter eternity with you, as you tap your watch for me being notoriously late." The last line drew a soft chuckle from the crowd, which broke the silence away from the sniffles and cries heard throughout. Eleanor stepped back and joined the family back in line. Anna grabbed her hand as she stared at the casket, sobbing over the loss of her brother and best friend.

I blotted my eyes with a handkerchief from my pocket and looked into the crowd, who was doing the same. The priest continued with his service and final prayers. As a violinist played a familiar song in the background—it sounded like the classical aria "Dido's Lament"—an early memory of Judge Mason crept into my thoughts. We had recently moved in with Anna and Herman and were only living there a few weeks. One afternoon, Anna had to take Frankie to the doctor for a sore throat while Herman was at work. I was home alone, sifting through some of the books in Herman's library when I heard a knock at the door. It was Judge Mason. He was dropping off some paperwork for Anna—an updated will I think—and he asked if I wanted to take a ride with him to finish some errands. I left a note on the counter for Anna should she return early, and joined Judge Mason for his errands. I didn't ask where we were heading, but knew I was in good hands.

Our first stop was at the food kitchen downtown. He was bringing some canned goods that people donated to the courthouse and wanted to drop them off himself. I carried a bag to help him as he greeted the volunteers and homeless men and women in line at the food kitchen. He pulled two aprons down and threw one at me. "Put this on, Cookie," he said, as he jumped in and started helping serve the food. "Grab those tongs and add a roll onto each plate," he whispered between discussions with people waiting in line. Everyone was so gracious and kind, and Judge Mason treated them as if they were his actual family. I watched in awe as he shook people's hands and asked how they were doing with sincerity. He hummed songs as he scooped hot meals onto people's plates.

After about an hour and a lull in lines, Judge Mason said it was time to go. Back in the car, he mentioned that he heard from Anna that reading was one of my favorite hobbies. "What's your favorite hobby?" I asked him.

"Funny, you should ask, Cookie. We're headed there right now." We pulled into a music store and I followed him inside. He scanned the store with his eyes and let out an "Ah!," while directing me to come along. He pulled out the piano bench and slid inside, and invited me to sit next to him. "You asked what my favorite hobby was. Well, this is it. I love to play the piano." As soon as the words left his mouth, he started touching the keys. He played the most delightful classical song I had ever heard, which I later learned was one of Vivaldi's "Four Seasons," as I watched in amazement. By then, the store clerk had come over. He stood next to us as he watched Judge Mason play with the passion of an on-stage performer. After a few songs, he rubbed his hands together. "My fingers sure are getting old." He got up, thanked the clerk for letting him play, and we left the store.

"That was amazing, Judge Mason. I wish I had talent like that. I can't even carry a tune," I said with a laugh.

"Well, Cookie. You know you can do anything you dream of, right? It just takes a little hard work and practice. Do you think you and Frankie would be interested in joining Eleanor and me for a classical concert in a few weeks? We have four tickets for a show in Hartford and we would love it if you girls joined us."

For the next few years, Frankie and I joined Judge Mason and Eleanor for a classical concert. We would get dressed up and join them for a fancy dinner at a steakhouse downtown that had cream linen napkins and waiters donned in black bow ties. Then, we would skip across the street to the theatre and enjoy the sounds of classical music. We felt like grown-ups and always behaved. Frankie and I came home late and full of energy. The next morning, we would share all the details with Anna and Herman at breakfast. It was a yearly tradition that got cut short by his fight with Anna after my graduation party. I wholeheartedly regret not seeing one last concert with him before his death.

As the crowd at the cemetery started moving in closer to the casket, I realized it was time to say our final goodbyes. I watched as people threw carnations and roses onto Judge Mason's casket. Some wept. One man grinned as he tapped the top of the casket with his palm. "Bye, old friend. Until we meet again," he said before walking away. The man wearing the Harvard cap removed it from his head and smoothed his hair before placing it on top of the casket. The tattered hat looked like it was about fifty years old. He must've worn it almost every day since he graduated from college. I found it so interesting that this man would leave his broken-in cap to rot away in the soil. But then I remembered how loved Judge Mason was and it all made sense to me.

I walked forward and placed a single red rose onto his casket. I whispered low enough that no one could hear me. "Thank you for believing in me. Thank you for instilling the importance of family. And thank you for being honest with me about Dad. I know you only wanted the best for me and my sisters and I promise to make you proud."

I turned and walked towards the car and held my head high as a wave of emotions washed over me. I realized just how lucky I was to know a man as marvelous as Judge Mason.

Connie used her finger to dab a muted shade of mauve lipstick onto her lips. She pursed her lips together and let her eyes linger at her reflection for a few moments after she finished getting ready. Connie's soft dirty blonde hair rolled down her neck and fell onto her shoulders. Her eyes were the color of slate and appeared sizable against her tiny face. She enhanced them with the darkest mascara she could find in Barb's makeup drawer. She was a beautiful girl—who looked more like a grown woman today—as she stood ready for her first official date with Jo's brother, Scott.

Scott recently graduated high school alongside Dottie. He

started an apprenticeship to become an electrician to follow in his father's footsteps. He was popular and bright and close to his sister and parents. He had tanned skin and hair as black as embers, with broad shoulders and a larger than life quality to him. His charm delighted her and his conversations were always engaging. He reminded Connie of all her father's good qualities, with none of the bad.

She had met Scott almost eight years ago when she and her family first moved to Tucson. At first, he would ignore Connie altogether, but over the years, the two became great friends. The turning point in their young relationship was the weeks and months following her encounter with him at the roller skating rink. That's when she could sense Scott's flirtation starting to grow. One morning at school, Connie hunched against her locker. She was upset about a grade she had gotten in math after trying so hard. Scott happened to be walking by and stopped to check on her when he saw the look on her face. He offered to tutor her and, soon enough, during a rather exhaustive study session, he leaned over to kiss her. However, they were still young and Connie was also interested in another boy from her grade, so she asked Scott if they could remain friends. She also didn't want to upset Jo. She was her closest friend and the person Connie turned to when things were hard—at home or otherwise.

Years passed and Connie's adolescent and high school relationships came and went. But, she always somehow made her way back to Scott. Recently, she was at Jo's house and brushed up against Scott in the hallway on the way to the bathroom. She looked back at him over her shoulder with her big gray eyes and smiled. He stopped in his tracks and whispered to her. "What are we doing, Connie? I'm not playing these games anymore. Either you want me or you don't. Which is it?"

Surprised, she retorted, "Well, Scottie, I wouldn't object if you asked me out on an actual date. I've just been waiting." Her eyes locked into his and she brushed a piece of hair out of his eye.

A soft smile overtook his face, replacing his stressed expression. He put his arm on the wall next to her face. "Will you go on a date with me, Connie?"

"Next Friday. Pick me up at 7," she said before walking into the bathroom and closing the door behind her. She leaned against the bathroom door and celebrated to herself without making a sound. Connie couldn't help it—she was buzzing with excitement for her first official date with Scott.

After Connie finished getting ready for her date, she strolled out to the living room where Dom and Barb sat. "Wow... you look pretty," Tommy said, as he broke away from his toy truck to hug her leg. He was a sweet little boy with brown hair and a pudgy belly. Tommy adored Connie. "Can I come with you and Scott?" he asked, his round eyes looking up at her from the ground.

Connie smiled down at him. "Next time, sweetie."

"Well, hubba hubba. Don't you look like a million bucks? Our baby is all grown up, Dom!" Barb exclaimed as she admired Connie, who was blushing. Barb let her borrow a short-sleeved dress that showed off Connie's petite, but curvy, figure. A few seconds later, Scott knocked at the door with flowers in his hands. "I'll take those," Barb said, as they waved goodbye from the house, watching as Scott opened the car door for Connie.

"Take care of my baby," Dom yelled as Scott started the car and drove away.

The two grabbed milkshakes and headed to a drive-in movie right outside of Tucson. This was the place to be on a Friday night after school and they often ran into each other there when a new movie premiered. Tonight, the weather had cooled once the sun went down. Connie tried her best to focus on the western film on the screen, but her heart almost pounded out of her chest when Scott scooted over and put his arm around her. She glanced at his hand out of the corner of her eye—it was shiny from the popcorn butter. Sure, Connie and Scott have kissed before, but something felt different about tonight and she wanted it to be perfect. Little did she know, though, that she could have been wearing a paper bag and no makeup while enjoying a first date in the school cafeteria and it would have felt just as perfect to him. Any date would be perfect with his dream girl, Connie. Approximately 45 minutes into the movie, she turned her head to kiss him.

He kissed her back while his hand sweetly held the back of her head. They spent the next few hours cuddling under a darkened sky—a sky illuminated only by the large projector screen in front of them.

When Scott drove her home, he walked her inside to make sure she was safe. Dottie stood in the family room, gripping the note about Judge Mason's death in her hand, while holding back tears. Dottie looked like she hadn't slept in weeks. She held up the note to show Connie and said, "Hi, Connie... Hey, Scott. I hate to tell you this, but Judge Mason died."

Connie doubled over as tears streamed down her face. She grabbed the note and read it before instinctively jumping into Scott's arms. Dottie stood next to the new couple, as she watched her sister turn to Scott for comfort instead of to her. She felt alone and continued to cry. Yes, she was sad over Judge Mason's death and the fact that she hasn't seen him in many years. But the pain she felt from Connie's rejection and her own loneliness was excruciating.

16

Dottie

June 1953

Dear Cookie and Frankie,

First, thank you both for the "well" wishes about my graduation. I can't believe I'm 18 and high school is over. As you
know, I am starting college in the fall. I would like to work
with children one day. Maybe even kids like us? I guess we'll
see…

But that's not the real reason I'm writing to you both today. I want to share more exciting news with you——Scott
asked me to marry him! We have been inseparable since
our first date, but even earlier than that if I'm being truthful. I have never felt this way before and I know with all my
heart that he is the person I'm supposed to be with forever. He brought me to Old Tucson where there was a Wild
West show complete with Can-Can dancers. He somehow
worked his magic and had one of the dancers hold my dain-

ty gold ring. The music went quiet and a dancer called him up on stage. That's when he asked me in front of a crowd of cheering onlookers. It was so thrilling and romantic!

We decided we will get married at the end of the summer in a small ceremony surrounded by family and friends. We don't have much money, but we want to make it as special as possible. Scott has been working full-time for a year now and has put away some money for us to start our new life together. I wish I could afford a fancier wedding dress, but I found one at the local department store that will suit me just fine. I'm simply so excited about marrying Scott that the details——and what we can and can't afford——don't matter.

Now the most important question: can I expect both of you to make the trek to Arizona once and for all? I want you both to stand beside me and Dottie as I say my vows.

All my love,
Connie

Frankie peeled the note out of the envelope, her jaw dropping as she began to read further down the page. I suspected this news was coming based on her previous letters, but the note confirmed it—Connie and Scott were getting married! Frankie grabbed my arm and we squealed in delight. Even though Connie was only 18, she was mature and ready to get married. She wanted a husband and children since she was a little girl. Based on what she told us about Scott over the years, he was her perfect partner and we were over the moon.

"We're going to Arizona!" Frankie screamed as kicked her legs like a Can-Can dancer, mimicking what she read in Connie's letter. By now, Anna had joined in the foyer. Frankie handed her the note and Anna beamed from ear to ear.

"I'm so happy for your sister, girls." She said with tears in her eyes while clutching the letter over her heart. "And I'm happy for YOU. You finally get to see your sisters after how many years? Five, six?"

I had tears in my eyes. "It's been nine years since we saw their faces. Right here in this exact spot." I wiped the tears off my cheek and grabbed Frankie. "We're going to Arizona!"

So much has happened since we last saw each other. We all began and graduated high school. Our family situations evolved. Dottie and Connie gained a new step-mother and half-brother. Anna lost her brother, Judge Mason, and we all lost a role model in him. Frankie and I finished nursing school at the local college. From what we've heard, Dottie got in a bit of trouble. Frankie won art shows. We all experienced new places, like The Grand Canyon and New York City. Connie got engaged to her high school sweetheart. And I met Ray.

Before we knew it, nine years had passed and brought us to today. The possibility of a reunion now feels more than a fleeting idea or a few words at the bottom of a letter. My sisters are now grown-up women. We survived the storm and will once again hold each other in our arms. I looked up towards the ceiling and closed my eyes, hoping that Judge Mason was looking down on this moment.

"I have an idea!" Frankie exclaimed before retreating to her room, leaving Anna and me to chat. She offered to help us as we began planning our trip out west.

Frankie pulled a sketchbook out of her drawer and began drawing. She's been around enough wedding dresses at this point that she could draw them in her sleep. She started sketching—first the shoulders, then the bosom and waist, and finally the puffy tulle skirt that grazed the ground. Frankie would design Connie's wedding dress and—with Anna's help—get it made to surprise Connie for her big day. Although Frankie hadn't seen Connie in many years, she knew everything about her. She was confident that she could design a dress that would fit her personality and petite frame with perfection. She drew, her hand moving at a rapid pace, almost as if it had a mind of its own. Her pencil marks were precise as she made broad strokes across the paper. Her hand turned black from the charcoal as she turned her pencil to the side to shade the skirt. About an hour later, she put her pencil down and softly blew the paper. Turning her head to the side, she smiled as she admired her work. The dress was intricate in design and bubbly yet refined—perfect for Connie. Frankie wanted nothing more than to make this dream a reality.

A few minutes later, she heard the chatter between me and Anna get louder as we walked up the stairs and towards her room. "Anna! Cookie! Come in. I want to show you something," Frankie yelled from her bedroom.

"We were coming to check on you, Frankie. We want to know what your bright idea is," I said as I took a seat on the bed. Frankie told Anna to take a seat next to me and instructed us to close our eyes.

She grabbed the sketch and held it in front of us. "Open your eyes."

My eyes grew wide as I took in the beautiful drawing in front of me. Anna gasped at its beauty. It didn't take long for us to learn what Frankie's idea was. "Yes!" Anna exclaimed. "Let's do it!"

In the weeks and months that followed, we led our lives as normal but spent every spare moment preparing for the wedding and our trip out west. Anna took charge of turning Frankie's vision into reality. She found the perfect seamstress. Several times a week, she'd go visit the woman and check on the progress. The woman mostly spoke Italian, but they didn't need to communicate much because her execution was flawless. Frankie was adamant that she wanted to pay for the fabric and the seamstress' time, so Anna let her. Anna called Mary to get Connie's measurements. Mary promised to keep the surprise a secret and cried to Anna about what a beautiful gift that would be. She told us that Connie had bought a tea-length white dress from the local department store that she liked, but seemed disappointed that she couldn't afford a more intricate dress.

Anna also wanted Connie's day to be extra special. She hemmed and hawed about what she could do for Connie from afar. Could she contact a local florist and get a bouquet made for her? Could she hire a string quartet from the university to play at the ceremony? None of that seemed right to her. She had an aha moment when a shipment came into the shop that contained piles of bridesmaid dresses. One specific dress caught her eye as it complemented Connie's newly designed gown. The answer of what Anna could do for Connie was right under her nose the whole time. She offered to gift the bridesmaid dresses to me, Frankie, Dottie, and Jo to wear in the wedding.

We booked train tickets and secured the dresses, and Frankie and I were set to make the voyage to Tucson. After going almost ten years without seeing one another, our reunion was long overdue. But now, we were days away from seeing our sisters in person to celebrate Connie's wedding. Judge Mason's words echoed in my head—we were on our way to creating new memories together. Together, at last. Together with my sisters.

After Dottie graduated from high school, she began waitressing to earn extra money. She wanted to save up and buy a car so she didn't have to walk to and from work. Today, though, Mary offered to pick her up after her shift and drive her home. She waited outside as she watched other people come and go out the front door of the restaurant.

Mary had company today as she waited. Her new boyfriend, Phil, sat in the passenger seat. She met Phil at the meat market in town one afternoon, where the two bonded over their choice of beef cuts. Phil worked at the local university as an accountant. He was quiet but had a dry sense of humor that made Mary laugh. Although she wasn't looking to date, she grew content with Phil and enjoyed his company. She was in love again for the first time in many years.

After about twenty minutes of small talk, Mary excused herself to go inside and check on Dottie's whereabouts. A minute later, Mary walked back outside with a blank look on her face. Dottie never showed up at work that morning for the breakfast shift.

Mary drove to Dom's house while trying not to panic. She jogged to the door and knocked repeatedly, praying someone would answer. Mary felt strange knocking on the door of a home where she used to live with her family. Barb opened the door in her bathrobe. "Oh, hi, Mary. What's going on?"

"I'm looking for Dottie. Is she here?"

"No, she's not here. I thought she was with you. That's

what she said before she left last night. Here, come inside."
She waved her hand for Mary to come in. "Dom's not home."
Mary turned to look at Phil who was still waiting in the car.
She held up her finger and mouthed "one minute" to him as
he nodded back in agreement.

"Hi!" Tommy was playing with his toy plane on the floor
and he looked up at Mary. He was a friendly boy and Mary
couldn't help but take a liking to him. She was bitter for a
long time that Dom decided to have a child with Barb after
years of not being able to conceive. Over time, though, she
learned that leaving Dom and starting over was the best thing
that could have happened to her. She was no longer angry at
the situation and got along fine with Barb the few times of the
year they saw each other.

Barb began unrolling the rollers in her hair and placing them
on the table. "Don't worry too much about Dottie, Mary.
She's probably with a friend. I had a feeling she was lying last
night about where she was going. She left the house late and
was acting suspicious." Connie walked out of the bedroom.

"Hi," she said as she greeted Mary with a hug. "Dottie isn't
with you? I thought the three of us had plans to go look at
shoes for the wedding today!" She stomped her foot out of
frustration.

"No, sweetie. I came here to look for her as she never showed
up for work today." It was now late morning as Dottie's usual
shift ended after the breakfast rush.

"Typical Dottie." Connie slumped down on the dining room chair and crossed her arms in disappointment. She held her hand up and looked at the ring that was present on her left hand. She got distracted as the light caught the tiny diamond. Her frown turned into a tiny smile as she thought about Scott. "Well, what do we do now?"

"Any idea who she's with, Connie?" Mary asked as she joined Barb and Connie at the table.

"I don't know," she said with a shrug. But Connie knew where Dottie was, and even though she was annoyed beyond belief, she didn't want to rat her out. She had found her way back to the guy she met at the college party, George. At first, George was fine and agreeable, but over time, his fearful temper began to rear its ugly head. He would snap on Dottie and put her down. He would poke fun at her body and then ask her to sleep with him in the next breath.

Dottie would often cry in her bedroom after seeing George. Connie was always there to comfort her. She would stroke her hair and tell her she deserved better than him—but Dottie never listened to her. Connie felt like she was losing her sister. If it wasn't the drinking, it was George and the blatant disregard for her self-respect.

Dom even caught wind of George's aggressive behavior. He threatened to confront him if Dottie didn't stop seeing him, so she lied and said it was over. That's when the sneaking out started. She would tell them she was with Connie or

Mary. Or she would say she was working. But, she was always with George. Dottie even lost a different waitressing job a few months ago, but she told her family she left because they weren't giving her enough shifts. It turned into a vicious cycle of lying and missing work. She drank with George and they became explosive, but Connie would always be there to pick up the pieces. She was nervous about the path Dottie was taking, as she had been for a few years now. And Connie was moving in with Scott after the wedding. She was nervous about leaving Dottie on her own in such a vulnerable state of mind.

Mary went outside to tell Phil it would be a little longer in case he wanted to leave and pick her up later. He came inside instead and sat at the table with Barb and Connie. Connie's frustration grew as she realized her wedding was only weeks away and she had a lot left to do. She could have been running errands, treating herself to new shoes, or going over wedding details with Scott and his parents. But no—instead she was stuck waiting until whenever Dottie decided to return home. Barb pulled out a deck of cards and the four played while Tommy busied himself with his toys in the family room.

Soon enough, a disheveled Dottie walked into the house. Her frizzy hair hung in front of her eyes and her hands were shaking enough that her keys jingled, creating a melodic sound. She didn't even notice her family at the table at first as she leaned down to kiss Tommy's forehead before stumbling into the dining room. When she looked up, she saw four sets

of eyes staring back at her. She immediately burst into tears—
her sunken eyes turned pink as she sobbed. As she walked
closer, a bruise became visible on her cheek.

"Dottie!" Mary jumped up and grabbed her on either shoulder. She hugged her out of relief but soon pulled back. "I was
worried sick about you. What happened?" she questioned as
she lifted her chin to get a better look at the bruise. "Are you
okay, dear?"

"Please don't worry. But... but... George and I had a fight."
She put her head down out of shame, as she knew she had lied
to everyone about still being with George. "I'm okay though,
I promise. It looks worse than it is."

Connie jumped up out of her seat. "Wait until Dom hears
about this. He's going to kill him. Heck, I want to kill him.
Did he just drop you off here, Dot?"

"No. A friend picked me up." She still had tears running
down her face. "He didn't mean to hit me." By this time,
Barb yelled for Tommy to head into the bedroom that he still
shared with his parents.

"I know you're an adult, Dottie, but you are not to see that
man again. You are defending him after he so clearly hurt
you." Mary decided at that moment it was best not to lecture
Dottie. She pulled her into her arms instead and let Dottie
sob onto her shoulder as Barb, Connie, and Phil looked on.
Dottie smelled like stale smoke and alcohol as Mary whispered
into her ear, "I told you I wanted more for you, Dottie. I love

you, sweetheart."

Connie stood up and hugged them both. She sighed and said, "Cookie and Frankie are going to be here in a few weeks. Do this for them. Do this for me. You need help, Dot, and we are here for you every step of the way. Promise me that you will try?"

Dottie stared at Connie. A semblance of a smile washed over her face at the thought of seeing Cookie and Frankie for the first time in so long. But, she felt humiliated. She let her life spiral out of control and this was the first time she was able to see how bad things have gotten. She made a vow with herself at that very moment to get better.

"I promise," Dottie said, as she wiped the tears off her cheek. Her spirit was so beat down that she didn't even believe herself. But she sure as hell was going to try—her sisters were worth all the effort Dottie had left to give.

17

The Wedding

"All aboard!" Frankie and I turned around to wave back at Anna and Herman before boarding the train. The porter helped us with our luggage, which included a large trunk that held Connie's wedding gown and four bridesmaid dresses. We were headed to Arizona for Connie's wedding and, more importantly, to reunite with our sisters. I stared at the ceiling most of the night and couldn't sleep from anticipation, but the day was here and we were on our way.

After handing the conductor our tickets, we were shown to our sleeping car. He pushed the door open and I was pleasantly surprised to see our cozy living quarters for the next few days. White linens and downy comforters adorned the tiny, but comfortable looking, beds. On the other side of the wall was a compact indigo sofa with two striped yellow pillows. It felt nautical, like the seaside restaurant in Mystic that Ray once took me to when we first started dating. There were fresh-cut pink tulips gathered into a vase atop the table in the corner that cast rose-colored shadows onto the walls. Next to the sofa was an entrance to our private bathroom. I poked my head inside to see miniature bottles of shampoo and lotion, as well as some extra-plush folded towels. An oil painting hung on the wall—a field that was so lifelike, its straw and grass textures almost jumped off the canvas. The gilded frame seemed almost out of place in an otherwise casual cabin. But I didn't mind. All the comforts from home were somehow tucked inside this space.

"The restaurant car opens in two hours, but please feel free to join your fellow travelers for a drink in the tavern car as soon as you're settled. Enjoy your trip, ladies." The conductor tipped his hat as he backed out of our room. Frankie shut the door behind him and collapsed onto the bottom bunk bed. "This is heaven."

"I guess that means I get the top bunk?" I giggled and tossed my book onto my bed. "What do you say we freshen up and go for a drink?" Frankie nodded. I reapplied my lipstick in the mirror and admired my graduation pearls. I smoothed my gloved hands over my short-sleeved navy jacket that was belted in the middle over an a-line matching skirt. Frankie wore a similar set, but in a taupe striped pattern, with a matching beret. Frankie slipped out of her loafers and into black heels. "Let's go, Cookie. Don't forget your purse."

We made our way to the tavern car and grabbed a seat near the bar, which was starting to fill in with other passengers. Another group of four young ladies sat next to us—impeccably dressed and in deep conversation. One of the girls burst into laughter "Don't be so serious, Syd," she yelled as she took a sip from her martini. She caught my eye and winked. She had Dottie's fighting spirit, and I couldn't help but think of my sisters. When we first got separated from each other, I used to daydream of the day we would first get together again. I thought we would be late teenagers and would meet up in a beachy location for a weekend of laughter and reconnecting. Connie would flirt with the boys on the towel nearest us on the sand, and Frankie would give them the cold shoulder. I never imagined Frankie and I would be taking a train out west for our youngest sister's wedding day. And I certainly never thought it would take so long to see them again.

As I sipped my drink, I imagined what Dottie and Connie looked like today. We hadn't seen many pictures of the girls over the years but they undoubtedly look different from when we last saw them as children. Would they look like Mom or Dad? Would they look like spitting images of us? Would we walk right by them at the train terminal because we didn't recognize them?

Through the smoky tavern car, I saw a few men in Army uniforms playing cards a few tables over. I immediately thought of Ray. He is set to come home from abroad at some point this year. In mere months, I could be in his arms once again. We can bring his letter to life as our date plays out in the cold streets of New York City. Between seeing my sisters and having Ray home again, I could barely keep my thoughts straight. I wanted everything to be perfect. I wanted me and my sisters to be perfect again.

Frankie nudged my shoulder. "Earth to Cookie. Whatcha thinking about over there?" I must have been daydreaming. "You almost knocked my drink over."

"Oh. Sorry, Frankie. I was thinking about the girls. Do you think it'll feel weird to see them again?"

"Weird? Why?" Frankie popped up a few of the mixed nuts into her mouth.

"I guess I mean we used to be inseparable and then we got separated. Will everything look different now? Will we be strangers?" I glanced down at the menu to see what was worth ordering, but pushed it away as I couldn't seem to focus on anything else. My drink sloshed around in its glass, dripping onto the tabletop and seeping into the paper menu.

"No. I don't think so, Cook. You'll see. We will pick up right where we left off."

Frankie's levelheadedness put me at ease and I sighed. "I hope you're right, Frankie."

After a few restless nights, the day was here—we were hours away from arriving in Arizona. After breakfast, we spent the rest of the morning getting ready in the small bathroom attached to our train cabin. Frankie and I swayed to the sounds of Dean Martin and some doo-wop hits as they echoed over the loudspeakers. As I got ready, I thought about the weather report that showed 90 degree temperatures in Tucson. I opted for a linen canary yellow belted dress with matching peep-toe heels. I pushed my hair back with a floral scarf and added cherry red lipstick to finish the look. Frankie wore a white sleeveless button-down shirt tucked into high-waisted teal cropped pants. She borrowed a polka-dot scarf from my bag and tied it around her neck.

After packing my belongings, I sat on the sofa and tried to remain calm. I was more nervous that I thought I'd be—I wanted to make my best impression on our sisters and their families. Frankie joined me and we stared ahead in silence. We flipped through a magazine until the train whistle blew—the telltale sign that we were close to our destination. Frankie popped up and stumbled as she caught her footing. She grabbed my hand to help me stand and then hugged me. She lingered for a few minutes as I hugged her back with all my might. I was so glad to have Frankie by my side.

Soon enough, the train stopped and we stepped onto concrete. Frankie nudged me and said, "I'm so glad to step foot on solid ground again." I nodded in agreement and took a deep breath of Tucson air. A pleasant porter offered to help us with our luggage and trunk once again as we made our way towards the terminal.

We rounded the corner—there Dottie and Connie stood clutching hands and antsy with excitement. As soon as our eyes met, we lost all control and sprinted towards each other. We collided into a four-way embrace, like we did when we were kids. I barely had a chance to look at them before we hugged, and I closed my eyes to savor the moment. The soldiers from the train whistled as they walked by. A few others huffed as they tried to make their way around us, but we ignored all the noise. There was nothing in the world that could peel our eight arms off each other. Nothing felt better than this.

"Umm, ma'am?" The porter cleared his throat and brought us back to the present moment. "Are you all set with your bags?"

I nodded my head and apologized to him for making him wait. I tipped him and said, "Yes, sir. We've got it from here." The girls and I giggled as we pushed the heavy cart through the terminal and outside. At one point, Connie stood on the cart, gripping the pole with her hands, as it rolled down the sidewalk. "They're hereeee," she shouted, which garnered some lackluster cheers from onlookers. The heat was dizzying, but Dottie and Connie seemed so accustomed to it. Sweat gathered on the back of my neck as the heat beat down on my hair. Frankie was using her train ticket as a fan, and I know she was feeling the Arizona heat, too.

A handsome young man who I assumed to be Scott was leaning against a car. He looked tall, with broad shoulders and dark gelled hair. His smile widened when he spotted us and he jogged our way to help with the bags, first sticking out his hand to greet us. "I'm Scott. Nice to meet you. You must be Cookie." He took off his sunglasses to look at me and shook my hand. "Yes. It's nice to meet you, Scott! This is my sister, Frankie." He shook her hand and gave Connie a quick kiss before helping us get to the car. "I've heard a lot about you two, ya know?" He smiled as he got us situated in the car. "What's in the trunk, anyway?" He struggled as he lifted the trunk into the car and started laughing. "It's not a dead body, is it?"

"Just a few surprises for Connie, that's all." Frankie beamed as Connie's face lit up in anticipation. She was stunning with fair skin and saucer-sized dark blue eyes that almost looked gray. Her face resembled Mom's, but her hair was lighter than all of ours. The sun reflected off of her hair's light waves that were tied in a neat ribbon. She was the same Connie I knew as a little girl. I knew she'd grow into a beautiful woman.

Dottie's once plump face was thin with dark features. Her sunglasses hid her eyes, which made it hard for me to sense her expressions. She had a small chip in her tooth that I don't remember being there and I wondered how she could have done that. She had thick makeup layered onto her face and rouge plumped up her cheekbones. She was attractive too, of course, but she seemed to be hiding something underneath it all.

Dottie, Frankie, and I piled into the spacious backseat as Connie joined Scott in the front. Although we were staying downtown in a hotel, he first drove us to Dom and Barb's home to greet everyone. Since the wedding was only days away, we couldn't wait to show them the surprises inside the trunk, either.

Barb, Dom, and Tommy were waiting for us on the front porch as we arrived. Tommy ran up to us and introduced himself as soon as we stepped out of the car. He was far from shy, that's for sure. Connie patted his head and shooed him back to the steps. Dom jogged over, gave us hugs, and proceeded to help Scott unload the trunk and baggage and carry it into the house. Barb followed and hugged us. Her eyes were warm and genuine. She told us to follow her inside and started pouring iced tea. "You girls must be thirsty from that long trip!"

"Thank you," we said in unison as we gulped down the tea. It was hotter than I even imagined it would be in Arizona, but the fan gave us some relief as soon as we stepped inside. My skin felt warm to the touch and the blush on my cheeks seemed unnecessary, as I knew my face was flushed. I could tell everyone else in the room was used to this heat aside from Frankie and me. I watched as Dom and Scott plopped the trunk onto the floor in the living room. Frankie and I looked at each other. It was time.

Frankie put down her drink and walked over to the trunk. "First things first. We have a surprise for you, Connie. It's been so hard to keep this a secret." Everyone gathered in front of the trunk as Frankie unlocked it. I pulled out the bridesmaid dresses first to throw Connie off the surprise. "Look! It's your bridesmaid dresses. All the way from Connecticut." I held one up to myself and swayed to show off the layers. The dress was bright white with large gold polka-dots scattered throughout. The polka-dots shimmered as I moved around. It was tea length with cap sleeves and contained layers and layers of netting in the petticoat. "I hope you like them. We brought accessories too! Gold shoes and tiny hats!" I looked at Connie's face, which was blank. "You... like them, right?" Frankie questioned.

"Like them?" Connie responded. "Girls, they are divine. I can't believe you and Anna did this for Scott and me." She had tears in her eyes as she squeezed Scott's hand. "Thank you so much. Really."

"Well, that's not all," Frankie said as she reached deep into the trunk. She pulled out a plastic dress bag and handed it to me to hold. "There's one more small thing. Scott, maybe you should go outside so you don't see this."

She began unzipping the bag as white tulle and lace spilled out, revealing Connie's wedding gown. "This one is for you." The dress Frankie made was exquisite, down to every detail. It was pure white—like an angel's wing—and contained dozens of wispy layers of tulle that pooled onto the ground. The top of the dress had intricate lace that dripped down the sides as well. It had a modest v-neck that crisscrossed in the front and attached to flowy short sleeves. The back of the dress contained

a hundred satin-covered buttons and the same delicate lace from the front. It was a classic gown that you would see in the window of Dior, with details only Frankie could come up with. It wasn't just a dress; it was heaven-sent.

Connie darted towards the dress. She needed to touch it. "You bought this too? All for me?" Connie sniffled as she cried.

"Well, the thing is... she didn't buy it, Con. She designed it herself. All with you in mind. She bought all the fabric, too, and found the perfect seamstress to create it for you from top to bottom. It took weeks and weeks." I said as I pulled a piece of paper out, unveiling the original design from Frankie's sketchbook. The charcoal sketch looked almost identical to the dress hanging in front of us. Frankie outdid herself.

Barb and Dottie dabbed their eyes and everyone watched in awe as Connie wrapped it around herself. A few seconds before, Mary knocked at the door and let herself in. She almost fell to her knees when she looked at Connie. "What's this? Is this your wedding dress?"

"It's all mine," Connie said, as she twirled around the room. "Frankie and Cookie brought it for me. Frankie designed it and then got it made especially for me! It puts my sales-rack little white dress to shame, that's for sure!" She turned toward me and Frankie. "Thank you, girls, from the bottom of my heart. How can I ever repay you?"

"We're here with you. That's more than enough. Plus, it's the least we could do!" Frankie responded. "Now, let's put that dress on you to make sure it fits." Connie led Frankie to the bedroom so she could try the dress on.

Meanwhile, Mary put her arm around me and squeezed my waist. "You have no idea how much you being here means to these girls," she said as she kissed my forehead while we waited. "It was tough keeping this secret, but she had no idea!" Connie emerged from the bedroom wearing her new wedding gown that was fit for a princess. Not only did it accentuate her figure like it was sewn right onto her, but it brought the radiance out of her. Her smile that day was something I'd never forget. She spun around while her family looked on. "Well, how do I look?"

Dom, a man of little words and emotions, had tears in his eyes. "You look beautiful, baby." Tommy ran up to her but Barb stopped him before he could touch her with his sticky iced tea fingers. "I think you look like you came out of a fairytale," he said as he looked up at her, awestruck. Dottie stepped forward to fluff out the back of her dress. "Con, you look like a million bucks. Now let's get you married!"

Over the next few days, the four of us ran around town getting last-minute errands done. Dottie and Connie also took the opportunity to show us the sites of Tucson. Connie brought us to the cute house she and Scott would be renting after the wedding. We drove past the university she was attending in the fall. I admired the Spanish architecture of the buildings downtown and the flat roads with a mountainous backdrop. We went downtown to the shops and even drove to the desert, which was truly magnificent. The rolling, sandy hills were dotted with flowering bushes and big spiky cacti, some of which towered over ten feet tall. A cotton-tailed rabbit stopped to check us out before hopping by. Frankie couldn't help herself—she brought her sketchbook along and made a picture-perfect sketch of a cactus. Dottie and Connie watched in admiration as Frankie did what she did best.

The night before the wedding, Dottie asked us if we could stop by the bakery to put the final touches on the cake. She and the owner, Filomena, made Scott and Connie's wedding cake that morning. Dottie was a woman of few words—she only spoke so far when we asked her direct questions. Connie, on the other hand, was a chatterbox and filled any silences.

But, in the bakery, Dottie was in her element. She was confident and poised as she tied an apron on and got to work. She danced around the kitchen with joy on her face as she finished decorating the two-tier cake with pastel pink sugar flowers and edible lace. As she added one last flower—a blue rose for good luck—she smiled and dusted her hands off. "Frankie, can you open that refrigerator door for me?" Dottie placed the cake on the shelf and closed the door behind her. "I think we're good here." She was beaming with pride at how the cake turned out. "Should we head to the hotel?"

The four of us retreated to our hotel room to settle in for the night. It was thrilling to have a night to talk and catch up, without any distractions. I wanted to talk about life and how things were going for them.

"How about a drink?" I asked as I took four glasses out of the cabinet. The girls gathered on the couches. Connie glanced over at Dottie who had already hopped up to help me pour some drinks.

"How about a toast? To Connie on the night before her wedding. And to us." Frankie toasted and we all clinked glasses in celebration. There was an awkward silence after the glasses stopped ringing. "So, Dottie. Tell me about the bakery. You're pretty much running it now. It's like your dreams came true!"

"Oh yeah. You can call it a dream come true. I come home covered in flour and can barely make ends meet." She rolled her eyes and then laughed it off to lighten the mood. "I'm trying to have Filomena expand the business so we can focus on custom orders—much like the wedding cake we created for Connie. That's where I want to take it, but if she doesn't agree, I might have to start a business of my own. I can see it now—the words Dottie's Cakery splashed across the side of the building. Now, that's my real dream." Dottie looked hopeful as she imagined a bright future in the cake business.

"Wow, that sounds amazing, Dottie. That's the exact career I imagined for you when you were a little girl and told the world you wanted to be a famous baker. I can see you making it happen, too." I leaned back and took a sip of wine.

"Yeah, right," Connie chimed in. "Dottie can barely make it to work on time and she wants to run Tucson's most successful cake business. Give me a break." I could feel the tension between them as Dottie glared back at her. Frankie appeared nervous as she adjusted herself in her seat and took a gulp out of her cup.

"Shut up, Connie. Mind your own business. Why do you care, anyway? You won't even be around soon!" Dottie stood up and tipped her glass backward, drinking every last drop in mere seconds.

"Oh, sure. Drink up, Dottie. Is that part of your business plan?"

"Hey, now," I interrupted before Connie could continue. "What's going on? Why are you girls fighting like this?"

"You wanted to see the real us, right? You want to see what life is like in good ol' Tucson without you and Frankie. Well, here I am. Every messy bit of me. Oh, and let me introduce you to Connie. She's the perfect child." Dottie poured herself another drink. The glass was so full that the alcohol dripped down the sides onto the dresser. "Aren't you glad you came all the way here?"

"As a matter of fact, I am glad I came all the way here. All I want is to be next to you girls. To erase the past and start fresh. But that's not possible and this is the best we could do."

"I guess the best you could do isn't good enough." Dottie finished her drink and wiped her mouth in one swift movement. She tucked her purse under her arm and left the hotel without another word. The rest of us sat stunned.

Frankie spoke up. "Connie, what the heck was that all about? What have we been missing?"

Connie sighed and took a small sip from her glass. "You girls have no idea. Dottie is going to ruin her life if she doesn't get it together. First, it was the drinking. Then, the partying. Now, it's her horrible relationship with her stupid boyfriend, George—who is NOT invited to my wedding, by the way. She better not dare invite that man." She was fighting back angry tears. "Dottie somehow managed to turn into Dad. But she doesn't see it. I try to help her, I do. I listen to her cry when she's had enough. I tell her I'm there for her, but she always falls back to old patterns. And let me tell you, Dom and Barb have had enough of it. They have Tommy there. They told her one more slip-up and she's on her own."

I shook my head in disbelief as I wondered how we missed this. We write almost every single week. We talk on the phone sometimes if we're able. But we somehow overlooked such a large part of Dottie's life. I grew embarrassed as I thought about our letters. Frankie and I drone on about art classes and fancy New York City trips while Dottie is suffering in silence. I stood up and jogged towards the door to chase Dottie before she left. I removed my shoes and called out for her as I ran down the hallway and entered the elevator barefoot. As soon as the doors opened, I saw her. She was staring out of the window in the hotel lobby into the flickering headlights on the dark road. I caught my breath and put my shoes back on, and grabbed a seat nearest her.

"I'm sorry, Dottie. I'm so sorry. I didn't know any of this. I didn't know you were struggling. I would have been here in a minute."

Dottie's eyes were red and swollen as she began to answer. "But that's the point, Cookie. You're not here, and I know it's not your fault. But me struggling shouldn't be the reason you jump on a plane or a train to come to see me. This should have never happened. We shouldn't be thousands of miles away from each other." She paused. "And I can't believe I somehow ruined this trip that I've been dreaming about for months." She cried into her hands as I put my arm around her shoulder.

"You didn't ruin anything, Dottie. We're going to have a wonderful time at Connie's dream wedding tomorrow. We're going to stand beside her and support her as she says her vows. And we are never, ever going to go this long without seeing each other again. Promise?"

"I promise," she said as she pulled a handkerchief out of her purse to wipe the tears. "That sounds like a plan."

We took our time walking back to the room. Dottie opened up about life and her drinking, as I simply listened and took it all in. When we got back to the room, Dottie apologized and hugged Connie with all her strength. We spent the night reminiscing and talking about anything and everything. Life felt normal for those few hours, as we acted like children. We traded in the cocktails for orange soda from the vending machine in the hallway. And Dottie's eyes got clearer as the alcohol left her system. She was ready for a change. I wondered what—if anything—we could do to help Dottie begin to heal.

The next morning, we woke up and immediately started getting ready. The room was buzzing with exciting energy—when Mary showed up with the dresses, it all started to feel real. Jo, Barb, and Tommy also made their way to the hotel. We giggled as Tommy practiced his slow march down the hallway, taking his role of ring bearer to heart. We did our hair and makeup and laughed our way through the day in preparation for the ceremony.

When Connie walked into the room wearing her wedding gown, I got teary. Our baby sister was getting married today, and we were all together again. As rocky as things got last night, I wouldn't trade being in the presence of these women for anything. My smile grew wide as we watched Connie whirl around the room in a gown that Frankie put so much love and care into. It looked like a cloud as she danced in and out of the sunlight, the shine of her skin reflecting onto us. "Oh! I almost forgot!" I exclaimed as I unhooked the pearl necklace from around my neck and placed it onto hers. "Your 'something borrowed'!"

The ceremony took place in a small church in Tucson, with tall wooden pews and stained glass windows. Incense and several candles burned on the altar and filled the air with a rich pine-needle scent. The priest talked about the sanctity of marriage. He brought special attention to the loved ones who were no longer with us, especially our mother and father. There wasn't a dry eye in the house as we remembered them. I imagined them looking down on the day while beaming with pride at Connie's relationship with Scott and the love that was overflowing out of the pews. Frankie and I held hands as Connie and Scott said their vows in front of their loved ones. They sealed their marriage with their first kiss as husband and wife. Connie glowed on the altar, and I knew she was ready to be Scott's wife.

Later that evening, our gold heels got a lot of use as we danced the night away. One of Scott's friends asked Frankie to join him during a slow song. We smirked as she blushed and took his lead on the dance floor. I took a break from dancing to stroll around the room. I wanted to take it all in: the mesmerizing scent of fresh flowers mixed with the vanilla bean aroma from the wedding cake, the heavy feeling of romance in the air, and the joy I got from seeing Connie so happy. It was intoxicating. I scanned the dance floor to look for Dottie, but she was nowhere in sight. I made my way to the bathroom where I bumped into her in the hallway.

"Hey! Are you okay? I was looking for you. I want the next dance..." I chuckled, but Dottie's face was grim. She was shaken.

"I'm okay, yeah. Sure. Let's dance." Her eyes were anywhere but here. Just then, a man stormed around the corner and exited out the back door. My senses were telling me it was George.

"Was that...?" I started.

"George?" She finished my question. "Yes, it was him. I told him he couldn't come but he insisted on meeting me here. I'm lucky Connie didn't see. She would have been so upset with me."

"Okay. Well, he's gone now. Let's brush it off and get right back to the dance floor before she notices." I pulled her into the bathroom and began fixing her makeup. "Here, put this on," I said as I handed her a tube of lipstick. "It'll brighten you right up!" She followed my directions. "So, does this mean you and George are together?"

"I broke up with him. Well, I tried to, anyway. He has this way of pulling me back in." I kissed her on the cheek. Dottie didn't need another lecture from me in this wedding hall bathroom. I grabbed her hand and led her out onto the dance floor, where I saw the smile return to her face.

Connie was none the wiser as we celebrated her and Scott's wedding well into the early morning hours.

Saying goodbye to our sisters was even more difficult than I had imagined. I spent the train ride home thinking about the highs and lows of our trip. I thought about Connie and the grown-up confidence she exuded. I couldn't believe she now had a husband who was carrying her over the threshold of their new home any moment now. I reflected on Mary and Dom and how—although their love faded—their love for my sisters never did. And I contemplated all the reasons why Dottie turned towards the bottle to make it through life. I felt restless as I tossed and turned in my bed, but didn't say a word to Frankie. I knew deep down, though, that she felt the same way as she reflected in her own bed.

When we arrived in Connecticut, Herman was waiting for us with open arms at the terminal. It was surprising to not see Anna with him but chalked it up to her being busy at the bridal salon. We talked about the trip the whole ride home, both of us conscious to leave out the complicated parts. We picked up a sweatshirt for him from the University of Arizona that had a logo from their law school blazed across the chest. I knew he'd love it. Herman's ears perked up when we spoke about Tucson's scenery, so we indulged him on our trip to the desert. He loved hearing about the lizards and rabbits that roamed around. "Did you see a roadrunner?" he asked with a chuckle. Frankie told him about the cactus she drew that she left for Connie as a wedding gift for her new home. We spend the next few minutes talking about how spiky cacti really are.

We pulled in our driveway around thirty minutes later and began our sluggish walk to the house—we were utterly exhausted. As I walked, I fumbled in my purse to ensure I had everything. For some reason, I had this nagging feeling I left something behind on the train. I lifted my head and was startled by a male figure sitting on the front steps. I rubbed my eyes and blinked out of shock and confusion to make sure I was seeing clearly.

It was Ray. In the flesh. Standing right in front of me. And somehow even more handsome than I remembered him several years ago. I stopped dead in my tracks, not knowing whether to believe it.

"Hi, Cook," he said as he stood up.

"Is this real? Are you here?" I felt like I was drunk.

Ray chuckled. "It's me. The love of your life."

"What... are you doing here? You weren't supposed to be home for months!"

"Well, I had to ask you something in person," he answered as he walked towards me and bent down on one knee. "Cookie, will you marry me?" He pulled a custom made diamond ring set in platinum out of his pocket and slipped it onto my trembling finger. I looked down in amazement, hoping I wasn't dreaming. "...Well?" he asked. My pulse sped up and I took a deep breath. I think my whole body was shaking.

"YES!" I shouted. "Of course I will!" I leapt into his arms and planted the biggest kiss onto his lips. Herman and Frankie cheered from the driveway as Anna stepped onto the porch, giddy with excitement. She cried as she applauded our big news and I knew she stayed home to help Ray with the surprise.

This was real and Ray was home. All felt right in the world. Well, except for one major thing. I continued to hug Ray and tried to be present but the heaviness of the Arizona trip hung over me. I had a bad feeling about Dottie.

18

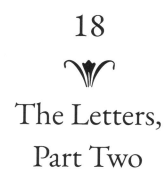

The Letters,
Part Two

September 10, 1953

Dear Dottie and Connie,

I am writing to share the most exciting news that Cookie and Ray got engaged! Would you believe that Ray was
waiting for her at home on the front steps when we arrived
home from the Tucson trip? He pulled the most beautiful
diamond ring out of his pocket and dropped down to one
knee while we watched! Cookie was in shock, but she happi-
ly accepted. They have decided to get married in a few short
months at the end of November. Anna has already started
planning a grand affair. I wouldn't expect anything less

from her.

I would love to have you both join us for the wedding in Connecticut. I know it might be difficult, but Cookie would love to have you here. We'll be in touch.

With love,
Frankie

September 11, 1953

Dear Cookie and Frankie,

There's something I want to share with you both, but you must keep it between us. Dottie would kill me if she found out I shared this with you. I feel like it's my obligation, though, especially after you both heard our argument in the hotel room that night.

Days after my wedding, there was an incident involving Dottie. I don't know all the details——Scott and I went away for a few days for a honeymoon——but it seems as if Dottie's bad decisions have caught up to her. She was at home watching Tommy. When Barb came home from work, Dottie was passed out in a drunken stupor on the couch, and Tommy was nowhere to be found. Barb woke up Dottie in a panic and the whole neighborhood must've heard her screaming. Luckily, she found him a few houses down. He had seen a ball roll by the window and went out the front door to find it. Dottie had no idea where he had gone because she didn't hear him leave.

I thought seeing you both would have a positive impact on her mindset. I never expected something like this to happen right after I told you girls that Dom and Barb have had it with Dottie's behaviors. But, this was their last straw, unfortunately. They asked Dottie to move out until she could get her life in order. And I'll give you one guess about where she went? She found her way back to George and is now living with him. It makes me wonder if they were ever done in the first place, or if she lied to me about that too.

I'm at a loss for words. I hope by some miracle she comes around. I will keep you updated, but please do not reach out to her yet.

Writing in confidence,
Connie

September 27, 1953

Dear Cookie,

Please accept my apologies for writing such depressing news in my last letter. When I wrote it, I did not yet receive Frankie's letter announcing your engagement [I will get to that news in a few short moments]. I am mortified to have potentially ruined an exciting time for you.

I am happy to report that the last few weeks have been eye-opening for Dottie. I have seen her quite often. She is remorseful of the incident that happened with Tommy and has been throwing herself into work at the bakery to make a name for herself. I know it's too soon to tell, but I do feel like I've seen a change in her. I will, of course, keep you updated on that matter, but please share this news with Frankie.

Now, back to your big news! Dottie and I were so thrilled to hear of your engagement to Ray. And to hear how he did it? How romantic! We can't believe he was waiting for you on your front steps when you arrived home with the ring in his pocket! Anna must have helped plan the timing of the engagement. Did she give him hints for your ring, too? We have been hearing about this wonderful man for years now. He seems like your perfect match, Cookie. We cannot wait to meet him.

However, I have some good and bad news about that. Dottie will be able to attend your upcoming wedding. Unfortunately, I won't be able to make the trip. I will be there in spirit, though. I am glad you chose a short engagement because I cannot wait to hear all the details upon her return. It will be marvelous, I just know it.

Now, the good news. I do have a good excuse for not coming to Connecticut. Scott and I recently found out that we are expecting! Little old me, bringing a little bundle of joy into the world... can you believe it? There's nothing I want more than babies of my own. I hope we can raise our children to be kind and close to one another, just like us.

I haven't been feeling too well, so my doctor instructed me to stay close to home. Nothing to worry about, girls, but Scott also wants me to stay put until this baby is born. I've also been attending some classes so I can gain some college credits towards my social work degree. I am determined to finish, even though the baby might put my plans on hold for a little while. But, that's life, right?

Please enjoy your special day. If you thought I looked beautiful as a bride, wait until the crowd sees you, Cookie. Their jaws will be on the floor.

Sending my best to you and Ray,
Connie

October 1953

Dear Connie,

I wanted to send you a quick note to thank you for the "well" wishes regarding my upcoming wedding. I, for one, am thrilled you are not coming to the wedding, because that means Dottie, Frankie, and I are going to be AUNTIES! There is no one more deserving of the beautiful life you are making for yourself with Scott. I am so happy I could cry [Well, I may have already cried——only a little].

Congratulations to you and Scott. I am so happy for you, Connie.

P.S. I was so relieved to hear the news about Dottie. We have been thinking of her day and night.

Love,
Aunt Cookie

November 29, 1953

Dear Connie,

Our sweet Cookie is a married woman! Her wedding was last night and I couldn't wait for a second more to tell you about it——and there's so much to tell. Before I begin, I wanted to share some bits and pieces about Dottie, who is sleeping soundly next to me. She has been so helpful and attentive to Cookie since she arrived a few days ago. She stepped up and she seems to be doing so much better. Her eyes are clearer and she looks much healthier than the last time we saw her. She even bonded in the kitchen with Anna and taught her how to make her famous cookies. She's headed back to Arizona by train tomorrow and I will say, I'm going to miss her. That's the Dottie I knew and loved so many years ago, and it was nice to see that side of her again. I knew it was in there somewhere, after all...

Now, let's talk about the wedding, starting with the dress. As you know, Anna owns a dress shop. But every time she got a new shipment in, she decided none of them were good enough for Cookie and her wedding. This went on for weeks! Until one day, she surprised Cookie and brought us to Manhattan to shop at one of the most exclusive bridal salons in the country. They served bubbly champagne in crystal stemware. She wore a white silk robe while she tried on dresses. And since they knew Anna so well, they even shut the store down to other shoppers. I'll never forget this experience——we felt like movie stars!

Every dress Cookie tried on was exquisite, but our breath was taken away when she walked out wearing "the one." It was a thick and silky ivory satin peau de soie gown. Close your eyes and picture this: long sleeves extending right past

her wrist and a collared v-neck to show off her decolletage.
The bodice was slim and fitted to the hip and flared out to a
full a-line to hit the floor. And then there was the train——
it floated behind her for what seemed like the whole length
of the store and was made from the same fabric. No beading or lace, but just luxurious flowing fabric that fit her
frame and made her look like a million bucks. As soon as
she stepped on the platform and they topped her off with
a layered tulle veil, we knew it was the dress she would wear
to marry Ray. Cookie is so effortless. Even with her hair
tied back in a simple ponytail with a fresh face, she looked
like she could step right off the platform and walk down the
aisle. And the funny part is that we would all think she spent
hours getting ready! That's Cookie for you! Now, I know
I'm biased, but your dress and her dress topped my list as
the most beautiful gowns I've ever laid eyes on. On her wedding day, Cookie carried our parents' Bible down the aisle.
She took it from our childhood home when we were there
that day packing up our things. When Anna was cleaning
out a closet, she found it in a shoebox amongst some photos and letters and gifted it to her the morning before the
wedding. This floored Cookie because she had forgotten all
about the shoebox——especially the Bible. The only jewelry she wore was her perfect diamond ring and a set of pearl
studs Ray gave her that matched her necklace.

The wedding itself took place last night——as you

know——on a warm November evening. Unseasonably warm, I should add. We were all so worried that it would snow. Well, everyone except Cookie who seemed to instinctively know the weather would be perfect. This was the Saturday after Thanksgiving and all the guests seemed to be in the holiday spirit. We first had a formal Catholic ceremony at Our Lady of Lourdes church downtown. There were enormous white and red poinsettias flooding the altar. Dottie, Ray's two sisters, and I stood on the altar next to Cookie as she said her vows. We wore high-neck champagne-colored gowns that seemed to foreshadow the champagne we would consume all night. And much like your ceremony, the priest spoke about our parents and how they were watching down and celebrating alongside us. It was perfect. Our Cookie was divine.

After the ceremony, we all headed to the wedding venue, which had twinkling lights strung every which way at the entrance. Inside, it looked like a wintry dream. A crackling stone fireplace roared and set the tone of the evening. Everyone sat at long tables with evergreen garland and candles splayed down the center. Instead of traditional dinner and dancing, Anna chose to do a formal five-course meal for the guests complete with wine and champagne that flowed all night. I couldn't get over the taste of the roasted Cornish hen I had for dinner with whipped mashed potatoes. We spent the night drinking, eating, and laughing. We connected. And the cake was incredible——Dottie didn't make this one but she even gave it rave reviews. A French pastry chef made it and it weighed 75 pounds. One of my favorite moments of the evening was sneaking off with Anna to have a piece of vanilla cake with chocolate mousse filling and a steaming cup of French drip coffee.

At the end of the night, Cookie and Ray changed outfits and left the venue to catch a plane to Miami, Florida. And somehow, the night continued for the rest of the wedding guests. The men smoked cigars and the women kept warm by the fireplace. It was a superb evening. The only thing that was missing was you, but your ears must have been ringing because we talked about you all night. I kept thinking about how different your weddings were. Yours had dancing and great food and was a bit more casual. Cookie's was formal and full of champagne. Yet, they both embodied your and your husbands' personalities with perfection! I could skip weddings altogether in the future knowing I already went to two of the best weddings I'd ever see in my lifetime.

Well, Dottie is stirring next to me so I better go. I'm sure she will tell you every last detail when she gets home. I hope you're feeling well. Please write soon, Connie.

Love and wedding bells,
Frankie

꙳

Honeymoon 1953

"Greetings from Florida"

To my lovely sisters Connie and Dottie [who should be back
in Arizona any day now],

   I am writing this postcard from the sunny beaches of
Florida. The hotel staff put a sign on our door that read
"Just Married" and that's when it all started to feel real. I
don't know if you had the same feeling, Connie? I'm in
paradise with my new "husband." I saw a group of women at
the hotel bar yesterday sipping cocktails after spending all
day getting kissed by the sun and I had a great idea!

   We should plan on meeting in South Beach next summer for a girls' trip. It's central to both Connecticut and
Arizona. Connie, you can bring the baby. And we can relive
our Tucson trip and just focus on each other and our new
bundle of joy.

What do you say?

Your newly married sister,
Cookie (Mrs. Cookie to you)

December 1953

Dear Frankie and Cookie,

I'm still spinning from Cookie's wedding. It was the most
fun I had in some time [aside from Connie's wedding
weekend]. This felt different though because it was the first
weekend in many years that I didn't have even one drink.
Not even a glass of flowing champagne. Not even a chilled
martini from the bar. My mind was lucid and although it
was hard, it felt good. I felt good.

Dom, Barb, and I had a long talk and we made up [finally].
We talked about me moving back home or maybe getting a
place of my own in Mary's apartment complex once I saved
up some more money. I still live with George. He has been
fine but it's not the life I want to live. I want to have a happy relationship like Cookie and Connie. Once I get on my
feet, I know I will find that, but for now, I am focused on
becoming the best version of me. I am what's most important right now.

Mary's boyfriend moved in with her and the two seem
content together. She left the bakery job on good terms to
spend more time at home, which brings me to my next topic. Filomena hasn't been feeling well. She trusted me with

running the business in its entirety until she gets better. She has given me a raise and I get to make more decisions. The extra money made it possible to quit my waitressing job and focus on the bakery, which was my dream all along.

I don't want you to worry about me anymore, girls. I know we had our ups and downs in Tucson when you were here, but I'm feeling more and more like myself every day. I have my sisters to thank for that.

Take care,
Dottie

February 1954

Dear Dottie [Please show this letter to Connie when you see her]:

It was lovely to catch up over the phone over the holidays. It was nice to hear your voice and you sound so great. It was all I needed for Christmas. In fact, my whole year was made because I got to see you and Connie. I agree with Cookie that we should try to meet up in South Beach this summer. I'm on board. Do you think you'll be able to get away for a long weekend?

On a different note, I have been thinking about something a lot lately. Isn't it funny how a small decision can change your life completely? Like that sad story of the plane crash that I saw on the news lately——I'm sure there was a man or woman who missed the flight because their car broke down on the way to the airport and is alive today because of it. Or, another woman's decision to go grocery shopping on a Saturday instead of her usual Sunday. It might have led to her reaching for the same loaf of bread as the man she would soon call her husband.

Life is a series of moments and little decisions that bring us to where we are at this very moment. If you and Connie didn't move to Tucson, she wouldn't have met Scott. And Dom and Mary would have remained in a loveless marriage instead of finding their soulmates. And who knows what would become of us if our parents were still here? I don't mean to bring you down, but it's something I have been thinking about and I wanted to share it with you. I want to make sure we continue to share our lives as we get busy from work or marriage or kids.

On a lighter note, I am going with some friends to Boston this weekend to check out the Isabella Stewart Gardner Museum. It has a variety of European, Asian, and American art that I want to see. I've never been to Boston before. Maybe I can convince the newlywed [Cookie] to take the trip with us...

Love,

Frankie ("L'Artiste")

April 9, 1954

Dear Cookie,

I hope Anna or Frankie was able to pass the good news along to you! Connie had her baby! It's a boy! His name is Robert Antonio. She wanted to honor Dad so she used his name as the baby's middle name. She and Scott have been calling him Bobby, though. How cute!

Connie is feeling well but is still sore. When I went to visit at the hospital, Scott said that she did amazing even though he almost passed out. Imagine a big, strong guy like Scottie almost passing out in the room? Before I held the baby, I watched as Connie handled the baby. She was gentle and soothing as she rocked him to sleep. She is a natural mother. When she handed the baby to me, I couldn't help but stare into his round bright blue eyes [he got those from Connie, didn't he?]. He looked like a little angel. I swear I can see Mom and Dad's faces in his. He's perfect, and I can't wait for you and Frankie to meet him.

I wanted to tell you, too, that Connie and I talked a few weeks ago [before she went into labor] about Cookie's suggestion to meet for a girls' trip in South Beach. Connie had some requests. First, she said she would be more comfortable if we waited until the baby was at least six months old. She would also prefer to bring Scott along to help with the baby. Otherwise, she is thrilled to come! And for me, I asked Mary if she could come back and help with the bakery for a few days if I gave her enough notice. She said it wouldn't be a problem. With all of that being said, I think we should plan on meeting there in October.

Lastly, I wanted to tell you that I'm still sober. I truly think that you saved me from a destructive path. I was involved with the wrong crowd but seeing your faces for the first time gave me a new perspective. I'm forever grateful for the time we got to spend together at Connie's wedding and again at your wedding, Cookie. You are the most important people in my life. I promise to make you proud.

Your sister,
Dottie

19

Dottie's Cakery

Summer of '54

Dear Frankie,

I received a call this morning that Filomena passed away. I expected her to recover in full from her illness, but her condition worsened over the past few months.

Filomena's niece called me to tell me the sad news. She stated that Filomena spoke about me every chance she got——Dottie, this and Dottie, that. She knew I would make it big one day. And the unexpected news: she said Filomena left something for me in her will. She gave me the address for the lawyer handling her estate and asked me to come in this week.

Please pass along the news to Cookie. I hope all is well in Connecticut.

Love,
Dottie

I felt the car come to a stop. Ray turned off the ignition and whispered with a laugh, "I hope that blindfold is on tight, Cookie. No peeking."

I nodded my head in anticipation. "I can't see a thing, I promise." At our apartment earlier, Ray announced we had to make a detour before our lunch date with Anna and Herman. He went on to say it was a surprise for me, something that has been in the works for months and months. I was intrigued. Whether a surprise date, a piece of jewelry, or even a slow dance in the middle of a store, Ray always had a surprise up his sleeves. He explained that he needed to make up for the lost time when he returned home. But I never needed him to make up for anything—marrying him was the easiest decision I ever made.

We got out of the car and he stood behind me as he escorted me forward. "Watch your step," he said, as he led me up a few steps. The ground beneath me changed from grass to a hard wood-like surface to a plushy material. "Ray, I can't take this anymore. Where are we?" I begged as he placed my hands on my shoulders.

"You sure you're ready?" he asked, knowing my answer. He began to untie my blindfold and it fell to the floor. We were standing in the living room of an empty house. It was a quaint ranch with a white stone fireplace and teal carpet. Through the cutout, I saw a kitchen that resembled the one I grew up with. Natural light shone through the windows and reflected off the metallic hardware of the new appliances. "Look, Cookie. These pieces of mail all have your name on it." He grabbed the first letter in a pile of envelopes off the mantle and handed it to me. My first name, Loretta, was printed in all capital letters across the front in marker. I opened it to find a letter from the bank congratulating us on our new home. I glanced up at Ray who was beaming from ear to ear. "This is our house," he said. "It's brand new... all for you, Cookie." I hugged him in disbelief as I took it all in. This is our home, together. "Oh, and Cookie. Take a look at the other letters."

In each envelope was a separate note from each of my sisters congratulating us. Ray reached out to each of them to secretly share the news ahead of time. Connie's note read: "Cookie and Ray—Sending many blessings to you as you embark on your next journey in your new home." Dottie finished her note with "...And make sure there is a spare bedroom all set up for me!" Frankie simply stated "It was hard keeping this secret from you, Cookie. Which holiday will you be taking over?" It felt good to feel my sisters' presence with me that afternoon as Ray showed me around the home.

I stopped at the kitchen sink and ran my hand over the cool white porcelain as I admired the view of the wooded back yard from the window. A weeping willow stood tall in the center, its branches dancing in the summer breeze. I felt an overwhelming sense of calmness wash over me as I imagined myself drying dishes after a card game with our friends. Little did I know that would be a place where I spent a lot of time reflecting and daydreaming in the many years to come. I teared up as we made our way into each of the three bedrooms, as I imagined the family that would soon fill these walls. Every soft step on our walkthrough solidified my decision to spend the rest of my life with this man.

I sat on the edge of the tub in the bathroom, the same way our mother would when Frankie and I would pile in together before Dottie and Connie were born. She would lean over and crack open the window while we splashed around. More water would end up on the floor than on our bodies, but Mom never seemed to care. I could still imagine her crossed legs as she smoked a cigarette and blew smoke rings into the air. The rings faded into the air as she would take another puff. I swore I could smell her signature Chesterfields as I sat there. She would twist the cigarette into her glass ashtray to put it out—each butt held a pink stain from her lipstick, which always stood out against the ash. She would then pour a cup of lukewarm water over my hair to rinse it. Then she would hand me the cup and I would wash Frankie's hair. Each of us remained silent as we enjoyed those few moments of pampering in the bath. And afterward—every single time—she would unplug the drain and sing while we giggled:

"Cookie and Frankie in the tub.
Mommy pulled out the plug.

Oh, my gracious! Oh, my soul!
There goes my babies down the hole!
Blub! Blub! Blub!"

I cracked the window a smidge before walking out of the bathroom to let the phantom smoke dissipate.

I walked back down the hallway to find Ray sitting on the counter in the kitchen. "Ah, I almost forgot one thing," he said as he jumped onto the floor and opened the refrigerator door. On the shelf was a single bottle of champagne next to two chilled glasses. "We have to have a proper celebration!"

He was about to twist open the top of an expensive bottle of champagne when I blurted out, "Ray, wait!" He stopped right before the cork exploded into the ceiling.

"What is it?"

"I don't want you to open that expensive bottle of champagne yet!"

"Yeah, I see that, Cookie. But why?"

My eyes sparkled in the afternoon sun. "Well, you're not the only one with a life-changing surprise today."

"Oh?"

"I can't drink the champagne, Ray...I can't drink it because... we're having a baby." Ray's eyes lit up as he pulled me towards him, cradling his hands onto my belly.

"We're going to be parents!" he exclaimed before popping open the bottle anyways in excitement. Champagne splashed onto the linoleum below our feet. He took a swig and looked me in the eyes. "I'm going to be a father. I'll make you proud, Cookie. You're going to be the best mother. I know it." He kissed my forehead before continuing. "It's a baby girl in there, you know that right?"

"Why would you think that? We won't know that until the baby is born!"

"I don't know, Cookie. I guess I feel it deep inside. And I know the perfect name for our little girl: Donna Marie." He leaned down and kissed my stomach. "Hi, my Donna girl. It's your daddy. I'm going to take good care of you forever," he said with a loving smile.

I smiled and looked around as Ray talked to our unborn baby like they were already the best of friends. Without a shadow of a doubt, I know Ray's words were sincere when he said he'd take care of the baby and me for the rest of our lives. Here, in this empty house, that would soon turn into our family's buzzing home.

Dottie glanced around the room at the mounds of legal books lining the walls of the stark lawyer's office. She perched herself on the edge of the leather club chair, which felt sticky against her warm skin. She waited in anticipation for the lawyer to enter the room.

Filomena's niece called about a week ago and gave her the address of this law firm. She asked if Dottie could come in this week to handle a few things relating to the bakery. She was nervous and avoided the trip altogether until Connie convinced her to go in and see what he had to say. Meanwhile, a sign—presumably hung by Filomena's niece—hung on the bakery's door that read "On Vacation," leaving Dottie to let her mind wander about her fate.

A lawyer in a navy three-piece suit with a striped handkerchief neatly folded into his vest pocket and a young woman walked into the room in tandem. He held a manila envelope in his hand and dropped it onto the desk in front of Dottie, which startled her.

"Hello, Dorothy. Do you know why you're here today?"

"Honestly, sir, I have no idea. Filomena's niece told me to come in and speak with you." Dottie picked at the skin around her nails.

"As you know, Filomena Rossi, unfortunately, passed away about a week ago. She was my client and I handled her estate and business matters, including that of the bakery. He removed paperwork from the envelope and shuffled through it as he continued. "I'll cut right to the chase, Dorothy. Filomena named you in her will."

A puzzled look washed over her face. "She did? Why would she do that? Filomena had nieces and nephews."

The lawyer laughed at her bluntness. "Yes, she does have

other family members, of which she did leave pieces of her estate too, as well." He turned a piece of paper to face Dottie and pointed to a row of text. "She left you the bakery and corresponding business accounts."

Dottie's face turned white as she tried to process what the lawyer was saying to her. Her mind was a jumble and this was the last piece of news she expected to hear today out of this stranger's mouth. "The bakery?" Her mouth was dry. The woman standing in the corner ran over with a glass of water and placed it on a coaster in front of Dottie. She smiled up at the woman, who peered down at her through thick, horn-rimmed glasses, before retreating back to the corner of the room.

"Yes, Dorothy. Filomena owned the building—including the apartment above the shop—the bakery business, and the baking equipment. She had no loans and everything was paid in full. She also left you a sum of money in a bank account that will help you in your transition to become the owner." He pointed again to the paper to a line item where the amount of money in the bank account was highlighted. "She wanted you to have everything relating to the bakery. She spoke highly of you over the years. Your abilities as a baker impressed Filomena. She did not doubt that you would handle her business with care. Do you understand?"

"I... I understand," she said. She was halfway telling the truth.

"Wonderful. I'm going to need some signatures and then we can send you on your way with the key and all the paperwork you'll need to get started. You'll have to come back in about a week to pick up some remaining ledgers and tax information. We can go over any of your remaining questions then."

Dottie spent the next hour or so reviewing and signing paperwork as the woman from the corner looked on as a witness. The lawyer took the time to explain each piece of paper as she signed to ensure she understood the full responsibility. At one point, Dottie looked over to the stocked bar cart at a bottle of scotch. She shook the negative thoughts out of her head and brought her mind back to the present moment.

Dottie signed the last paper and placed the pen down on the lawyer's lacquered desk. She was now a business owner with a good amount of wealth backing her. She held her head a little higher as she walked out of his office while holding the key. Dottie felt proud and humbled that this woman entrusted her with her lifelong business and earnings. Her mind raced with ideas as she drove to the bakery.

When she arrived, she pulled off the "On Vacation" sign and crumpled it into a ball. She turned the key to unlock the front door, locked it behind her, and turned on the lights. Everything looked different as she walked through the space. She ran her fingertips across the counter and over the glass case, where last week's pastry was still chilling inside. She made a mental note to clean everything out of the case. The bread boxes were empty but the smell of bread still lingered in the air. Above the register hung a dingy price list. It reminded her of Filomena, as she insisted on changing out the letters for the special of the day. Even as it became harder and harder for her to climb the steps of the ladder, she refused to let Dottie help her. It was something she'd always remember about Filomena—her work ethic and determination... and, at times, her stubbornness.

She walked into the back and flipped on the light switches to illuminate the room. The stainless steel working space was immaculate. Dottie liked a clean kitchen and it was therapeutic for her to wipe down the surfaces after a hard day's work. She made her way to Filomena's office—now, her office—which was a small locked room attached to the kitchen. Filomena's paperwork was stacked in a pile on her desk. On the wall hung a lone picture of Dottie standing in front of the cake she made for Connie's wedding. Dottie had no idea that the photo existed. She certainly never expected it to be hanging on the wall by itself in Filomena's office.

Dottie stared at the black and white photo of herself for a few more moments and thought about that day. That was the day before Connie's wedding. Later that afternoon, she chugged drinks in the hotel room before running off and later apologized for her actions. It was the night she thought long and hard about the path her drinking was taking her down, while her sisters lay asleep beside her. She slept next to Connie that night, who smiled on her pillow as she dreamt of her upcoming nuptials. Dottie recalls watching Connie's sleeping face in the darkness as she remained wide awake. She hoped one day that her life would soon fall into place as her sisters' lives were beginning to, too.

She sat down on Filomena's office chair and put her elbows on the desk. She continued to stare at the photo as a smile made its way onto her face. She wrote the words "Dottie's Cakery" on a piece of blank paper and pinned it to the wall next to the photo. Her life was falling into place. First, due to her sobriety that began soon after Filomena took this photo, which she attributed to her sisters' visit. And second, because of this bakery of which she was now the proud owner. Her wildest dreams were coming true right before her eyes. She vowed right then and there to leave George once and for all. She would go there to pack her belongings and move into the vacant apartment upstairs that now owned. She wanted nothing more than to make Filomena—and her sisters—proud of the woman she knew she would become.

20

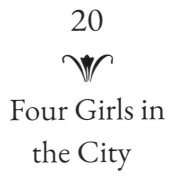

Four Girls in
the City

Room 904

To: Cookie, Frankie, Dottie, and Connie:

"Hello from Connecticut"

I called ahead at the hotel because I wanted to send you
something to start your girls' weekend off with a bang. A
bottle of cheap champagne was the best they could do.
Oh well, it'll all taste the same after your first glass.
Enjoy your trip to Miami.
P.S. Miss you already, Cook. Be safe.

From,
Ray

I tapped on the door with the back of my hand and put my

ear up to listen for any movement inside. Frankie stood beside me as a large grin spread across her face and we waited. We arrived in Miami much earlier than expected and decided to surprise the girls at the hotel instead of having them meet us at the airport. We were staying at a glitzy hotel on Miami Beach that overlooked the world-famous white sand beaches. Once the taxi signaled onto the coastline boulevard on the drive to the hotel, Frankie lowered the window and stuck her head outside. She showed the giddy excitement of a child on Christmas morning. The warm coastal air bounced off her cheeks as she closed her eyes and put her head back to face the hazy sun. The city's skyline buzzed by and the tall buildings reminded me of the times I've spent in New York City.

My sisters and I said we would get together more and we managed to pull it off—a little over one short year after our weddings last fall. Frankie could only take a few days off from work, so it was a quick weekend getaway for us. Meanwhile, Dottie, Connie, Scott, and baby Bobby arrived several days ago for a longer stay. Dottie's focus has been on the bakery, but she trusted Mary to run things for a few days so long as she checked in often. Luckily, money no longer felt as tight for her and she was able to get away on a whim. And for Connie, she was taking time away from courses to savor time at home with the baby for as long as she could, which means she also had some free time. I wanted to wait until my three-month check-up with the doctor before flying. Although Ray was nervous, he knew I needed more time with my sisters after our last trip left me uneasy. I hadn't told the girls I was expecting yet, and I thought this would be the perfect weekend to do so. I slung my rather large tote bag over my shoulder so it covered my growing stomach until I could reveal the news.

A few moments later, Dottie opened the door and squealed in excitement when she saw us. As soon as we stepped inside, we could see the view of the ocean in the backdrop. The shades of blue from the water and sky blended together—the only thing that differentiated them from one another was the puffy white clouds that crawled across the sky. Palm trees shimmied their bright green leaves like maracas. The shutters were open and a salty breeze swept through the room, almost knocking the hat off my head. The October weather was perfect—it was sunny and toasty without the intense South Florida heat. We dropped our bags and hugged our sisters, but Scott and the baby were nowhere in sight.

"Where's this beautiful baby boy we've heard so much about?" Frankie asked. "I have been dying to grab his little cheeks!"

"Look over there," Connie said as she pointed out the window towards the beach. "Those two little specks are Scott and the baby. He wanted to take the baby for a walk before you got here so he would go down for a nap. We weren't expecting you sneaky girls for a few hours!" She swatted my arm and grinned. "We're so happy to see you." Connie's wavy hair looked bright against her sun-kissed skin. She was glowing.

"I can only hope that motherhood looks as good on me as it does on you, Con!" I removed the bag from my shoulder and rounded my hand over the loose fabric that covered my stomach to expose my small bump. I posed for a minute while I waited for the girls to catch on.

"You're having a baby!" Dottie exclaimed as a trail of happy tears rolled off her cheek. Connie chimed in to correct her. "*We're* having a baby!" The two raced towards me as they tripped over each other, wanting to be first in line for a congratulatory hug.

"Thanks, girls! I wanted to surprise you. It was tough to keep this one under wraps. Especially with this gossip queen over here." I pointed to Frankie who put her hands up to cover her mouth.

"I could barely contain my excitement," Frankie said. "Pretty soon, babies will fill this whole hotel room. One can dream, anyway!"

"Ray maintains that it's a girl. I don't know what drove him to such a conclusion."

"Maybe he's praying for a little one as perfect as you, Cook," Connie said. "My little boy is going to have a cousin. I can't believe I'm saying that out loud! It feels like yesterday that the four of us were playing on the sand on the beach that day..." Connie's voice trailed off. "That was the last time I was at the beach if you could believe it." She, of course, was referencing that day... the one we tend to avoid bringing up in discussion. In fact, none of us have ever brought up the day our parents died in conversation.

Dottie turned to walk towards the kitchen. She poured herself a glass of water as she hung her head. She held up a note next to a bottle of champagne on the counter. "Cookie," she said to break the silence, "Ray sent this bottle of champagne to the hotel room for us. What a guy! Not that you can drink. And not that I drink anymore, either." She laughed.

"More for us. Right, Connie?" Frankie said as she grabbed the note to read it. "We'll have to open it before we go out later. Any idea of what we want to do tonight?"

"I saw an adorable oceanfront restaurant a few blocks away. I thought we would do that and then follow it up with some dancing. Scott is staying here with the baby so I'm all yours." Connie shimmied across the room in her striped top and white sailor shorts. "Four girls in the big city!"

This trip already felt different than the last. We all seemed more comfortable in each other's presence like no time had passed. Connie looked relaxed and Dottie appeared especially healthy. Her skin was rosy and plump. The whites of her eyes were clear and focused. I felt the four spirited wide-eyed little girls within us again. The girls that I longed to be near for so long.

We spent all afternoon lounging on the patio next to the pool in a spot where we could also see the turquoise waves crash into the white sand. Soon enough, Scott and the baby returned from the beach to join us. That's when Connie's spirited baby boy, Bobby, stole our hearts. I watched in admiration as she held him on her hip. Connie—the colicky baby I'd hear screaming through paper-thin walls that grew into a temper-tantrum throwing toddler with a stutter—was now an impressive young woman with an easy-going temperament. My baby sister wasn't a baby anymore. She was a wife and a mother who was on her way to becoming a social worker. She wanted nothing more than to help little boys and girls from Tucson who grew up just like us.

Frankie asked us if we wanted to take a walk down to the ocean. She wasn't a strong swimmer, but the water always drew her in. When we would take walks along the brook at the country home, Frankie splashed water everywhere as she stepped in and out of the water. A half-mile hike to the lake would take hours and water soaked her pants up to her knees. We'd gaze out into the water and take it all in—the scenery and serenity of the sprawling lake. Frankie would take off her socks and shoes, roll her pant legs up, and step into the clear water. She would walk in until water covered her ankles, but not a step further than that. As much as bodies of water appealed to her senses, she feared them.

So when we made our way down to the water, it shocked me that Frankie removed her cover-up and headed into the waves without a second thought. The ocean mist sparkled against her skin as she immersed her body into the depths of the blue waters. She waited for a wave to crash into her thighs and then dove in as we watched the bubbles float into the air.

Dottie looked at me with furrowed eyebrows. "Does Frankie even know how to swim?"

"Apparently, she does," I answered as Frankie emerged from the wave. Her slicked-back dark hair trailed behind her.

She turned back to wave to us. "It feels like bathwater," she said. "Come in!" Connie was standing off to the side in her own world as she dipped the baby's toes into the water. His toes curled under him and he let out a belly laugh. Dottie and I shook our heads.

Frankie waded in the water and floated further and further away from the shore, which prompted Dottie to yell. "Okay, Frankie. It's time to come back now." She waited a few seconds before becoming agitated. "Come back NOW, I said."

I nudged Dottie's shoulder with mine. "She's okay. She can still touch the bottom." Frankie waved again, indicating that she couldn't hear Dottie yelling over the sounds of the crashing waves. Connie stepped her way over with the baby to join us.

"What's going on over here?" she questioned. "I didn't even know Frankie liked to swim." The three of us—and the baby—looked on as Frankie rode waves back towards the shore and then swam out further again to catch them. It was almost as if she was reliving a childhood moment that she never got to experience when she was a young girl.

A larger wave formed and knocked Frankie underneath the water as it barrelled towards the shore. I could no longer see her, and the blood rushed through my body as I made a few steps forward into the water. "Do you girls see her?" I begged.

Connie picked up the baby and put him on her hip. "I don't see her, Cookie." The spot where Frankie last was floating was quiet and still.

"FRANKIE!" Dottie let out a blood-curdling scream and rushed into the water in her swimsuit cover-up. She barely took a breath before she dove into the sea and emerged a few seconds later to scan the surface of the water. "Do you guys see her?" She screamed up at us. The waves were choppy and strong, which made it hard for Dottie to take full breaths of air. She dove back under the water.

I gasped in relief as Frankie came up for air about twenty yards to our right. She was breathless and appeared fatigued, but she was okay. Dottie spotted her and took aggressive strokes towards her. She latched onto Frankie and pulled her towards shallower waters. The two women trudged through the water and onto the sand, where Frankie collapsed onto the beach. A few seconds later, she began to laugh. A loud, roaring cackle followed by, "Boy, now I know why I don't like to swim." She stood up and brushed the sand off her legs and body.

"Are YOU kidding me, Frankie? You could have gotten

yourself killed out there!" Dottie shoved her, leading Frankie to almost fall to the ground.

"What's your problem, Dottie? It's not like I meant to do that! I got tired and the waves were too much for me. Why are you so upset?"

"You have no idea. None of you have any idea. A million memories came rushing into my mind when Frankie went under."

"We have no idea?" Frankie retorted. "You don't think we remember that day, too? We were ALL there."

Dottie sighed and closed her eyes. "But you guys don't know everything...." Her voice was quiet, barely comprehensible amongst the hostile waves.

"Dottie, what are you talking about?" I took a step towards her and put my hand on her shoulder. "What does that mean?" Connie and Frankie stepped forward, too.

"There is something I've been keeping from you. I held it inside for so long. Something from the day Mom died." My mouth dropped open. "Mom took me to the bathroom at the beach a little while before it happened. She had a fearful look in her eyes and I knew something was off. She grabbed a bottle of pills out of her bag and shook them into her mouth. She swallowed them without a second thought. She didn't even close the bottle; she threw it back into her purse and the pills fell everywhere. Then, she took out a scratch piece of paper and a pen and scratched a few words across the paper. The note said: 'You made me do this. You'll never see my face again. Goodbye forever.' I thought it was so strange. Who was she writing to? Where was Mom going? She had a cold look that I'll never forget. Then she looked at my scared little eyes in the reflection of the mirror and said 'Mommy's leaving, honey. But, shh, don't tell anyone. It's our little secret.' She kissed my forehead and led me back to the beach blanket where you were playing. She slipped the note into Dad's shirt pocket. That was right before she went for her last swim."

Frankie, Connie, and I stood there speechless, as the sandy wind and sea foam swirled around us at the shore. "Mom killed herself. It wasn't an accident," I stated.

"How could you not have told us this before, Dottie? I lived in the same bedroom as you for almost ten years and not a word!"

"I wanted to protect you all from it. I held it inside and I buried it in the depths of my memory. Until a few minutes ago when I watched Frankie's life flash before my eyes. I blame myself for everything. I could have stopped her."

I shook her gently by the shoulders. "Don't be ridiculous! You were a little girl. There was nothing you could have done. Mom was sicker than we thought. I can't believe you held it inside..."

Dottie backed away from me. "You girls all led perfect lives and then there was me. Little ol' Dottie, the alcoholic. The cookie-cutter version of her father. Holding onto this horrific memory. Wondering if I could have stopped it. Seeing Mom's scorned face when I close my eyes at night. Thinking about the chicken scratch on that note. Watching Dad's face as he read it after Mom already went into the water. I need to be alone for a minute," she said. She walked towards the hotel. Her steps were heavy as she sunk into the sand with each movement until she got to solid ground. She jogged towards the entrance and disappeared out of our sight.

I plopped onto the sand and rested my elbows onto my weak knees. I couldn't stand for another minute. I closed my eyes, leaned back, and rubbed my stomach. Dottie's words rushed into my head like a tsunami and I couldn't think straight. I took a big breath in through my nose and held it for a few seconds before releasing it.

"You okay, Cookie?" Connie asked before sitting down next to me. I nodded and smiled at Bobby. He was cooing in excitement as he watched the waves crash against our feet. Frankie grabbed a seat on the other side of me.

"Where do we go from here?" Frankie asked. She was gazing out into the water, which appeared calmer from this vantage point. I continued to take deep breaths as I looked far into the ocean. The sun was starting to cast its orange and pink hues across the sea as it inched towards the horizon. We sat in silence and breathed in the salty air.

Connie popped up and started making her way up the beach. "Where are you going?" Frankie asked before grabbing her things and helping me up so we could follow her.

Without turning around, she said "I can't sit here and pretend nothing happened. I need to talk to her."

We ran into Scott in the lobby. Connie pulled him along without saying a word and we crammed into an already full elevator. Scott opened the door to our room—room 904—and Connie pushed him out of her way to get inside.

But Dottie wasn't there. The breeze blew through the room as we searched for her in the bedroom and bathroom. Scott perked up when he discovered a note on the counter. "Uhm, Connie," he said as she stopped to walk towards him. "Dottie said she went back to Arizona." He passed the note to Connie, which read: "Girls, I can't do this. I need to get back to my bakery. I don't want a lecture about this. I don't want to talk about it. I'm sorry.—D." Her suitcase wasn't there any longer. Scott looked up at us. "What the heck did I miss?"

Later that night, Frankie, Connie, and I went out to dinner as originally planned. Scott stayed back at the hotel with the baby to give us a little breathing room. We walked down the promenade in silence with our heads hung low. We were all deep in thought about what we learned over the course of the afternoon.

We weren't four girls in the big city. We were three girls, lost and emotional, full of what-ifs. My mind was clear enough to know that the weight of our parents' deaths could not rest on the shoulders of a ten-year-old girl. Someone who didn't know what suicide or death was. Someone who couldn't feel the strain of our parents' tumultuous relationship wearing away at our mother's heart. Someone who shouldn't have had to bear witness to the behavior of a mother who was spiraling out of control and needed help. I worried about Dottie. Where was she right now? What was she thinking?

We continued to walk. The bright lights of Miami illuminated the sidewalk and reflected off the expensive cars as they buzzed by. A fire engine charged down the street, its sirens blaring into space, but it didn't faze us. Nothing could scare the three of us anymore, or so I imagined.

I thought about Dottie and the way her life unfolded. She held onto the heaviness of what she heard and what she saw. That heaviness led her to drink—to numb the pain that lived so deep inside of her. It was the pain that caused her to run to a man who harmed her. The burden that sat atop a loveless relationship that she felt was all she deserved. Dottie thought that was as good as she would get out of life. Much like our father, she found solace at the bottom of a bottle. She found emptiness in her heart when she was sober. She felt fear in her mind when it ran wild during times of silence.

I knew right then that what I thought earlier was not reality. When I saw Dottie and Connie's faces, I made the mistake of assuming we were somehow unscathed. That things were different than they were in Tucson. Things weren't better; they were merely covered up. Dottie was sober now. She was a business owner. She was out of an abusive relationship. She was thriving. Yet, this all left me fearful for her. I worried that conjuring up these deep memories would bring her back to where she started. I worried that life would continue to be cruel to Dottie once again.

As we neared the restaurant, I thought about Frankie's drawing and how I remembered it. I pictured four women who had it all—walking in lockstep as lights of the cityscape flashed around them and lit their path. But in the real-world on this hot October evening, our paths were dim. The street was buzzing, but we were anywhere but present. Our arms were not linked. They were stuck to our sides as we shuffled down the littered sidewalk. Although we didn't say it out loud, we all wondered what the future held—for our relationship and for each other.

21

❦

Tucson's Rising
Star

March 1955

Dear Cookie,

You must be ready to pop any day now! Are you past your
due date? Remember to breathe in and out——you will do
great, Cookie!

Also, I wanted to tell you that I ran into Dottie yesterday.
We were both grocery shopping at the store. I had the baby
with me, and she was alone. I watched her as she navigated
the produce section. She looked good actually, but something was off. She almost seemed out of it. She didn't even
notice me when I was standing a few feet from her. I tapped
her on her shoulder and she turned around. She had a look
of shock on her face. She instantly started to cry and so did
I.

I can't believe it's been nearly five months since we all last
spoke to her. This is the longest we've ever gone and I've

been sick over it. We are all still sisters at the end of the day. We need to push ourselves to get back in the groove, just like old times. She agreed to meet me for coffee at the diner during the week to catch up. She said there was something she had to tell me, anyway, and she was glad we ran into each other.

Good luck,
Connie

I pushed open the door to the nursery without making a sound. Ray was holding the baby against his chest with closed eyes, as he swayed along to the soft music that was playing on the portable radio. I had just finished catching up with my friend from school, Martha, who lived a few streets away from our new home. Even though it was March, she took a bun- dled-up stroll to our house with her two little boys to drop off a basket of warm blueberry muffins. Friends always seem to know when you need a pick-me-up. I placed a muffin down on the dresser, which startled Ray. He opened his groggy eyes and smiled at me as pure joy radiated off him. "Have some- thing to eat," I whispered, as I pulled the baby into my arms and took a seat on the rocking chair.

Ray was smitten with her the minute he laid eyes on her. She looked tiny and fragile in the hospital bassinet but that didn't stop Ray. He would scoop her up—his hand larger than her whole body—and look deep into her sparkling brown eyes. I almost thought I could see a genuine smile on our baby's face as she gazed back at him, but I don't think it could be possible for an infant of only one day old.

We had an eventful start to labor. My water broke while we were at Anna and Herman's house for supper. I sat on the club chair in the foyer as they all ran around the house in different directions. Grabbing keys, packed suitcases—whatever they could get their hands on. They nearly forgot me as they rushed out the door. As Ray slid across the foyer, his eye caught mine and he skidded to a stop. He chuckled and jogged towards me, lifting me to a standing position. "Let's go have this baby, Cook," he said as he helped his waddling wife get to the running car.

Luckily, the delivery went smoothly and Ray was right all along. I gave birth to a beautiful and healthy baby girl. When they placed our baby on my chest, an overwhelming sense of love and contentment washed over me. I smiled down at her. "Welcome to the world, our precious little Donna. We are so happy you're here." Ray wiped a single tear from his cheek. I knew he'd be a great father.

Ray's mother and siblings were the first to visit us at the hospital the day after the baby was born. Our room was stuffed to the brim with balloons, stuffed bears, and colorful bouquets. Today, Anna, Herman, and Frankie stopped in since I was feeling much better. Ray took Anna and Herman downstairs to get a bite to eat, leaving me to catch up with Frankie while the baby slept. "Wow," she said as she hovered over the bassinet in admiration. "Do you think this is how Mom and Dad felt when they saw us for the first time?"

"Of course," I replied. "With all of their faults, they loved us so much. Don't you remember the way he would soothe Connie? She felt so safe in his arms."

"Speaking of Connie, did she also send you a note to say she ran into Dottie?"

"Yes. And I'm glad they are going for coffee to smooth things over and move forward. Seeing my baby made me miss Dottie so much. I think Donna has her eyes."

We sat and observed the baby while her chest moved up and down as she rested. After a few minutes, Frankie broke the silence. "I have some exciting news for you."

"Oh? And what's that?"

"Remember how I've been thinking about making a change and quitting my job at the nursing home?"

"Yes. Did you quit?"

"Well, not exactly. The morning before I was supposed to have an interview for the entry-level job I saw posted at the art museum, the museum coordinator called me to cancel. They were dealing with a big leak in the ceiling that might ruin the art. I was disappointed but figured they would call back eventually. So, instead of calling out sick like I originally planned to go to the interview, I begrudgingly went into work and started making my rounds. I was in one of my patient's rooms when I heard a soft knock at the door. A handsome man, maybe 28 years old, asked me where the supply closet was. I walked him to the room and it turns out he was filling in for the person who usually delivered the medical supplies. His name was Marshall and I instantly liked him."

"What? That's great, Frankie. How come you didn't tell me all this?!"

"I wanted to make sure it was something before I told you about it. Marshall took me out on a date last weekend and we hit it off, Cookie. I like him. I really like him. He's sweet and attentive. He was initially quiet but opened up after a while. We are going out again tonight for dinner. I know it's too early to say, but I think he might be the one." She paused to rock the bassinet because the baby started stirring. She fell right back to sleep. "I can't stop thinking about the note I sent to Dottie a few years ago now. I wrote about how small decisions can change your life. How life is a series of moments that bring us to where we are at this very moment. I would have never met Marshall if I went for that other interview that day. You would have never married Ray if I didn't agree to that blind date so many years ago." She laughed and rolled her eyes to lighten the mood.

I thought about this sentiment for a moment. "And Dottie perhaps wouldn't have gone through so many hardships if she never knew the true story behind Mom's death." We collectively let out a deep sigh just as Ray returned to the room.

"I just saw the nurse in the hallway. Sounds like we're ready to go home!"

My thoughts fell back to the present, as I rocked in the chair with the baby. Her sweet breath warmed my neck. The phone started ringing, and Ray took a bite of his muffin and scurried to the kitchen to answer.

I could hear Ray as he spoke. "Oh, hi, Connie... Yes, she's here... Yep, our baby Donna is healthy and beautiful... Okay, hang on just one minute. Let me grab her."

Ray rushed into the nursery to tell me Connie was on the phone. "She said it was urgent." I stood up with the baby and walked to the kitchen to pick up the receiver. "Hi, Connie. What's the matter?"

"First of all, congratulations on your baby girl," she said. "Ray said she's beautiful and healthy. And he was right—it was a girl after all. My little Bobby has a new baby cousin to play with..."

I interrupted her. "Thanks, Connie. We'll get to all that, but I'm worried. What's the urgent news?"

"I had coffee with Dottie yesterday. And... and. Well, Dottie's sick, Cookie. She just found out." I handed the baby to Ray. My hands were shaking and I nearly dropped the phone. Connie continued to talk about Dottie's illness and what she learned. She talked about an upcoming doctor's appointment that Connie was taking her to. It all sounded gibberish to me; all I heard was that something was wrong with our sister. And I wasn't there for her.

I hung up the phone and put my head into my hands. I wept over the counter as Ray rocked our baby who now woke up and began to cry.

Dottie polished a smudge on the stainless steel counter. She stepped back and admired her work after cleaning the bakery from top to bottom. Today, a reporter from "The Arizona Daily Star" was coming to interview and photograph Dottie and her bakery. A few weeks ago, she received a letter stating she would be featured as "Tucson's Rising Star" in the newspaper and that a reporter would come to discuss her business.

This news flattered Dottie—she put her heart and soul into the business after Filomena left it to her. She refreshed the menu, began serving freshly-brewed drip coffee, and—most importantly—marketed her custom wedding cakes to all of

Tucson. There were varieties of cannolis with a special fillings each week. The customers' favorite was the lemon ricotta. She also began layering fresh whipped cream and fruit into her cakes. Strawberries, raspberries, peaches, and even sugared pears brought a freshness to her desserts. She worked around-the-clock after the bakery closed. She drove to college campuses and handed out flyers. She worked with an ad agency to create colored posters that showcased her cakes. Everywhere she went, she would spark up a conversation about Dottie's Cakery.

And her efforts worked. The bakery was busier than ever. She hired someone to work in front, while she focused on growing the business. She met with customers to design the cake of their dreams and got imaginative with her creations. Dottie received so many calls about wedding cakes that she had to start turning people down! That is, until she hired another baker who was almost as skilled as she was. Mary and Barb even filled shifts as needed. Everyone recognized Dottie's talents—she was Tucson's Rising Star. She had everything she ever dreamed of.

But, Dottie's trip to Miami was emotional and draining. Her dark thoughts almost clouded her sobriety when she placed a bottle of whiskey in her cart while out shopping. As she stood in line to check out, she spotted a Dottie's Cakery flyer pinned to the wall behind the cashier. She took a deep breath and handed the liquor to the woman behind the counter and left the store. That same day, she found a local church that offered alcohol counseling and turned to them for support. She never gave in to her temptations. It was then and there she decided to put her energy into her business and make a name for herself. And, although she missed her sisters with everything inside of her, she knew she had to focus on herself. It was up to her and her alone to do everything she could to forgive herself, heal, and move forward. Dottie was close to making amends, though. She knew her sisters would be proud of her successes—both on a personal and professional level.

The reporter walked through the front door, which caused the bells to jingle. Dottie grew nervous. She took one last glance at the spotless kitchen and shoved the folded towel she was holding into her apron. "Hello! I'm Dottie," she said with confidence as she introduced herself to the reporter and photographer. The reporter was a young woman with tortoise glasses and coiffed blonde hair. The diamond hanging off of her finger sparkled under the fluorescent lighting every time she moved. The photographer, a middle-aged man with a camera strapped around his neck, was quiet and tried to remain part of the background as an observer. The reporter motioned for him to grab a seat at the table next to her. Dottie poured steaming cups of coffee and placed them on saucers with tiny floral spoons to stir in the cream. Both the reporter and photographer admired the plate of goodies in front of them. Dottie handpicked mini samplings of her favorite desserts—including a crusty sfogliatelle, a creamy cannoli dotted on each end in chocolate chips, and a few crumbly biscottis—and arranged them on a doily-lined plate. They looked delectable. "Go ahead! Dig in!" she exclaimed as she removed her apron and joined them at the table.

They spent the morning engrossed in conversation, like the reporter was an old friend. Dottie shared with enthusiasm the details of her shop and her wedding cake strategy. Her regular customers shuffled in and out, sometimes interrupting the interview to greet Dottie. She would smile wide and wave to them, as the photographer snapped candid photos of her staff in action. A proud look cast over her face as she watched customers carry her signature bright yellow boxes wrapped in pink string. This was a new touch she added to the bakery to rebrand and modernize it. The reporter's face lit up as she jotted down some notes about the bright colors of the box. Dottie couldn't wait to read that detail in the article when it came out.

"So, I have one last question before we go. You have such a forward-thinking direction for your cakery. You're getting more and more into wedding cakes and other custom wedding details. Who was the inspiration for this beautiful shop and your new-found strategy?"

"Well, that's an easy one. My sisters, of course. I created a custom wedding cake for my sister Connie's wedding. I baked every ounce of love I had into that cake, and I think she felt it.

The whole guest list felt it! She was so happy when she saw the cake I designed for her and her husband, and I knew I had to share this gift with the world. My sisters are my inspiration for everything I do here. I have them to thank for always believing in me and loving me no matter what. Look up there—that's a drawing my sister Frankie did of us many years ago." Dottie had taken the sketch from her old bedroom and got it framed to hang in the shop. Dottie looked at it while daydreaming of the next time they would get together since Miami didn't exactly go as planned for the four of them. She was determined to recreate that photo with her sisters and she knew better times were ahead.

After the reporter and photographer left, Dottie went into the kitchen and began prepping her space for the next morning. She was feeling light-headed—perhaps because the only things she consumed were sweets and coffee all day. She lined up everything on the counters, the same way she did every day. She couldn't handle a messy kitchen and thrived on organization.

Dottie went into her office and pulled out her book to go over her upcoming orders. Opening the binder, she turned to today's date. It had her handwritten notes and to-do lists ready for her to take on. The longer she looked at the paper, the more light-headed she got. Flashes of light flickered in her peripheral vision and her eyes stopped focusing. A few seconds later, Dottie lost consciousness and collapsed to the ground, sending the papers on her desk into a flurry around the room. Her employee heard the noise from the front and sprinted to her aid, but Dottie wasn't responding. She called 9-1-1 and waited beside her—Tucson's fallen star—for the ambulance to arrive.

Dottie woke up—confused and fatigued—right after the ambulance arrived. "Put me down! I'm fine," she demanded as they moved her onto the gurney to bring her to the hospital. The days and weeks ahead would prove that Dottie wasn't fine. She needed the support of the people she loved most— her sisters, who were always on her side for better or worse.

22

The Story of
Our Lives

March 1955

Dear Dottie,

I wanted to write and let you know that I'm thinking of you.
It's been a long six months. I wanted to give you your space
after Miami. I know your main focus has been on growing
the bakery and making a name for yourself. There's no
doubt in my mind that you'll be successful because you have
the drive and passion to make it happen. But, no matter
what, your sisters love you and we're here for you.

   With that being said, I'm sorry I couldn't join Frankie
this time for a visit to Tucson. Your new baby niece, Donna
Marie, is here and needs me. I promise I will come to see
you as soon as I'm able, though.

   Sending you my thoughts. I love you, Dottie. I truly do.

Your sister,
Cookie

A few weeks after we got the news from Connie, Frankie and her new boyfriend, Marshall, flew to Tucson to visit Dottie. I couldn't travel yet, as I had just had the baby, but I felt comfort in knowing that Frankie didn't have to go alone. We felt it would be best if one of us were there for any further news that was uncovered about Dottie's health.

Ray reached over and grabbed my hand that was folded in my lap. We were driving to his mother's house for our first outing since we had the baby. Donna was sound asleep and let out a comforting whimper. She wore a pink crocheted dress and matching bonnet that Ray's sister knit for her, along with the tiniest mary-janes I've ever seen. A change of scenery was what we needed today. There have been many sleepless nights since we returned home with the baby, but Ray made it all easier. He let me sleep while he got up to feed her. Once, I woke up and found him sitting at his desk. He was punching numbers into his adding machine while Donna slept on his shoulder.

I must have been deep in thought. "Everything okay, Cookie?" he asked as we pulled into the driveway. His mother's house, a sprawling white ranch on a few manicured acres, emerged from behind some trees as he put the car in park. I looked over at him. "I was thinking about these last few weeks. Between the news about Dottie and bringing the baby home, it's been a roller coaster of emotions. I'm bursting at the seams with love and sadness all at once. I'll be happy to see your family. It will be a nice distraction."

Before he got the chance to reply, Ray's mother and two sisters, Peggy and Rita, met us in the driveway. They were so kind to me and made me feel like I was part of the family, like I've been a fixture for many, many years. Marrying into a big family was always something that appealed to me. Aside from three siblings of his own, Ray had lots of aunts, uncles, and cousins, most of whom lived in the area. We followed them inside, and Ray's brother, Marty, was sitting on the couch. He reminded me of Ray—he had the same chiseled jaw and a similar build—but he wasn't as relaxed. He always seemed a little stiff. "Congratulations are in order," he said, as he handed Ray a drink. The two of them clinked glasses and he turned his ice blue eyes towards me. "Hi, Cookie," he said with a nod.

The baby started to stir and Ray's sister, Peggy, perked up. "Can I hold her?" she asked. I nodded and she lifted the baby out of her seat. "Cookie, should we heat up a bottle for this beautiful baby?" Peggy's daughters were playing with their dolls in the other room. She was a natural with children. We went into the kitchen and warmed up a bottle. Rita, Ray's other sister, joined.

We caught up on each other's lives. We talked about the cold weather and the new house. We talked about our children and their extended family, which was also now my extended family, too. Then Peggy lowered her glasses and asked, "How is your sister, Frankie?" Her auburn hair was pulled back into an updo. Her hand was on the hip of her forest green belted dress.

"She's great. Thanks for asking. She's in Arizona right now visiting our other sisters."

"Oh, that's right! You have two other sisters out there, right? I only met Dottie."

"Yes. Dottie lives there and also our youngest sister, Connie. She has a little boy named Bobby. He's the sweetest little boy," I responded, as I watched Peggy feed the baby. Rita sat at the table and smoked a cigarette. She was in her own world as she puffed clouds of smoke out of her lips.

"I've been meaning to tell you this, but your sister Dottie is quite the woman. I spent a lot of time with her at your wedding. She's so passionate about baking. And she had an old soul. Very kind."

"She is those things and more." I had a knot in my stomach as I thought about Dottie. In the weeks after learning Dottie was ill, we learned she had an auto-immune disease that was causing her kidneys to fail. She was meeting with the doctors this week to learn more and Frankie was luckily going to be by her side. Her blood work caused concerns amongst her medical team, but they are hopeful she will be with us for a long time.

As the day went on, we enjoyed the company of Ray's family. Ray's mother set out home-cooked Italian food and everyone picked throughout the day—the smell of thick and garlicky tomato sauce lingered in the air. I made myself a small plate of meatballs and salad and savored every single bite, even though I was trying to get rid of this baby weight. There were chairs scattered throughout the room and the vibe was informal compared to Anna's dinner parties. But this party was equally as fun, if not more. Peggy's girls performed for us and sang a made-up song about their teddy bears, who they put on full display in the center of the room. Ray cheered them on between drags of his cigar. Everyone took turns holding, feeding, and changing Donna. It thrilled me to see our little precious baby receive so much love.

A few of Ray's mother's friends and cousins showed up unannounced. Dinner turned into an hours-long game of bridge and laughter fest. The dirty jokes flowed—some of them even made me blush. But everyone was having such a great time and I think it was all because of Ray's mother. She was a well-known and respected woman around town, and loved entertaining. Everyone was relaxed and looked at-home in her big, but cozy, house. Soon enough, spilled liquor and dropped ashes created a mess on the floral tablecloth. But no one seemed to mind. Peggy and Rita couldn't stop laughing as their brothers wrestled around on the carpet. "Cut it out, you two," Ray's mother joked as she bit a cigarette between her lips and smiled. She was a pistol and loved to tell stories from earlier years when Ray and his siblings were young. I tended to be more reserved, but I couldn't help but take it all in.

I realized as I watched the beautiful chaos around me that I would never be lonely again. I grew up with three sisters, but we didn't have an extended family. When our parents died and I went to live with my foster parents, I remember feeling true loneliness for the first time. I wasn't used to having my own bedroom. I wasn't used to the quiet that came with a house not filled with four screaming girls.

I learned from my sisters, and I think they learned from me, too. I was there the first time Frankie rode a bicycle. I watched as Connie jumped into her first puddle and splashed mud all over our clothes. I saw Dottie pick eggs shells out of her first cake. And they watched as I fawned over my first crush. They hung onto every word as I read aloud to them every single night before bed in the darkness—a dim lantern illuminating my face as I read.

We worked together to cook, to clean, and to pitch in around the house. We would argue over stolen toys and clothes, and somehow that was one of the things I missed the most. I would take a million throw-down fights with my sisters if it meant forgiving each other and waking up in the same room for the rest of our childhoods. We were a team and we stuck up for one another with fierceness. If someone felt hurt or left out, we stepped in to fix the situation. We were inseparable. Until, of course, we got separated.

We were all adults now. Some of us had families of our own. Connie had a husband, son, and a best friend turned sister-in-law with whom she shared her deepest and darkest secrets over her teenage years. Frankie was a nurse, an artist, a dreamer, and my other half. Dottie finally found herself before it was too late—although time will tell what the future holds. And I found love in a bowling alley with a man named Ray. He built me a home, and we had a little girl; perhaps, the first of several children. His family welcomed me with open arms and brought me out of my shell. I know when I'm old and gray and look back over my life, some of my greatest memories will be with them. There will come a time when the years spent at home with my sisters would be a short blip in the course of my life. No matter how long I live, only a few short years would be spent living under the same roof as Dottie and Connie.

But I know in my heart that I'll always need my sisters, no matter how often I see them or feel their hands in my hand. I plan on saving every one of their letters, so one day, when I'm feeling the distance between us, I can read the old pages and feel close to them once more. And as time goes on, I'll add to my collection with letters from my new sisters-in-law, my husband and our children, my friends, and even from our grandchildren. These letters will tell the story of my life.

Soon after landing in Tucson, Marshall pulled the rental car into a gas station to fill up the tank. He went inside to pay and came jogging out a few minutes later, holding several newspapers in his hand. "Look who it is," he shouted. Frankie rolled down the window and outstretched the paper in her hands. There it was—a large black and white portrait of Dottie. The headline "Tucson's Rising Star" splashed across the top of the page. In the photo, she stood next to an electric mixer with her apron on and was placing a slice of cake into a scalloped box. In the background, Frankie swore she could see the drawing she made when she was a kid framed and hung on the wall. Dottie looked happy and well, even though the picture was taken a few hours before her collapse. The caption under the photo read: "The owner of Dottie's Cakery, Dorothy "Dottie" Cipriani, attributes her success to her sisters." She's shown here putting the final touches on a slice of her signature cake." Frankie read the article with pride. She had no idea that Dottie had been so successful, and she couldn't wait to share the news. She asked Marshall to grab a few more copies to bring home to Connecticut.

Connie waited outside for Frankie to arrive and almost knocked her over when she ran across the yard to hug her. She also welcomed Marshall into the family, even though he and Frankie had only been dating for a few weeks now. "Do you think you're ready for all of the craziness?" she said as she squeezed his shoulders to greet him. They all walked inside to find Scott playing on the floor with Bobby. "Well, we don't have much time to waste. The party is in a few hours!"

Connie decided to lift Dottie's spirits with a surprise party in her honor. It seems that the entire city of Tucson was buzzing about her after being featured in the local newspaper. Connie wanted to show Dottie how talented and special she truly was. Instead of focusing on the sadness surrounding her illness, the girls thought it would be best to distract her with a celebration.

Marshall and Scott conversed in the living room while Frankie sifted through her bags for something to wear. She removed her sketchpad and pencils and placed them on the dresser. Frankie changed into an emerald green dress and blotted her face with powder. She applied mauve lipstick and pursed her lips into the mirror. When she walked back into the living room, Marshall stood up and grabbed her hand. "You look marvelous, Frankie." Frankie blushed at the attention.

"Wow, Frankie. You do look great. Shall we head to the bakery to see Dottie and throw her off the scent of this party?" Frankie nodded and the two women got into Connie's car and headed to the bakery.

After Dottie's collapse, she stayed in the hospital for a few days as she recovered. Mary stepped in to help with the bakery until Dottie was strong enough to get back to work. It was hard for Dottie to relax; she had been working since she was a young girl and the bakery was her home. But she knew it was important to focus on her health and find out what was wrong with her. Several days of scans, blood work, and other tests concluded that Dottie had lupus, which caused a myriad of side effects. Dottie always thought the pain was from being on her feet and working too hard. She was set to meet with the doctor in a few days to discuss her illness further. She wanted to get a sense of what this news meant for her quality of life moving forward. She sulked at first. She wondered why this happened to her—she had worked so hard to stop drinking and put herself first. She felt sad, but as soon as she saw the orders stacked up on the counter after returning to work, a wave of gratitude brushed over her. She was determined not to let this news stop her from becoming what she always dreamed she would be.

After a short drive, Frankie and Connie opened the door to the bakery to surprise Dottie. She hollered out of excitement and ran towards them for a group embrace. Dottie looked different. Despite being sick, she looked happy. A little distance after an emotional Miami trip was what she needed to feel close to her sisters once again. She felt the weight lift off her shoulders after sharing what she had been holding onto for so long. Through her support groups, she finally realized that Mom's death wasn't her fault. Nothing could have saved their mother from her demise. If it wasn't that day at the beach, it was another day—her death was inevitable. Releasing buried memories and lots of tears over these past six months helped her begin to heal. "I'm so happy to see you, Frankie. You have no idea! I'm sorry for what happened in Miami. I never wanted to hurt any of you."

"I'm sorry, too, Dottie. My strange urge to go swimming that day brought up so many scarred emotions for you. I should have known better."

"To be honest Frankie, getting that off my chest and into the open was what I needed to begin to move onward and upward." She paused. "Speaking of which, how do you like my new bakery?" She extended her arms and a wide grin spread across her face. She nodded towards Frankie's drawing hung by the entrance. Dottie looked back at Frankie, puzzled. "Frankie, would you look at that? You're wearing almost the same dress that you drew yourself wearing in that drawing. Same color and everything. What a strange coincidence."

Frankie looked down at her dress and back up at the drawing. "Wow, isn't that funny? I think it's meant to be."

Connie laughed and said, "So, Dottie, how did the cake for my sister-in-law come out?" Connie commissioned Dottie to bake a cake for her surprise party but said it was for Jo. She knew Dottie preferred her own baking and wanted to somehow include her in the party-planning process, even though it was a surprise.

"Ah, come in the back and let me show you. I was just putting it into the box." We walked to the back and Dottie created a three-tier cake with brushed gold frosting. It had mini edible pearls scattered throughout that resembled polka dots.

"It's perfect!" Connie exclaimed. They wrapped up the cake

and Dottie helped put it in the car. "We'll be back to get you in two hours for dinner. Make sure you look as nice as our gorgeous sister, Frankie, would ya?" Dottie nodded and headed back inside, none the wiser about the party they were throwing in her honor.

Connie and Frankie drove to the restaurant where they were holding the party. Connie and Scott had eaten here a few weeks ago and loved the atmosphere and food. As they were leaving, Connie noticed a magical courtyard in the back with a stone patio and an array of Arizona flowers and plants. Twinkling lights were strung throughout the space and lit up the sky. As soon as she saw it, she knew she had to book it for Dottie's party.

They were cautious as they carried the cake inside, careful not to drop such a beautiful work of art. They walked around the courtyard to make sure every detail was perfect. Several business owners from around town were coming, as well as their family and friends. Connie even hired a singer to serenade Dottie. He sang some hits from the early '50s by Buddy Holly and The Four Aces. They hoped the party would reflect the celebration Dottie deserved. After they finalized the menu with the manager, Connie and Frankie sat down at the bar and each ordered a cocktail. They relished in this time together—they couldn't remember the last time they spent time together alone. Connie teased Frankie about Marshall and saw a twinkle in her eye as she gushed about him. Frankie and Connie bonded and reminisced about the dress Frankie designed for Connie.

Soon enough, it was time to go pick up Dottie. As they left, some of the party guests started to arrive, including Scott, Marshall, and Bobby. They took their time getting to Dottie's apartment—they wanted to ensure the guests settled in and were ready for the surprise. When they pulled up to the bakery—where Dottie also lived in the apartment above—they saw Dottie inside the shop straightening up. They watched her for a moment. She had on a mustard-colored dress with a white belt and white gloves that stopped at her wrist. She pinned back her curled hair. She looked dazzling. She spotted us and waved through the windows of the bakery before flipping off the switches and locking the door.

Frankie turned in her chair to face Dottie, who was sitting in the backseat. "You look like a million bucks, Dottie. How do you feel?" The girls hadn't addressed the elephant in the room yet, which was Dottie's health.

"I'm feeling great actually. I've been having some off days since I fell that day, but I think I'm going to be okay." It was a relief to hear that Dottie felt that way. When the sisters first found out that Dottie had collapsed and was sick, they panicked. They couldn't help but assume the worst about her prognosis and livelihood. But over the weeks, they had time to think rationally and digest any news that came in. The scare reminded them of the importance of family, and that each of their lives was precious. There was no time to hold grudges or be mad—they were in this life together, no matter what was thrown their way.

The three sisters—Dottie, Frankie, and Connie—walked into the restaurant. Connie told Dottie there was something she wanted to show her before they sat down for dinner. Dottie followed behind as the waiter opened the doors that exposed the back patio. "SURPRISE!" The crowd yelled as a stunned Dottie stepped outside. Dottie turned towards Connie and Frankie, who were glowing with pride. "This is all for me?" she asked.

"We're here to celebrate you: Tucson's brightest and most beautiful star," Connie answered. "Now, go mingle with your guests!"

Dozens of people smiled at her and cheered her on as she greeted her family and friends and waved to acquaintances from around town. In the center of the crowd was Dottie's gold cake, which was the anchor of the party. She pointed at it and said "You guys tricked me into baking a cake for my own party? No time off, I guess!" and her guests erupted in laughter. The glow from the twinkle lights reflected off the gold hue of the cake and made Dottie's eyes glisten.

Dottie linked arms with her sisters as they moved through the party. In their vibrant dresses and coiffed hair, they stole the show—but it was the smiles on their faces that were magnetic. The dream they all had in their mind to recreate the picture Frankie once drew in Miami never came true. Instead, here they were, six months later and minus one sister, but the sentiment remained. They were three sisters who appeared to have it all to the outside world. But on the inside, they were working through a myriad of complex emotions—pain, joy, sickness, love, and deep scars from their pasts. They were three sisters—four, including me—trying their best to stay connected and create new memories. All in the hopes that, someday, these new memories would overshadow the darkness from their younger years.

And for the first time, they realized their pasts didn't define them. It did, however, meld them into the strong and complicated women they were today. Dottie, Connie, and Frankie looked up as the clouds parted—exposing a magnificent Tucson night sky. Constellations danced as a silver moon flickered above, flooding light into the otherwise deep dark atmosphere. They squeezed each other's hands as they all noticed the same bright stars. Two exceptional bright stars twinkled overhead—illuminating their paths forward to brighter days.

23

The Last Letter

I think about my mother. I think about my father. I think about my sisters.

I think about what our lives could have been.

I continue staring at my face in the mirror, as the droplets of water roll off my cheeks and onto the counter. My once taut face is filled with deep lines that spread across my cheeks and forehead. I tug at the skin for a moment to smooth it out, but notice the lines and crepiness of my fingertips, too. Aging is a beautiful—but funny—display of nature and time. It felt like only yesterday that I was a young mother laughing as my four children played in our hilly backyard.

I made it a point to laugh every single day—at Ray's jokes, at my children's and grandchildren's antics, at my friend's stories, and my sisters' clumsiness. With each laugh, the lines of life around my face deepened. Lines put there by love and laughter, tears and sorrow, over 80 long years that went by in the blink of an eye.

It feels like only yesterday that my sisters, my parents, and I were headed to the beach on that fateful Saturday morning. I used to block out the painful memories that come along with this day, but I welcome the thoughts on this still evening. Instead of replaying the day's actual events over and over in my head, I sit on the edge of the bathtub and close my eyes. I stay there for what feels like an eternity as warm tears fall from my closed eyes. It's so quiet that I can hear each one as it drops onto the tiled floor.

I grabbed the robe on the back of the door to help with the chill in the air before sneaking into our bedroom. I glanced at Ray, who was still sound asleep as he always does, before pulling down the box of letters from my closet. I closed the door behind me and snuck down the hallway into the kitchen.

The letters slowed over the years. We never missed a Christmas or birthday card and spent countless hours on the telephone. But, the full-length written stories became few and far between. I still remember the way it felt to receive a new letter from my sisters. I would always be able to spot their letters amidst the pile of bills on the counter because of their pastel envelopes. Sometimes Dottie or Connie would doodle on the back. Stars and hearts, that sort of thing. I would open the envelope carefully with Herman's letter opener, making sure not to disrupt anything inside. In the early years when we were much younger, the letters were plain, but we all got creative as time went on. Connie even started to use scented stationary—rosewater, strawberry, or vanilla—that would fill my nostrils as soon as I pulled the letter out of its envelope. Few feelings came close to that thrill—especially on days when I missed the little things about them.

I placed the box of letters on the table, and with a sigh, opened the lid. There was a five-dollar bill and a folded letter on top of the pile. It read:

Dear Dottie,

Please give Vinnie the $5 I've enclosed in the envelope. 'Five bucks for our favorite five-year-old.' Happy Birthday, Vinnie. Auntie Loretta and Uncle Ray send their love. The kids say 'Happy Birthday' too [Donna, Lorraine, Karen, and Ray, Jr.]. We hope you have fun at the birthday par-ty——what's the theme? I can't believe he is five years old, Dottie. Where does the time go?

Connie told me you haven't been feeling well lately. I'm sorry to hear that, Dottie. Your strength is admirable. Do you remember that time when we were little when I had a stomach bug and I couldn't stop vomiting? You must've been, what——5 or 6? I was up and down all night with chills and body aches. You crept into the kitchen and came back with a small saucepan. 'You can throw up in this, Cookie,' you said as you placed it on the floor on my bedside. Then you rubbed my hair and patted my face with a towel. You never left my side and I swear you made me feel better.

You always made me feel better, Dottie. You were my little caretaker. You cared so deeply for your sisters. You always put us first, and I hope you know how much you mean to me. You were my shining star far before you were Tucson's shining star. Do you know I still have that newspaper clipping hanging on the wall of my mirror? I look at it when I have a bad day or when I'm feeling low. Your smile always makes me feel better, like it did when you handed me the saucepan that night. I hope this letter makes you feel bett-

The letter ended mid-sentence and I never sent it. A few minutes later was when I got the news that Dottie had passed away. She was only 35 years old. Her only son was a mere 5 years old. Dottie battled an auto-immune disease for many years that eventually shut down her kidneys. She had good days and bad days. On the good days, she continued to run the bakery (with the help of Mary and Barb who helped her every step of the way). She even met her husband, Greg, on a good day when he came into the bakery. He was in search of the perfect pastry for his girlfriend. He left the bakery without a pastry, but instead with a piece of paper with Dottie's phone number written on it. He broke up with his girlfriend later that night and called Dottie the next day to take her out on a date. They had their only son, Vinnie, soon after. His coming into the world filled so many of Dottie's good days.

But, unfortunately, the bad days were horrible. She was sick. She was tired. She was scared. She would lay in bed in excruciating pain. Greg would sit by her side as she received dialysis for her failing kidneys. Much like Dottie, Vinnie was a caretaker, too. He would put cold face cloths on her forehead and rub her back as she slept. He would cry when she would cry.

Frankie and I were lucky enough to have seen her months before she died. We rented a multi-passenger van and—along with our husbands and the kids—drove across the country. We spent time doing nothing at all. We sat on blankets in Connie's backyard as we watched our children run and play, as we once did ourselves. We reminisced about anything and everything we could remember from our youth. Our first kisses. Our group dates. We left Dottie's dark times out of our conversations. The times when we thought we were losing her in the same way we lost our father. That week we spent in Arizona was one of the best weeks of my life. Dottie felt great—or so she said—and we laughed so hard we cried. We stayed up late. We held hands. We created the missing moments from our childhood. We were in our thirties, but it felt like we were young girls again as we skipped through the sprinkler in our shorts and bare feet.

My sisters all passed away before me. Dottie was the first to die at a painfully young age. Frankie died in her sixties of congestive heart failure. She never had any children, but Marshall was the love of her life and a blessing for our family. Frankie was the best aunt to my children, and the day she died was bittersweet. She was sick for many years before she died, and life support restricted her quality of life. She couldn't speak because of a tracheostomy tube, which was tragic for someone who loved to talk as much as Frankie did. She communicated through written notes on her handheld chalkboard. When she died, I knew she would finally rest easy. It didn't help me from feeling heartbroken over losing my best friend.

Connie died only a few short months ago of no particular cause. She had lived out her final years in an assisted living facility in Connecticut. Her children settled in the Northeast after going to college here and she followed. I remember the day her moving truck pulled up to our house after she and Scott drove here from Arizona. "We're ba-ack," she screamed out the window. They bought a house a few miles away from me and I was lucky enough to see them often.

My relationship with Connie grew to be so special over the years. I was so thankful that her family chose to settle here so she could be with me and Frankie again. I was there the moment Connie took her final breath. I found peace in knowing our sisters would soon greet her in heaven. I asked Ray if he could drive me to the beach the morning after Connie died.

I couldn't help but think of how easy walking through the sand used to be, compared to how it felt that day. Ray held my arm as I inched my way down the beach—almost losing my balance and definitely losing my breath on the walk down. I dipped my toes into the water and looked out over the calm sea. Ray pointed to our left. "Look at that," he said as three seabirds swirled in harmony in the sky. They came to a halt right in front of us and circled calmly on the still water off the sound. One looked over at us and screeched out of its bright orange beak. I couldn't help but think that the seabirds were my sisters—free and floating in the open waters. They were together again in their favorite place and playing like children as the waves rolled underneath them.

I sifted through more and more letters that night as Ray lay asleep in our bed. Amid the letters was my diary from my childhood. The last entry I ever wrote was from the night before my wedding. I tossed and turned all night and woke up to write. It was the last night I slept in Anna and Herman's home. I know they would have been proud of how my life turned out.

I turned to a blank page and stared at the lined paper. I picked up a pen and began to write:

Dear Diary,

I'm writing this letter from my kitchen table. I'm sorry it's taken me almost 57 years to write again; I guess you could say that I have been busy. I have four children and four grandchildren that are my world. Ray is the same blue-eyed gentleman that I beat in bowling when he was still a high school student. He still surprises me——only these days, it's with flowers or my favorite meal instead of jewels from the diamond district. Sometimes, I stare down at the engagement ring that still fits my weathered fingers and wonder how I ever got so lucky. My first granddaughter, Cherie, always asks me to try it on. I told her that it's hers to keep one day when I die, as I knew she'll cherish it forever.

My kids are the loves of my life. They kept me on my toes throughout the decades, that's for sure. I'll never forget the 1970s. My daughters Donna, Lorraine, and Karen wore bell bottom jeans and skirts so short that my parents would roll over in their grave! Donna was a pip——she still is! Ray loved watching her cheer at the football games, but I always got scared when they tossed her in the air. My middle daughter married in the 1980s when she was only 20 years old. I thought of Connie and how young she was when she got married. Lorraine was like her——mature and wise beyond her years. Karen gave me my other three grandkids later in life——Olivia, Emily, and Matthew. They brought me such joy———and a ton of laughs. My sisters would have loved those kids. And my son, Ray Jr., was my youngest. I used to worry so much when he first got his license. His friends would pick him up in their muscle cars and they would take off down the street. I never told him how I would stay up all night waiting for him to come home. As soon as I saw the headlights in the driveway, I'd sneak into bed and he'd be none the wiser.

After working as an X-ray technician for many years and taking off some time to raise the kids, I decided to go back to work after Ray Jr. was old enough to go to school. I always admired the school teachers that lived on my street so, one day, I drove about a mile down the road to Wendell Cross Elementary School to ask about a job. I was curious if I had what it took to be a teacher. What's the harm in asking, I thought? But the thing is, I walked into the wrong entrance and found my way in the school's cafeteria! I'll never forget how shiny the wooden floor was. It squeaked underneath my feet as I walked across the painted lines. A woman poked her head out of a door in the corner and asked if I was there to apply for the part-time lunch lady job. "Hours are 7 to 1. You interested? I could really use the help." So, I took the job without ever asking about becoming a teacher. And it was one of the things in my life that brought me the most joy. I loved helping the kids and befriending the teachers. I even got to keep an eye on my granddaughter

Cherie when she attended school there. I was so proud of being a lunch lady and took meticulous pride in my kitchen———I stayed late to shine the metal oven or pick crumbs off the floor, even though the custodian would sweep it again anyways. That little part-time job gave me purpose and took me into my late 70s until my knees started bothering and I needed more rest.

Raising kids without my own parents was challenging to say the least. It takes a village———which is where Ray's family came in. They welcomed me with open arms and became my best friends. My kids grew up with loads of cousins. There was never a quiet day in this house. If it wasn't my nieces and nephews running through the front door, it was my kids' friends. Some of their friends would even stay for weeks at a time. I always wondered where their parents thought they were... This was the kind of home I always dreamed of, with lots of love and action between the walls.

But the people on my mind most tonight are my sisters as I reminisce and read through the box of letters they've sent me. I read the first letter that Dottie and Connie wrote to me after they moved to Arizona. It's funny to read it now———a letter written by a 10 and 9-year-old———as it reads so childlike. But I'll never forget the way I felt the day I opened the mailbox to find the first letter ever addressed to me and Frankie. Dottie wrote our names and address on the outside and it seemed like it took her hours, as the penmanship was perfect and straight. It was invigorating and that feeling kept us writing to each other for many, many years.

Whenever I think about my sisters and imagine what they are doing in heaven together, my mind goes to the day our mother died. I remember their faces so vividly as they played in the sand that morning. This image is stuck in my mind——belly laughs, swirling in the sea, and at an age and a time before we became damaged by the loss of the lives we had with one another.

The truth is that our parents' deaths did affect each of us. We didn't always show it and the effects weren't always negative, but we all took something away from the tragic events of our past. But I know one thing for sure——I wouldn't be the person I am today if I hadn't experienced such a heavy loss at such a young age. Not only the loss of my parents, but the loss of my sparkly-eyed sisters. Their eyes dulled one-by-one when we became separated from each other.

It was this loss that was too much to bear.

Ray walked out into the kitchen and I put the pen down. "Everything okay, Cookie?"

"Actually," I began. "Everything is perfect now." He kissed my forehead and led me back to bed. I drifted off to sleep that night as my sisters' faces flashed across my mind. They were waiting for me, and it wouldn't be long before I was ready to see them again, too.

THE END

Southern Pacific Railroad Co.

GOOD FOR ONE TRIP ONLY

22139

To Tucson, A.Z.   From New York, N.Y.

ROUND TRIP SINGLE TICKET

Wedding Gown

HANDLE WITH CARE

Honeymoon in Miami

Our Kids

Tucson, A.Z.

The four of us

My Sister's Wedding

WATERBURY
SEP 10
1953
CONN.

List for Tucson trip:
- ~~Connie's wedding gown!~~
- ~~Bridesmaid dresses~~
- ~~Jewelry~~
- ~~Gifts for our sisters~~
- ~~Photos I found from the old house~~

* Don't forget the gold shoes and hats!

Cookie's
Memory Board

Loretta & Raymond

5¢ U.S. POSTAGE 5¢

Photo © 2021 Andy Lee Photography

ABOUT THE AUTHOR

Cherie L. Genua's first love is—and always will be—writing. Writing is the outlet that illuminated the most wonderful times of her life, while also helping her find the sunshine on some otherwise dark days. After facing a life-changing breast cancer diagnosis at the age of 34, Cherie co-authored the non-fiction book "Wisdom from Five Cancer Travelers: Lessons Learned" with others affected by the disease. She was declared "no evidence of disease" in 2019 and made it a mission to write and publish her first fiction novel, "Greetings from Tucson," inspired by her grandmother's story. Cherie lives in Connecticut with her husband, Matt, and their Portuguese Water Dog, Poppy. She holds a B.A. in English from Southern Connecticut State University and an M.B.A. from the University of Massachusetts Amherst.

Made in the USA
Middletown, DE
11 April 2023

28559196R00201